HIGH PRAISE FOR
**R.D. ZIMMERMAN**
and **TRIBE**

*"Tribe* tells a gay story of intrigue and deceit that drives the reader forward with compelling prose." —*In Touch*

"ZIMMERMAN IS A SUPERB WRITER, building suspense through genuine surprises while creating believable characters." —*The Ft. Lauderdale Sun-Sentinel*

"VIVID . . . A REAL PAGE-TURNING YARN . . . Along with deftly weaving unexpected elements from the characters' past and present, Zimmerman introduces a creepy religious cult, with suspenseful results." —*Q Monthly*

"The real test of a detective or mystery novel is its ability to hold the reader's interest and keep those pages turning. Zimmerman succeeds at this quite well." —*TriCity Herald*

"R.D. ZIMMERMAN IS A WONDERFUL WRITER OF SUSPENSE and surely the most original storyteller of the genre." —Sharyn McCrumb, author of *If I'd Killed Him When I Met Him*

"R.D. Zimmerman is one of the best of the new generation of thriller writers who use the form to entertain and enlighten us on the highest level." —Roger L. Simon, creator of the Moses Wine series

"ZIMMERMAN'S WRITING IS TOO BREATHLESS TO LEAVE YOU DISCONTENTED." —*Kirkus Reviews*

## ALSO BY R.D. ZIMMERMAN

# TRIBE

## R.D. ZIMMERMAN

Delta
Trade Paperbacks

A Delta Book
Published by
Dell Publishing
a division of
Bantam Doubleday Dell Publishing Group, Inc.
1540 Broadway
New York, New York 10036

ISBN: 0-385-32002-7

Manufactured in the United States of America
Published simultaneously in Canada

November 1997

10  9  8  7  6  5  4  3  2  1

BVG

# TRIBE

# PROLOGUE

*Evanston, Illinois*
*December 1973*

This was about sex.

They stood, the two of them, in the small bedroom on the fourth floor of the fraternity, the door carefully closed and locked, the desk light turned to the wall to dim its light. This was as private as things got at Northwestern University, or any college, for that matter. As intimate, as quiet. For days the two young men had been exchanging furtive glances, eyeing each other at the dinner table, peering down the hall, and, above all, staring in the shower room. And now they stood motionless in the narrow chamber, one next to the single bed, the other by the door, each of them silently daring the other to act first or at least say something, anything.

Sure, this was about sex, and it was making Todd sick. Brown-haired and handsome in a rugged, youthful way, seemingly always cool, even happy, his entire stomach now seemed to have caved in on itself, tightening his gut painfully. Oh, God, this wasn't what he wanted out of his life, was it? Hell no. He was the guy with the broad shoulders and quick legs, the captain of the frat-house intramural football team. All fall he'd been dating one of the cutest girls on campus. He'd worked so hard at making sure everyone liked him. Which they did. And now, biting his lip, he appraised the situation. There were clothes strewn everywhere: jeans on the bed, a gray sweatshirt tossed on a chair, socks and underwear all over the avocado shag carpet. But those were merely yesterday's clothes, and lanky Pat, his blond hair pulled into a ponytail, was still dressed. Thank God. Just get the hell out of here, Todd told himself.

But he couldn't force himself to move because his body was telling him something entirely different from his mind. It was as if there were two parts of him, each at war with the other. To be sure, this power that was surging in his loins was everything Todd hated about himself. Christ, he should just turn and run. Run right to his shrink. Or should he even tell his therapist about this? Would he be horribly disappointed in Todd, or would he merely shrug and turn up the electricity on the aversion-therapy gizmo and really shock the hell out of Todd whenever he visualized a naked, aroused man?

"I can't help it," said Pat, the first one to shatter the crystalline silence. "I . . . I want you again."

As much as Todd wanted to forget, they had done it before, twice to be exact. Todd now slumped against the door, horrified by what he felt, paralyzed with fear that others might find out, and yet overwhelmed with an animal urge to take this young Pat and wrestle him naked to the floor. He closed his eyes, clung to his silence. The walls up here on the fourth floor were so thin, nothing much more than Sheetrock and a coat of paint dividing the rooms. Everyone could hear them, couldn't they?

"I like doing it, you know, with guys. I can't help it. I . . . I just do. I mean, I just can't control it." Pat paused, shifted awkwardly on his feet, rubbed his right shoulder, and asked, "What about you?"

Todd opened his eyes, stared across the dimly lit space, and saw Pat's tempting image outlined in front of the single, large window. No. Don't get into this. Hold back.

"Oh, come on, loosen up," urged Pat. "You don't have to be so uptight about it. Have you been down at the gym at night? You should see all the guys down there. I mean, there's even a couple of guys from the club hockey team hanging around in the showers. And have you seen what's going on down at the beach? Man, everyone's got a sexual secret."

Todd had always wanted just one thing in life: to be straight. He'd have given anything not simply to have this torture subside, but to be normal and accepted. If his father ever found out what lurked in Todd's head and what he'd actually done a handful of times, dear God, the old Pole would really go into a rage. And if he'd been dipping into the vodka Todd would get the crap beat out of him. Perhaps even the belt.

"Fuck, it's happening right here too. Right at the frat house. I've done it with one of the other guys here, you know. Someone who's crazy for me." Pat pleaded, "Come on, say something."

"Listen, I . . . I . . ." began Todd, but then cut himself off when he heard one of the guys shouting downstairs.

"It's okay," said Pat in a soft, soothing voice. "The door's locked."

Right in front of him Pat started to lift off his sweater, pulling one arm from the sleeve, then the next. Todd knew this was the last moment he could escape, yet he stood there, both captive and captivated.

"Just relax," continued Pat.

In an instant the sweater was gone, one sleeve flung over the back of the yellow plastic molded desk chair, the other draping to the floor and onto a stack of biology books. Todd was paralyzed, his eyes fixated on Pat's hands as they slowly moved down his old plaid shirt, unfastening one button at a time and unveiling a perfect chest, that of a swimmer, sleek and smooth and muscular. Then finally the shirt was rolled off the shoulders and not flung, not tossed, but slowly dropped onto the green shag. His heart charging with lust, his mind churning with confusion, Todd stared at the long arms, the flat stomach.

"You like?" taunted Pat.

Sure, he did, but still Todd didn't move and couldn't bring himself to verbalize his lust. He stood rigid across the room, braided with desire and guilt. And then Pat started unfastening his jeans, the metal button at the top, the zipper. Todd swallowed, heard more steps somewhere down the hall, a voice or two, but paid no attention, unable to conceive that just on the other side of the old, battered door, over thirty frat boys were going about their business, some listening to Cat Stevens, the pensive few listening to Judy Collins, a couple of guys torturing a mouse, and a handful of others huddled out front around a grill, barbecuing some hot dogs on coat hangers as the chilly December winds gusted. No, all of that was another, distant world, totally blocked from this dark, carnal den. Todd felt the desire rising painfully in his crotch and watched transfixed as Pat continued his strip show, shedding his worn jeans, stepping out of them, and then standing there in his Jockeys, his own excitement more than evident. Oh, dear God.

Todd took a deep breath and realized he couldn't hold himself back anymore. He took a step forward, opened his arms. In an instant the nearly naked Pat was in his arms, and Todd clutched the other young man, pulling him against himself as hard as he could. No, he couldn't stop himself, never would be able to, and he ran one hand down Pat's spine and under the elastic band of his cotton underwear. If this is so wrong, thought Todd, his eyes drifting shut as he kissed Pat on the ear, why does it feel so right?

Pat groaned and said, "Oh, my God, you feel good."

Todd was so nervous, so excited, he could only moan, "Yeah."

Something hit the window. A branch, he assumed. Todd opened his dreamy, lustful eyes. Looked up. But instead of a wintry, spindly, leafless branch tapping the glass, he saw a figure pressing against the window and a shocked pair of eyes staring back at him.

"Oh, shit!" shouted Todd.

The face, that of one of his fraternity brothers. It was Greg, the guy from the room next door. Short. Stocky. Glasses. A big face. As if he were flying among the trees, he hovered right outside the window, looking right at Todd and Pat. Shot with fear, Todd hurled Pat back, pushing him out of his arms, trying to distance himself, desperate to make it appear that this was anything but a homosexual love scene.

"Christ," growled Pat, "he's out on the fire escape!"

Outside in the cold, Greg screamed the alarm: "Homo alert!"

A tidal wave of panic overwhelmed Todd. He saw his future. He knew what was going to happen. This was exactly what he'd been so terrified of. And now Greg knew the truth. He was going to tell everyone. Todd would be kicked out of the fraternity. He'd be shamed out of school. His parents would find out. This was the end.

The adrenaline coursed through Todd's veins. There was no doubt Greg had seen everything and recognized Todd, and in a mere instant Todd's body blossomed with sweat. He spun around, tripped over a shoe. Just get away. Just get out of here. And he half-fell as he clambered to escape. Reaching the door, his trembling hands fumbled with the lock.

Behind him, Pat was charging toward the window, furious and shouting, "Get out of here, you asshole! Leave us the fuck alone!"

Todd ripped open the door, glanced back one last time, saw Pat trying to lift open the window.

"Todd, I can't get the window up!" yelled Pat in a panic. "Help me!"

As Todd stood in the doorway, Pat turned around and their eyes locked. For an instant everything seemed to freeze in disbelief: Is this really happening? Overcome with terror, however, it never occurred to Todd not to run away, not to beat a cowardly retreat, and he darted into the hallway. Greg lived just there, in the room to the right, the one with the open door and open window. Hearing footsteps from that room—shit, who was in there?—Todd spun around and dashed the other way down the hallway. And immediately stopped. The next door, Kevin's room, was opening. A bunch of guys screaming with juvenile gusto was about to burst out.

"Get the faggots!"

"Pat's doing it with some guy!"

Todd guessed that these guys had been in on it too, perhaps listening through the flimsy walls. Right, they'd been on one side of Pat's room, Greg on the other. On a boring night just before finals it was a conspiracy to trap and rid the fraternity of queers.

There was a small door right in front of him and Todd heaved it open. Not a closet but a narrow staircase. The back stairs, totally dark. Todd was rushing so quickly that he missed the first couple of steps and tumbled forward. Catching himself on the railing, he paused, heard Pat slam his door as the herd of frat boys charged his room.

"Open the fucking lock, Pat!" shouted one of the guys as they started beating on the door.

In the dark Todd scrambled to his feet and raced down, not stopping at the third floor nor the second. He just had to get away. Away from the truth. When he reached the first floor he didn't head out into the main living room, where someone was watching television and others were playing Ping-Pong. No. He couldn't let them see him so panicky, so blistered with sweat.

The back door. He tore through the small hall behind the kitchen and then out the rear of the house. Hurling open the door, he was hit with a gust of frigid air. He closed his eyes, took a deep breath, and slumped against the side of the building, his right cheek pressing into the brick. Oh, shit. He clutched himself. There was no way Greg hadn't seen what was going on. There was no way Greg hadn't spied Todd nibbling on Pat's ear or caressing his ass. And there was no way Greg wasn't going to tell the entire world.

Opening his eyes, Todd stared at the frozen ground covered by a mere inch of snow. As he stood there, paralyzed with any number of horrific thoughts, something fell from above, slipping through the air and landing on the ground a mere foot or two from him. Not a snowflake but a chunky cigarette butt, hand-rolled and one end still burning an orangish-red.

Suddenly a scream cut through the cold night air. Todd looked toward Sheridan Avenue. Seeing nothing, not even a car, his eyes darted to the side toward a clump of trees. He heard it again. Another terrified plea. Following the sound more closely, Todd looked up. The fire escape was directly above him, a mishmash of black steel climbing back and forth the entire four floors of the fraternity. And way up there, right at the top, shadows were dancing in the night. He couldn't see, couldn't tell in the dark, who was up there, if there was one guy or two. Wait. He stepped away from the building and to his horror saw more clearly. Holy shit, someone was dangling and twisting from the fire escape, scrambling to hang on.

A figure that dropped free.

Dear God in heaven, they'd thrown Pat off the fire escape. Hurled him right out. Todd watched in horrified dismay as the figure hurtled downward, shrieking all the way, his shirt and pants flapping, his body arched and tumbling like that of a tragic diver.

And finally it ended, that moment that seemed to stretch forever. The cry ceased with a thud, followed by the deep, cold silence of the night.

Standing there in a helpless moment that lasted far too long, Todd stared at the body lying facedown not ten feet from him. Barely able to breathe, Todd understood that the guy was dead. It was the way the body was so horribly twisted and so pathetically still. Todd wasn't sure whether he wanted to vomit or scream for help. Or run. If they had done this to Pat, what would they do to him? Perhaps come after him and drown him in the frigid waters of Lake Michigan?

Wait, he realized, this can't be Pat. This person's fully clothed.

Trembling, Todd's feet slid through the thin snow as he moved closer. If not Pat, then who? Leaning forward, trying to see the face smashed against the hard ground, Todd saw the glasses, recognized the hair. Holy shit, it was Greg.

And the question that the campus cops would ask over the course of the next week was, thankfully, not whether or not Todd was gay, for the dead frat boy had carried that secret to his grave. No, the question they would ask was whether Todd had witnessed an accident. Or murder.

# 1

*Minneapolis, present day*

She'd seen him only once, but had thought of him every day since.

Back then he'd been a kid of eighteen with beautiful long, dark hair, a clear complexion, and a rugged jaw surfacing beneath the round cheeks. A shy smile, too, that showed off all those white teeth. Very cute. No, extremely cute. He'd been thin, his legs long and a bit awkward. And those eyes, dark with eyebrows that promised to be thick and striking.

Okay, okay, thought Janice Gray as she sat in her idling car, the heater on high. So she would recognize him. It was just that they'd met only that single time; one summer morning he'd just shown up at her law office, claimed he was passing through town, and they'd disappeared into the conference room for several of the most intimate, heated hours Janice had ever experienced or imagined. He'd gone on and on, even cried, this boy—he and a friend, he confessed, had been caught smoking pot and he'd run away from home—and had opened up to her in a way that had shocked her. In response she couldn't help but be as revealing as he, telling him all about the joys and tragedies of her life, of her legal practice, and finally, eventually, that she was a lesbian, which at the time hadn't seemed to faze him.

That was three years ago. Three and a half years, actually, and not a word or any news from him since. He'd just disappeared. Perhaps her honesty had frightened him. Perhaps she'd been too lawyerly, too probing. Perhaps she'd looked too formidable in her pretrial blue pinstripe suit that made her appear distinctly tight and conservative. Or maybe he'd vanished because he really couldn't handle the fact that she was a dyke.

Shit, thought Janice, hugging her dark blue wool coat around herself, it was too cold for this kind of thing. Early January in Minnesota was no time to be sitting in your car in some snow-whitened parking lot, waiting for a punk to show up. If he showed up. She shivered and rubbed herself, then wiped a film of fog off the inside of the windshield and peered out. It was a classic Minnesota winter night, the famous kind—fourteen below, the night sky clear, the air still and amazingly pure. A car drew in from the street, and two people got out and ran for the glaring lights and promised warmth of the supermarket.

A month ago she couldn't take it anymore, so she went out and bought the one and only Christmas card she was to send that season. Janice wrote a brief note inside, included a couple of photos, and then mailed it off to the only address she had for him, printing on the front PLEASE FORWARD. Ever since she'd dropped it in the mail Janice had wondered if he received it, and then finally at four this afternoon the response came. She'd been sitting at her desk, reviewing a case on a woman who'd been fired from a computer firm, when the call came. He was in town again, he told her, and he desperately needed to see her. They could meet tonight, right? Behind his pushy request she'd immediately sensed some sort of trouble—could it be drugs again?—but she was so stunned to hear from him that she didn't ask. Yes, she'd replied, for in truth she'd meet him anywhere, anytime. Eight this evening. Sure, the parking lot of Rainbow Foods at Lagoon and Dupont. Of course she knew where that was, right in south Minneapolis, right on the edge of Uptown, the trendy and popular neighborhood adjacent to the chain of now frozen lakes.

Janice tilted her rearview mirror and checked herself in the faint light. She'd changed after work and now wore jeans and a red wool sweater that complemented her deep-auburn hair. Perhaps they'd go out for coffee and he'd tell her what was up; they certainly couldn't sit out here very long. With any luck she'd get him back to her house. She dabbed at her makeup, tried to soften it a bit, for she didn't want to look like a hard-ass defense attorney who regularly went up against the top lawyers in town. She just wanted to look like her real self—a forty-two-year-old woman who was trim, her narrow face attractive, her mouth always ready with an eager laugh. She didn't want him to sense, however, the emptiness in her heart.

Janice's car windows were fogging up badly, and she turned a knob until the heater died and the defroster began to spew full blast. Glancing at the car clock, Janice saw that it was ten after eight. Maybe he wasn't going to show. On the phone he'd said there was something he had to tell her, but maybe he'd chickened out. Perhaps he was afraid or perhaps he couldn't bring himself to trust her after all.

The lights of another car swept off Lagoon Avenue and toward her, and Janice felt her stomach tighten. It was a small car, blue and old and rusty from countless winters. A kid's car? Probably. Studying the vehicle as it pulled into the parking lot, however, Janice couldn't really see much, for the windows on that car were mostly iced over as well. But there was just one person in there, wasn't there? Right. She saw a head of long hair but couldn't tell if the driver was a man or a woman. Her eyes trained on the vehicle, Janice watched as the car came to a stop some forty feet away. Though she had followed his directions and parked in the exact snow-filled corner, she wondered if she should climb out of her own car and identify herself, call out to him perhaps. She twisted around, saw a figure emerging from the other car, bundled in a thick nylon parka.

Damn, a young woman. Janice couldn't really see the face, but she could see a purse and—

Her entire car seemed to shake as the passenger door was hurled open. A large bundled and hooded figure descended rapidly into her car, and Janice tensed and threw herself against the seat. Reflexively, she grabbed the door handle, for more than anything it seemed that she was about to be accosted. The figure then slammed shut the door, sat there for a moment, and finally pulled back his large black hood.

"Shit, it's cold."

As was seldom the case, Janice was at a loss for words. He was no longer a boy but a young man, his once long hair now as short as if he were in the army. His baby face had melted away as well, he'd grown so that he had to be over six feet tall, and despite the overcoat she guessed that there were broad shoulders beneath that bulky parka. The shading of a beard lined his chilled red cheeks, and the eyebrows had indeed grown thick, just as she had imagined. She hadn't foreseen, however, the dark circles beneath his eyes.

Oh, God. Somewhere deep inside herself Janice moaned silently, and her entire body flushed with a deep, penetrating warmth. She had to have him, this Zebulun. She had to take him and hold him in her arms. She had to kiss this gorgeous young man and tell him how she loved him with every part of her being and that never, not for one moment, had she ever stopped thinking of him. And she had to tell him how she never wanted to lose him again.

Instead, attorney Janice Gray clenched down on her teeth and held herself in check.

"Hello, Zeb," she said.

They stared at each other in the faint light of her Honda Prelude. There was so much to say, so much to catch up on.

"Hi," he replied, his voice hesitant and low and deep.

"How have you been?"

He wrapped his arms oddly, nervously, around his waist and looked away. His profile silhouetted by the parking-lot lights, she was struck as much by his beauty as his seriousness. Every trace of boyishness seemed to have been eradicated, and this adulthood saddened Janice.

Finally he replied, "I've been better."

"You want to get a cup of coffee?"

Obviously disturbed about something, he quickly said, "No."

All Janice could imagine was that he found her disgusting. Watching as his hands fumbled around his waist—what the hell was he doing, did he have something hidden beneath the folds of his parka?—Janice felt her heart ripping in two. She shouldn't have come. This was far too hard, for she already sensed that he was going to disappear again.

"Zeb . . ." Janice clenched her eyes shut, forbidding herself to cry, telling herself that, no, she couldn't beg him to stay this time forever and ever. "What is it? Why did you call?"

"I needed to see you."

"But why?"

"I'm in trouble."

"What do you mean? What's happened?"

"I . . . I . . ."

He stopped his muttering, and Janice watched as Zeb slowly unzipped his parka with one gloved hand. He most definitely did have something stowed away beneath his coat, she realized as an awkward bundle began to emerge. Dear God, she feared, he's not going to hurt me, is he?

And then there was a slight cry. Janice couldn't believe it. The entire world seemed to stop.

"Beautiful, isn't she?" asked Zeb, a proud grin emerging on his sullen face.

"Oh, Lord," gasped Janice. "Is . . . is she yours?"

"Absolutely."

Zeb lifted a baby girl—a tiny thing not more than a few months old—from his coat. Bundled in a pink snowsuit, a pure white cotton knit blanket, and a white knit hat tied on her bitty head, the infant squirmed and cried until Zeb pressed his cheek to her face and cooed softly in her ear.

The young man turned to Janice and said, "Would you like to hold her?"

A weird sensation went charging through Janice, for she had never known that horror and joy could fuse together into an altogether new and bizarre emotion, a paralyzing one at that. She stared at this tiny baby girl—admired the dark curl of hair that hung on her forehead, her little nose, thin lips—and couldn't speak, couldn't move. Her own breathing started coming short and quick, and for a fretful second Janice feared she was having a panic attack, which she quickly dismissed when she realized her heart was pumping wildly and purely with unbridled happiness.

As he held her toward Janice, Zeb softly said, "Here."

A dam of tears broke from Janice's eyes, and she nodded. Yes, Janice wanted to scream, let me take this treasure, let me hold her and rock her and love her. And in the front seat of the Honda Prelude Zeb awkwardly passed the baby girl, and Janice took her and thought she'd never seen so beautiful a child.

"Oh, my God, I can't believe it. How old?"

"Four and a half months." Zeb pulled out a small can and a vial and set them on the dashboard. "This is her formula and her drops. She's fine, but she has to have these drops three times a day."

"She's perfect."

"I know. And I love her. With all my heart I love her."

"Of course you do."

"But will you tell her that?"

"What?" asked Janice, briefly looking up.

"If anything ever happens to me, will you tell her that?"

"Of course, but dear God, Zeb, don't talk like that. This child's an angel. She'll protect us all." Janice bent forward, pressed her lips against the silky softness of the baby's cheeks. "Zeb, she's . . . she's just so beautiful. What's her name?"

"Ribka."

"Ribka," repeated Janice, letting the name hang in the air. "That's a pretty name."

He hesitated, then added, "I wanted to name her after you, but it all got really complicated."

Janice could only manage to mutter a small "Oh."

All the pain, all the sorrow of Janice's life came rushing forward, focusing on the joy she now held in her arms. A sob rose from the deepest, darkest corner of her soul, and she held the little baby in her arms and cried and cried, for now she understood there were indeed miracles.

Zeb said, "Tell her every day that I'll be back soon."

Over her own crying, Janice barely heard. "What?"

"I'm in serious trouble. Don't come looking for me. Promise me that? Don't come after me. I just don't want anything to happen to the baby."

"Zeb, what are you saying?"

"I don't want them to hurt her. That's why I'm giving her to you."

Janice began to panic. What had he gotten himself involved in? Smoking a joint or two in your teens was one thing, but could it be anything more serious, could the problem have gotten worse, was he doing heroin? Oh, Christ, she thought, what if he's dealing?

Janice demanded, "Zeb, what the hell are you talking about?"

"I need to hide her so no one can find her. I've got some things to straighten out. Don't worry, I'll be around—I just interviewed for a job at a hospital in Edina."

The baby twisted in her arms and she glanced down, saw this infant and her dark curls, a greater gift than Janice could ever have hoped for. But then she heard something click, saw Zeb's thick, gloved hand reaching for the door. Who could be after him and what would they do if they found him?

Seized by panic, Janice awkwardly grabbed him by the sleeve. "Zeb!"

"I'm sorry." He turned toward her, his own eyes glistening with tears that would freeze as soon as he stepped into the wintry night. "Don't worry, I'll be back. Just don't come after me or they'll hurt her too."

"Who?"

"You don't understand, I'm just trying to protect her."

"Zeb, no!"

But she couldn't stop him, and the son Janice Gray had given up for adoption when he was three days old scrambled out of her red Honda Prelude and disappeared into the frigid Minnesota night.

# 2

The brilliancy of a Minnesota winter never ceased to remind Todd of the gray Chicago winters he'd left behind. Sipping his first cup of coffee of the day, he sat on his black leather couch, the dazzling light pouring in through the windows of his fifteenth-floor condo. Of course it was colder than hell up here in Minneapolis—the night before last the thermometer had dipped to twenty-three below—but the frigid temperatures came only when the arctic blasts cleared the skies of every bit of cloud cover. Not like Chicago, where the days stretched warmer perhaps, but dull and damp, Lake Michigan attracting winter gloom like a meteorological magnet.

The sun wasn't supposed to last forever though. Nor the cold. The frigid snap was due to end about noon today, according to every educated guess, of which there tended to be a great, great number in Minnesota. The clouds were supposed to move in, the temperature rise all the way to twenty, and then, of course, the snow was expected to come falling. Lots of it, which was all they'd been talking about at the grocery stores around town as people loaded up on supplies. Todd now glanced outside, and squinting he saw the distant bright sail of an ice sailboard go zipping across Lake Calhoun. He almost preferred the clarity of the cold to the expected heat wave.

Having gotten out of bed only ten minutes earlier, he stretched and yawned and rubbed his stubbly beard. He wore a large gray T-shirt, faded blue jeans, no socks. Now in his early forties, his light brown hair was just beginning to gray, and he took pride in being in almost as good shape as he was in his college days. Maybe today he'd go to the gym. Maybe not. He hadn't worked a day since his lover Michael had been murdered and the scandal of their relationship broadcast on all the media. And he didn't know if he'd ever work in television again, not because he hadn't had any offers but because that drive, that thirst, seemed to have evaporated. Hard to imagine that less than six months ago he'd won two Emmys, been the hottest TV reporter in town if not the Midwest, and was about to be offered the anchor position on Channel 7. And now? Perhaps this was a mid-life crisis. If that were the case, though, shouldn't he be in turmoil or at least experiencing angst of some kind instead of this subtle sense of peace?

He took another sip of coffee, then reached for the shoe box full of photographs that sat on the coffee table. Among the many things he wanted to accomplish in this, his first pause in his professional life—he'd taken his first job at a public television station just a week after graduating from Northwestern twenty years ago and had worked constantly since—was to sort through all these pictures and get them into some albums. He also wanted to paint the second bedroom that he used as his office. Get some new skates. And do some writing about what it was like to be closeted for so long in the television industry.

Pulling out a handful of pictures, he came to one of his father taken not long after he'd emigrated from Poland following World War II. There he was, strong and smiling, dressed in a suit, hair slicked back, square-jawed and striking. The man who'd studied in Warsaw to be a doctor and ended working in an automotive parts plant in Chicago. The man who'd castrated the family name from Milkowski to Mills. The man who'd married an American beauty and never spoken his native language again. He and Todd had some terrible fights, particularly in the latter vodka-sodden years.

There were pictures of their cat, the huge black one, Trix. The little brick bungalow in Chicago that was the family's first house. The big station wagon, all shiny and new. The trip to Yellowstone. His kid brother, Timmy, once so scrawny and shy, standing there in shorts and a Davy Crockett raccoon hat, now a stockbroker in New York. His mother, simple and sweet and beautiful. And young. Todd peered at the picture, shocked at how youthful she looked, her hair dark and thick, her face so slender. Now she lived in a trailer park in Florida, white-haired and happy, her own life having had a renaissance with the death of her husband. In the next bunch Todd fished out a handful of photos from college. His dad had been so proud that his oldest son had gotten into Northwestern, and there was a snapshot of them loading the car with Todd's things, another of them unloading the car, yet another of his mom and him and awkward Timmy on the front steps of the dorm. Oh, brother. He remembered his dad and that camera and that first day. Snap, snap, snap. It had been so embarrassing.

"What are you grinning about?"

Todd looked up, saw Steve Rawlins stumbling out of the hall and wearing Todd's white terry cloth robe. He was shorter, a tad stockier than Todd, and his brown hair was ruffled, his dark eyes puffy. Of all the things since Michael's death, this budding romance with the police detective had been one of the most confusing. Rawlins was more than good-looking. More than nice. But . . .

"Well, look who's up," said Todd.

"Some of us have to work, you know."

"Hey, I've been working. I made coffee."

There was no need to tell him where the mugs were, because Rawlins had been spending at least a couple of nights a week here for the last two or three months. And he would have been staying more but for Todd's reticence. Simply, now that Todd was out of the closet in a major-league way, he wasn't sure if a full-blown, monogamous relationship was what he wanted or needed right now. He'd never just dated around, let alone gotten to know himself as an openly gay man. So if this wasn't the time for these things, when would it be?

He asked, "What do you want for breakfast?"

"Just coffee," said Rawlins as he poured himself some. "I'm supposed to be down at the station in a half hour, so I'd better get in the shower. Will I see you tonight?"

"Actually, I'm busy." Seeing the all-too-obvious disappointment on Rawlins's face, Todd added, "I'm having dinner with Janice."

"I see."

The answer didn't seem to appease Rawlins. Which was part of the problem. Todd needed space. Time. Not guilt at not giving himself fully to Rawlins. So even though he was a tad resentful at explaining just why Rawlins wouldn't be welcome at dinner, he knew he had to. After all, Todd wasn't sure he wanted to lose Rawlins either.

"Sorry," Todd said, "but Janice has got a sitter so the two of us can go out. She specifically asked that I come alone—she promised she's finally going to tell me what's going on with her and this baby."

"Oh," he replied, his voice rather flat. "A good story there, I bet."

"All she's told me is that it's some client's kid. What I can't figure out is why she's gone so gaga over her."

"Maybe it's her maternal instincts flaring up." Rawlins came into the living room and kissed Todd on the top of his head. "Listen, you two go out and have a good time. I just can't get enough of you, but that's my problem."

"Thanks."

"So what are you looking at?"

"Old pictures."

"Of whom, old lovers?"

"Well, kind of."

With a laugh Todd reached into the box, sifted through a few more pictures, pulled out one of a blond girl. "Here's one—I dated Kathy in high school for about six weeks." Next he pulled out one of him walking down the aisle with a slender woman in a white dress. "Oh, shit, here's my wedding picture."

"No kidding."

Before Todd knew, Rawlins was perched next to him on the couch, pulling the photograph from his hand. There was Todd, looking so virile, so happy; he remembered thinking this proved it, if he was getting married he couldn't be gay. And Trish, tall and radiant, her dark hair flowing over her shoulders. They looked the ideal couple.

"She was pretty."

"Yeah, she still is too. I've seen her only a couple of times since we were divorced, but I hear she's doing really well. She's a pediatrician." Todd took a deep breath, knowing this was on his list of things he had to do. "I've got to write her. Or call. I mean, I never talked about my being gay, even though that's obviously why things didn't work out between us."

"She must know."

"I'm sure she does, particularly after Michael was killed." The story had not only made all the local papers but *The New York Times* as well. "Still, I need to set things straight."

"So to speak." Rawlins rubbed Todd on the back of the neck. "Man, I can't imagine you married."

"Those were my deep denial years. I was just trying so hard to be normal."

"But you're not. Hasn't anyone told you that you're deviant?"

"God, I was so stupid. Not only was I messing up my own life, but a lot of other people's too." Todd groaned, reached into the box of photos. "Look, here's an old picture of me and Janice."

It was a faded color snapshot, the two of them dancing at some frat-house kegger. They both wore bell-bottoms, their hair was long and free, and their faces looked simple, even pure.

"My favorite dyke," said Rawlins with a grin as he studied the picture. "Wow, you two were just a couple of kids."

"That was taken back at Northwestern when we were little boyfriend and girlfriend. Can you believe it?"

"My, what a curious and queer relationship that was. And look at both of you with those jeans—a couple of little hippies, huh?"

"We did have fun."

Rawlins stared into the box and asked, "What else you got there?"

Todd dug around and finally pulled up a large-group photo. "Here's a group photo in front of the frat house I lived in."

Todd looked at the big old brick building with the large terrace out front. All the guys were gathered there, the faces so eager, so young, so full of unbridled energy. Some of the guys were holding beers, others looked to be screaming, and most had long hair, scruffy clothes. Immediately Todd's eyes fell upon not his own face but another. And immediately a wave of shame swelled over him.

*It was cold and dark in the basement, and Todd didn't think the other guy was ever going to get there. He'd been waiting ten minutes already. Shit, he should just take off, get the hell out of here.*

*Several painful minutes later he finally heard footsteps descending into the basement of one of the journalism buildings. Furtive steps. Light and quick.*

*"Hi," said Pat, slipping into the shadows near Todd.*

*"You're late."*

*"I wanted to make sure no one saw me."*

*"No one did, did they?"*

*"No, it's okay."*

*"So how did it go?" asked Todd.*

*The police had questioned Todd that morning, Pat this afternoon, and Todd couldn't hold it in, the question that had been burning in his gut for hours.*

*"You didn't tell them anything, did you? They don't know, do they?"*

*"About us? No. What about you, what did you say?"*

*"Just that I went outside and heard something. Then I looked up and saw him falling. That's all. I didn't even tell them about the cigarette that dropped right in front of me."*

*Pat let out a deep sigh. "Man, I can't believe this."*

*"Pat, you didn't see anyone else out there on the fire escape, did you?"*

*"What the hell are you saying?"*

*The more Todd thought back on that night, the more he couldn't be sure that Greg had been alone outside Pat's window. That in turn made him wonder if someone hadn't come to their defense.*

*"I don't know. I'm not sure what I saw, but there might have been someone else out there." Knowing they could have only one possible ally at the fraternity, Todd said, "You told me you'd done it with someone else at the frat house, that, you know, you had sex with one of the other guys. Who was that?"*

*"What? Are you crazy? He wasn't out there, that's for sure," Pat defensively snapped. "I was right there, right inside. And Greg was by himself. He must have slipped, that's all. I mean, the fire escape was all icy."*

*"Yeah, it was."*

*"You know what they're saying about me at the frat house, don't you?"*

*Todd nodded. The word was that Pat was a homo. The frat brothers who'd been in Kevin's room were sure they'd heard Pat about to have sex with a guy. Definitely a guy because both voices were deep and low.*

*"Don't worry," said Pat, who for a moment seemed as if he was going to cry. "I won't tell them about you."*

*That was all Todd wanted to know. "Thanks."*

*"Just hold me, will you?"*

*"Pat, I don't think that's such a good idea. Something might happen."*

*"You mean like sex?" Pat stared at the cement floor, a dazed look on his face. "That wouldn't be so bad, would it? After all, this has been really hard, the cops and everything."*

*"I know, but . . ."*

*For fear of what it might lead to, he turned away. He didn't want to touch Pat or any other guy ever again. From now on it was going to be girls, only girls.*

*Seeing Todd hesitate, Pat asked, "You didn't tell the police what you told me, did you?"*

*Todd tensed and glared at him over his shoulder. "I told you I wouldn't."*

*"Good, then you don't have anything to worry about."*

*"But Pat—"*

*"Listen, I don't care what they call me back at the fraternity, I won't tell them it was you in my room, and I won't tell them that we've done it, had sex, you know." Suddenly his voice became stern. "I promise no one will ever know just as long as you do one little thing—suck me."*

*"What?"*

*"That's right—you have to give me a blow job."*

*"Now? Down . . . down here?"*

*"You got it. I'm just all stressed out. I need it." Pat opened his coat and started to unzip his jeans. "Trust me, you don't want to piss me off, especially not now."*

*All Todd wanted to do was run as fast and hard as he could. All he wanted was to scream out. To punch Pat in the jaw. But looking into his eyes, seeing the intent, the determination, Todd realized that he really didn't have an option, at least not if he didn't want the world to know.*

"So did you do it with one of the guys there in the fraternity?" asked Rawlins, studying the picture.

"Well . . ."

"I sense some genuine dirt here."

"Trust me, you don't want to know." Todd moaned, took back the photo, and buried it in the box. "Something really horrible happened back then."

"Don't hold out on me, man."

Full of remorse, Todd shook his head. "Maybe I'll tell you someday, but it was something truly awful. You know, the kind of thing that haunts you the rest of your life."

# 3

"Here, this is it," said Rick, seated in the passenger seat of the Pontiac. "Pull over."

He stared up at the house, a one-story bungalow nestled in the low hills on the edge of Santa Fe. She'd always been an early riser, and there were a handful of lights on this morning, which meant she was already up, probably getting ready for work. And probably alone. He knew she hadn't remarried, and if she was anything like her old self, Martha would still be a loner. She'd never had many friends, never much liked going out. Then again, he hadn't see her in nearly a decade.

Rick took his leather-bound Bible from the dashboard, closed his eyes, and bent his head forward in silent prayer. He needed information. Had to have it. And he prayed to God that his trip from Colorado Springs would be fruitful, for a child's life was at stake. He was a tall man with thinning hair and snowy-white sideburns, his long face ashen, and he just wanted what was best for all. What had happened was ridiculous, absurd, and with the help of the Lord Jehovah he was going to put a stop to it. Help me right this terrible wrong, he begged silently. Help me punish those who have transgressed my family.

He turned to the driver, Paul, a quiet, heavyset fellow with a mustache, a prominent member of The Congregation for almost five years now. When all this mess had begun, Paul, who'd worked for years installing security systems, had been more than happy to offer his help. Yes, agreed Paul. They needed to rescue Zeb and Ribka, they needed to bring them back into the fold of love.

"Is it doable?" asked Rick, studying the house.

Paul stared at the telephone wires leading to the low structure and said, "Of course it is."

"Good." Rick added, "And she shouldn't be a problem either. If she's anything like her old self she's easily intimidated."

Paul shrugged and reached for his briefcase, from which he took a small white plastic box and his pistol. "You never know."

"Right. I'll take the carrot," said Rick, slipping his Bible into the large pocket of his raincoat, "and you take the stick."

If things got nasty, then so be it. There was so much more at stake than this reclusive woman. And as the two men walked past a couple of tall cactuses and up the edge of her short drive, Rick checked up and down the street. It was too early, no one was out. No one had seen them thus far. He just prayed to the Lord Jehovah that they'd come to the right place, that he would get that which he so desperately needed.

Rick stopped at the edge of the carport and nodded to Paul, who, with the small white box in one hand and the pistol in the other, trotted along the side of the house and disappeared into the darkness. Rick looked up the street, saw a half dozen houses just like this—earth-colored homes with flat roofs. He peered the other way, saw another half dozen of the same. But no one was about, he realized with pleasure, for after all these years he would still relish the opportunity to punish her.

Less than five minutes later Paul reappeared.

"Everything okay?" asked Rick, his voice low and noting that Paul no longer carried the small device.

"Piece of cake. These one-story houses are never a problem."

Relieved that their first piece of business was taken care of, Rick silently led the way around the front of the garage and right up to the front door. Before Rick reached for the doorbell, though, he motioned to Paul to stand out of sight. The two of them would certainly be intimidating, whereas he alone might be able to get her to talk. He ran one hand back over his hair, straightened his shirt, and recalled how he had once loved her. She was, after all, the first to forgive his earthly sins, the first to embrace him with unqualified love, the first to show him the light of God. Taking a deep breath, he pressed the bell, and a moment later he heard a television silenced inside, some steps. Next the front light burst on.

"Who's there?" she called from behind the locked door.

"It's me, Martha. Rick."

A pause. "Who?"

"Rick, your ex-husband."

"Oh, Christ."

As if she had simply turned away from the door and was returning to her news show, there was nothing. Then a few long seconds later there was a fumbling of a lock, the twisting of a knob, and finally the dark wooden door, secured by a thin brass chain, eased back a few inches. Hesitantly she peered out, this handsome woman with the broad cheekbones, deepset eyes, and the red lipstick smeared across her full lips.

"Good morning. It's been a long time," said Martha, wearing a turquoise sweatshirt and her blond hair pulled back behind her head. "I just wanted to see what you looked like after, what? Ten years?"

"You look wonderful, my dear. Barely a day older."

"Well, it must be my worldly ways. Look at these bright colors I'm wearing," she said, pulling at a sleeve of her sweatshirt. "And lipstick too, not to mention eyeliner. Oh, and I even color my hair now, because after all, there's no sense in letting my gray show. What do you think—isn't my fall from God becoming? Don't I look just positively wicked?''

''Martha, please.''

''Christ, I wish I could say you look great, but you don't. In fact, you look like shit. You're going bald, Rick. And gray too. Look at your sideburns—they're completely white. You know, you look twenty years older than when I last saw you.'' She eyed him up and down. ''Of course the weight you've put on doesn't help. How much? Twenty pounds? Thirty? Wow, you've really let yourself go.''

''Martha, I—''

''Goodby, Rick. Sorry you came such a long way for such a short conversation, but I have to finish getting ready for work,'' she said, pushing the door shut. ''It's been nice glimpsing you. Hope I never see you again.''

He rammed his hand out, caught the door. ''Where is he?''

''Who?''

''Our son.''

''Zeb?''

''Yes, I do believe that's his name. Where is he?''

She shrugged. ''I haven't the faintest.''

''Martha, please, no games.''

''You can sure as hell bet he's not here, if that's what you're wondering.''

Rick felt his spine tighten, and he glanced down at the ground, ran one foot slowly along the concrete. ''You know he's kidnapped our granddaughter, don't you?''

''Really? How very interesting. I didn't know taking a helpless young child out of the clutches of a religious cult was called that. I thought it came under the category of rescue.''

''Martha, it's very serious. We're not only talking about the two most important people in my life, we're talking about the safety and health of a mere infant. I beg you with all my heart, if you love them as much as I do, then tell me what you know." He paused. "After all, he's taken her out of Colorado. We could have the FBI get involved."

"Oh, my, what a good idea." Martha smiled. "In fact, maybe I'll call them right now."

"Martha, I saved Zeb from drugs and Satan before. I can save him again."

"Knock off the bullshit, Rick. You might as well give up—he's never going back there. From what little I do know, I believe he was going to hide her somewhere. Somewhere you'd never find her."

"But he does have her, doesn't he?"

"Frankly, my dear, I have no idea."

"Then who does?"

"Maybe someone in Mexico, maybe one of his friends in California. Or Canada. He mentioned something about going up there." She looked at him wryly, gathered her courage, and said, "But that's a good idea, now that you mention it. I'll call the FBI and then they'll investigate The Congregation. Maybe they'd even shut down your fucking church, burn down your little compound of quackery, and put all you goddamn nuts in jail where you and your fucking god belong. I hope to hell—"

A huge mass began swirling to Rick's right and swept him aside. It was Paul, his fury erupting at the sound of her blasphemous words. And in an instant Paul and all his brute force were hurling against the front door. Under his sheer force the brass chain snapped in two and the door went hurling inward. Martha screamed as the door hit her in the face and threw her back onto the floor. Paul surged inside, zeroing in on her, aiming his pistol right at her forehead.

"Don't, Paul!" shouted Rick, rushing in after him.

"Go ahead, you fuckers!" screamed Martha, lying on her back, her nose bleeding. "Kill me! Isn't that what you wanted to do when I left? Go on, you goddamn Bible-thumping Jesus freaks, kill me! Now's your chance!"

"Shut up, Martha!"

"Eat shit, Rick!" She looked right up at Paul. "Don't listen to that bossy ass! He's always telling everyone what to do, how to act! Why do you think I ran away? I was looking for love and trust, a spiritual place, but that's not what I found. Your god is evil! Evil and awful! Go on, pull the trigger! If you kill me I'll meet the real Maker, and He's certainly not yours!''

Seeing Paul steady his aim, Rick jumped in, grabbed him by the arm. ''No!'' He nudged Paul back, shielded Martha. ''She still hasn't told us where he is.''

''And I won't! I could give a shit what you do to me. I took your beatings before and I'll take them again. I'm not telling you a thing about my son!'' She wiped her nose, grinned. ''You know what, Rick? I was the one who told him to do it, to take her. I told him if he had any brains he'd get the hell out of there. Your church is the biggest garbage pile I've ever seen.''

This bitch, Rick knew, was nothing if not resolute. He'd been married to her for almost eleven years when she'd broken with The Congregation and taken their young son and fled. He'd looked and looked, spending an entire six months driving around the country in search of them. Finally he'd hired an investigator, but that, too, proved fruitless. It was as if the two of them, Martha and the young Zebulun, had simply evaporated. He'd never stopped praying, however, and finally a miracle occurred: One day some three years ago his son Zeb just walked up the dirt road of The Congregation's compound.

But now Zeb was gone once again, his family was breaking apart one more time, and Rick knew it was because of this woman lying before him. This was the second time she'd done this, taken his son from him. He wasn't going to let her succeed.

Rick leaned down to her, lifted his right fist up to his left shoulder, then swung down, striking Martha on the chin as hard as he could, shouting, ''God have mercy on you!''

Martha cried out and wormed her way backward. Blood

now gushed from her bottom lip as well as her nose, and she clutched her face with her right hand.

"You're filled with the devil! You're desperately wicked!" Rick turned to Paul and shouted, "Watch her!"

He left them, stormed through the small living room, found a hall, and charged to the rear of the house. The first door proved to be a bathroom. The next a bedroom. He ducked in, saw her bed, her clothes, her makeup. And he tore through it all, flinging her clothes out of the closet, kicking her shoes aside, pulling her sweaters from a shelf. Then he turned to her small dressing table, and with one great holler he took his arm and wiped her cosmetics and brushes, her mirror and creams from the table and all over the floor. He couldn't believe it all, so many colors, so many vain items. And so many different kinds of fabrics—cottons combined with polyesters, wools stitched with elastic bands. Nothing pure. Nothing simple. Spinning around, he grabbed the salmon-colored sheets—they should be pure white!—from her double bed, ripped them loose, and then tore them in half. Next he dumped over her small bedside table, sending a clock radio, lamp, and a couple of books crashing onto the floor.

His righteous anger hotter than ever, he rushed out of the room, across the hall, into another small bedroom. He froze. There was a single bed on one side, some baseball posters on the wall. Of course this had been where Zeb had grown up. These were his boyhood things. Certainly he'd put together that plastic model of a plane hanging from the ceiling. Of course he'd written his high school reports on that little type-writer. Rick hurled open the closet door, saw books, a few clothes, some boxes, a baseball glove and bat. Dear Jehovah. All those years Zeb had been so close, right here in Santa Fe, and Rick hadn't known it. And then he wondered if this was where his son had first come with the baby. Perhaps. The thought drove him crazy with rage, and Rick grabbed the bat and smashed it all, the model, the typewriter, the radio, the lamp. When all of it lay in pieces on the floor, he stopped, his breathing fast and heavy.

But still he didn't have what he came for.

He dropped the baseball bat and charged out. Returning to the living room, he found Paul still aiming his gun directly at Martha, who was now on her couch, her head leaned back. Seated next to a small basket that contained the remote controls for the television and VCR, she pressed the corner of a small throw blanket to her nose in a futile attempt to stop the bleeding.

Rick pointed a finger right at her and in a voice like thunder from the mountain shouted, "Where is my son?"

In response her right hand shot out, the middle finger pointing high from her fist. "Up your tight ass!"

And Rick yelled, "Lord have mercy on you!"

"Likewise, I'm sure!"

He spun to his left, bursting into the kitchen, a small space, mostly white, a little table at the far end. His eyes darting around, he took it all in: the blender, the sink, the microwave. A steaming pot of coffee. Lastly he hit upon the small stack of mail on the far edge of the counter and next to the phone. He dove into the envelopes, his fingers desperately tearing through the electrical bill, some Christmas cards, a Visa bill, as well as—

Wait, he thought. His hands shaking, he thumbed back through it all, returning to one of the cards. He saw the postmark, noted the address on the back. Why did this look familiar? It was something Zeb himself had once mentioned, wasn't it? And then he ripped open the envelope, which contained a brief note as well as two photographs, one of a woman, another of a house. Of course, Rick realized. Why hadn't he thought to look there?

Out of nowhere a siren started screaming. Dear Lord, realized Rick, it was the burglar alarm.

He stuffed the envelope and its contents into his pocket, and by the time Rick rushed back to the living room Paul was upon Martha, batting a remote control out of her hands. All Martha did, however, was laugh.

"He's not so smart, is he!" she shouted almost gleefully to Rick. "I told him I was going to turn on the TV, but instead I took the remote to my alarm system. I hit the panic button, you assholes—the police are on the way!"

Rick strode directly toward her, raised his fist, and as Paul held her, struck Martha on the chin. A fresh spray of blood flew across the room, and hearing the crack of her jaw and the pitch of her scream, Rick was glad. She deserved all this pain and more. Unfortunately there just wasn't time.

Grabbing Paul by the arm, Rick shouted, "Come on, let's get out of here!"

"But—"

"Move it!"

As they charged out of the house Rick paused at the front door, glanced back, saw the battered Martha slumped on the couch and laughing hysterically. Or was she crying? Her blond hair was matted, her clothing wet with blood. Pathetic. Demonic. How had he ever loved her?

Never mind, he thought, turning and racing through the dull morning light toward the car. There was indeed a God. His God. And He was great, for He'd answered Rick's prayers yet again. Praise the Almighty Lord. It was He who had shown the postmark to Rick. He who was leading Rick to his fallen son. Praise God. Praise God. Praise God.

The two men rushed to the car, climbed in, and sped away. Two blocks later, just like any law-abiding citizens, they pulled to the side of the street and let the police car zoom by.

Watching it disappear in the rearview mirror, Paul asked, "Where to now?"

"Where?" replied Rick smugly as he patted his pocket. "Minneapolis, of course."

# 4

As Todd waited for Janice to return to the table at Florentine's, a trendy Italian restaurant on Hennepin Avenue, he stared out the large plate-glass window at the raging storm. The temperature had indeed jumped upward this afternoon, warming all the way to a balmy twenty above, the first time the temperature had topped zero all week. As also promised, the snow was falling with wintry gusto. Surely, thought Todd, sipping his red wine and watching as a whirlwind of snow came charging up the street, they were going to get more than the promised twelve inches. Maybe even fifteen. Yet while traffic on the whitened Hennepin was down noticeably, this restaurant was packed with yuppies wearing Moon-Boots and puffy, awkward coats and sweaters as thick as doormats. Rather than a quiet, candlelit haven, Florentine's was wild tonight, the pastas steaming, the wine flowing and flowing, people partying as the proverbial ship went down.

This was a great place to spend a deep winter night, but Todd realized he shouldn't have taken Janice here, not tonight. Much too noisy. Much too fun. Janice had wanted to talk, needed to most desperately. This thing about a client dropping a baby in her lap had clearly thrown her for a loop. In all the years since college Todd had never known Janice to get tripped up like this, to muddy the boundaries of her personal life with other people's dirty little problems. Then again, maybe the crisis was all about babies; perhaps it tapped into her despair at not having kids, which she had mentioned with increasing frequency in the last few years.

Well, he supposed, that would make sense, although he couldn't really sympathize. Having been married for a half dozen years, he could have a teenaged son or daughter by now, a concept he found frightening. Way back when, Trish and he had fortunately put off the kid thing. She'd been in med school. He'd been obsessed with his career. They'd been too busy. So when the marriage ended it wasn't very complicated—not even a cat to divide—and Todd continued to be thankful for that.

Todd checked his watch, wondered what was taking Janice so long. They hadn't been here more than ten minutes when she'd slipped off to call home and check on Jeff Barnes, their friend and infamous drag queen, who was also tonight's baby-sitter. Now turning around in his seat, Todd looked toward the rear of the restaurant and couldn't spot Janice, but did notice a few heads turning his way. So at least some people still recognized him, he thought, even though it had been months and months since he'd left Channel 7. And while for the first month or two after Michael's death Todd had dreaded going out in public, it felt okay tonight; now that he was out as gay he was no longer worried about what people were thinking.

Suddenly he saw Janice cutting through the tiny, crowded restaurant, and he admired her beauty all over again. Tall and slender, a narrow face that was dynamic and eye-catching, she was always full of energy. Tonight, though, the smile that usually paved her way through life was noticeably absent.

*"Janice, you look so sad."*
   *"I am."*

*"Don't be."*

Todd held her tight as they danced slowly to a Carly Simon song in the basement of Janice's sorority at Northwestern University. It was late and most of the other kids had drifted away, but Todd and Janice lingered as if they didn't want to let go of this night or perhaps their time in college. In a way, they both saw the future and they both sensed that this was the end of their relationship. Not only did Christmas break begin tomorrow, but after that Janice was taking off for a semester in Europe. Southern France to be exact, where she would study up on her French as well as drink in the sun and the wine. And then Greece, an entire summer of Mediterranean sun and topless beaches.

*"I'm going to miss you,"* said Todd.

*"Yeah, I'm going to miss you too."*

As they moved slowly to the song he ran his hand through her rich, silky hair and kissed the side of her head. Even though he sensed that their relationship had run its course, he knew this winter would be lonely without her. For a variety of reasons they weren't right together, the two of them, yet Todd felt deeply attached to Janice, as if they were mysteriously linked. And holding her now he felt calm for the first time since Greg was killed last week. Still shaken by the incident, Todd clutched Janice more tightly, tried to block out the image of Greg dangling from the fire escape. Just exactly who and what had he seen up there?

Janice kissed him on the neck and said, *"Debbie left today."*

Todd knew what that meant. Debbie was Janice's roommate. Which in turn meant that Janice had the room to herself for the night.

*"Would you like to come up?"* she asked with a sly look in her eye. *"We can sneak up the back stairs."*

He pulled back and looked into her eyes, took a deep, nervous breath, and replied, *"Sure."*

And as they turned, his arm around her shoulders, hers

*around his waist, Todd wondered exactly what she had in mind. They'd kissed a lot, they'd hugged and caressed and come close to doing it, but had somehow always fallen away from the actual act of intercourse. So would this final night together be it, the climax, per se, of their time together?*

As she sat down Todd asked, "How's the little tyke?"

"Don't call her that."

"Call her what?"

"Dyke."

"I didn't. I said 'tyke.' With a *T*."

"Oh."

"So how is she?"

"Fine." She sat down, took a sip of wine. "I'm not so good at this motherhood stuff, after all. I just worry all the time. You know, is Ribka eating enough, is her diaper wet, is she warm . . ."

"Don't worry, Jeff's not going to let anything happen to her."

"Yeah, well, that old queen better be watching her instead of playing around with my cosmetics. At least he's too fat to fit into any of my dresses, so he won't be messing with any of that stuff."

"Janice," began Todd, surprised to hear her talking so disparagingly, "what the hell's with you?"

"What do you mean?"

"You've just been so uptight ever since this baby's arrived. Listen, you've taken five days off to be home with someone else's kid. Don't you think it's time you do a reality check and get back to work? You must have tons to do."

"Tons and tons and tons."

"So what are you waiting for?"

"Todd, it's just not that simple."

He watched as she turned away, blotted her eyes, and asked, "Janice, what's this all about?"

She shrugged. "I've done some stupid things in my life."

"Funny, I was just saying something like that this morn-ing."

"No, I mean really stupid."

"Trust me, I know what you mean."

"God, I need to talk." She smiled sadly at him. "I just can't handle this. It's too much. Too big."

He reached across the table, took her hand in his. "Hey, doll, you're one of the most together people I've ever met."

"Thanks, but . . . but . . ." Janice started to say some-thing, stopped, then asked, "I wish I had kids, don't you?"

"You know, I really hate that question. It's just so loaded with technicalities."

"I mean, we should have had kids, the two of us together."

"My, there's a complicated thought for you." He glanced out the window. "Don't take it personally, Janice, but those two or three months we dated in college were some of the most awkward times of my life."

"Gee, thanks, butch."

"If I remember, you were the one who dumped me, went to Europe for a semester, and came back the following fall a so-called avowed lesbian."

"Oh, please, don't remind me." Her words hesitant, she added, "Oh, by the way—and no offense meant—there were a couple of other guys in there. After you, I mean. I guess I never told you that."

"No, actually you didn't."

He glanced again out the window, losing himself in thought, for whatever Janice had or hadn't done with whom or when, she'd certainly come to terms with her sexuality years earlier than he. Decades, actually. Todd, on the other hand, had done everything possible to avoid the truth and in turn complicate his life. As a matter of fact he was wishing he'd never gone into such a high-profile career as television. Ap-pearance. Image. What any and everyone thought. He now saw how television had simply perpetuated his deep-seated fears. Each time he stood before the camera some little part of him was wondering what people would really think of him if they knew the truth.

When he turned back he saw that Janice was clutching her white dinner napkin to her eyes and crying.

"Janice," Todd said softly as he squeezed her hand, "what's the matter?"

"Sorry, I'm having a meltdown."

"I kind of guessed that."

"Can we go?"

"No," he chided gently, "not until you tell me what this is all about."

"I will." She sniffled, eyed the noisy restaurant. "But I don't want to talk about it here."

"Okay, I'll get the waiter to wrap our order to go."

She nodded, blew her nose.

Todd stared at her and said, "But you promise me you're going to tell me everything?"

"Promise." She wiped her eyes. "Oh, Todd, there's something I've never told you, something that's been haunting me for years and years, and now I have a very real problem."

# 5

In his hotel room not far from the Minneapolis/St. Paul airport, Rick dropped himself onto the edge of his bed and stared at the phone. This was exhausting, all this gallivanting around the country, but for the first time he felt hope. Absolutely. The Lord was leading him to little Ribka, and soon he'd have his family back together and they could return to The Congregation, that safe and isolated island in this sea of madness. Oh, thought Rick, shaking his head, but this was a Godless nation, one full of worldly lies and rejected knowledge, idolaters and fornicators, and the sooner Zeb, Ribka, and he were back within the confines of the one true church, the better. There was safety there. True wisdom. And love.

Rick knew too well what it was like out here in this wicked world. Lost. That was what he'd been as a young man until some of his college friends and others from the Midwest invited him to join The Congregation. He'd been lost and on the verge of being swallowed up, just as was now happening to poor Zeb. So many years ago Rick had had a slovenly, Laodicean attitude, had wanted to give his life entirely to sin. But then, he thought remembering those terrible times, he'd turned his life around. He might have been born in sin, but long ago he had recaptured the true values and become a soldier in God's army, a believer who would always stand firmly on the promises. And if he could make right what was so wrong way back then, Zeb could well do the same now.

At least, thought Rick as he picked up the phone and dialed, he had some good news to report. Ribka, he was confident, would be all right. They were sure to find her. The blanket she'd been wrapped in, made from cotton grown right at The Congregation's compound and woven by the women there, would shield her from evil. After all, the blanket had been anointed by all of The Elders.

The phone rang, and a voice on the other end answered, saying, "Praise Jehovah."

"Yes, praise Him." Addressing God's Apostle and the leader of The Congregation, Rick said, "Good afternoon, Henry, it's me."

"Where are you? Minneapolis?"

"Yes, we arrived this afternoon."

They'd flown out of Albuquerque, having paid over a thousand dollars for their full-fare, one-way tickets. But money was the least of Rick's worries, for he'd been given more than enough from the coffers of The Congregation. All that matters, Henry had said, is Ribka. She has to be found, he had proclaimed, before Satan wraps his clever hands around her as well. Bring her back, that's all that matters.

"Paul and I are here," continued Rick, speaking into the receiver, "and I'm fairly confident the baby is too."

"Praise Jehovah!" The deep voice on the other end of the long-distance call turned away from the receiver and bellowed, "Honey! Honey, praise Jehovah, they've found your little baby girl!"

"No, wait, not so fast," Rick said loudly. "Henry? Henry, listen to me. Henry, can you hear me?"

"Heavens, yes. How is she? How is my little—"

"I said I'm pretty sure the baby's here. I'm almost positive

I know where she is. But we don't have her actually with us yet.''

"Wh-what?''

"Trust me, with God's vision we'll have her soon, possibly within a few hours. In fact, Paul's already scoping things out. Just be patient.''

"But . . .''

"Henry, as you say, Satan is wily.''

"Indeed he is.''

"So I must be cautious,'' continued Rick. "Don't worry, you and I have an understanding.''

"Of course.''

Fortunately, Rick went on to explain, they'd received yet another blessing, for they'd made it here just ahead of the storm that was now going full force. The snow was falling out of the heavens to no end. All manly movement had been severely hampered. And if they'd hesitated, even caught the next flight, Rick was sure they wouldn't have made it in, for if the airport wasn't already shut down, it would be at any minute.

Seated on the bed of his hotel room, Rick said, "Anyway, we drove by the house this afternoon and there was a diaper truck out front.''

"What?'' questioned the voice from Colorado. "A truck?''

"They were delivering diapers.''

"You . . . you think my little granddaughter's there because you saw a diaper truck?''

"That's right, Henry, but I—''

"Dear Lord help me, I don't follow you.''

"I know she's in there. There's more to it than that, but let me assure you that you have nothing to worry about.''

"Well . . . well, I hope so. My Suzanne here is a total wreck. An absolute wreck. She's hardly slept ever since her baby vanished.''

"I know, I understand, I feel the same way. After all, Henry, Ribka's my granddaughter as well.''

"True, but that worldly boy who started all this is your son, not mine," stated Henry, his voice thick with anger. "So where is that little bastard? He there too?"

"I doubt it," replied Rick, rising and starting to pace back and forth. "He could be nearby, but I'm fairly sure he's not at the house."

"I want him back here too."

"I know, Henry."

"We all do. The Elders are going to do something, perhaps even disfellowship him according to the laws of The Congregation."

"I am one of The Elders, you realize, and I couldn't agree more, something has to be done. He has to be marked. Our tribe must always be united and must always stand firm on its principles."

"Of course, but this is all our people are talking about down at the bakery," Henry said, referring to the cooperative business The Congregation ran to sustain itself. "There's ghastly gossip going on, gossip that's affecting everyone's work. Some are even saying that Zeb has never been more than a fringer, an unconverted sinner who has never believed in our ways."

"Tell them not to worry," insisted Rick. "Zeb's my son. He has shamed God the Father and God the Son, and of course you, Henry, God's Apostle. Zeb has given over for a time to Satan, and I'll take pride in punishing the boy strictly according to The Elders' decision."

"So be it."

Rick just hoped they'd be able to get Zeb back as well. Once they had little Ribka, though, they'd probably be able to lure him. His son was soft, Rick knew. He wouldn't be able to withstand not seeing his daughter. He'd certainly be consumed with worry, meaning, of course, he wouldn't come back merely to rejoin The Congregation and probably not to rejoin his young wife, Suzanne, either. No, Rick knew his son would return to the fold for one reason and one alone: his baby girl.

"I'm assuming Zeb hasn't called?" inquired Rick.

"You'd think he'd call Suzanne, his own wife. You'd think he'd let her know that her baby was okay, but, no, he hasn't."

"He will."

"Well, we've been waiting. And we have all the contraptions set up, everything you gave us."

"Excellent. What number am I calling you from?"

"Ah . . ." And then Henry read the caller identification number: "612–377–1267."

"Very good. And if he does call don't forget to tape record everything he says."

"I'm not an idiot," replied Henry curtly.

"Of course not, sir."

Rick went over to the window and held back the stiff curtain. It was already dark, the snow falling thicker than ever. Off to the right he saw the clogged freeway and a band of cars creeping along.

"With God's mercy this will all be over in a few hours," continued Rick. "I'll call you as soon as I have any news."

"And it better be good news, that's all I have to say."

In his one-story house a few miles south of Colorado Springs, Henry slammed down the phone and said, "He's as big an ass as his kid."

Shaking his head, he sauntered over to the large picture window that looked out over his precious domain. Oh, sure, they'd had any number of crises over the years at The Congregation, but this ranked up there with the worst of them and none had ever touched Henry so personally. His very own little granddaughter kidnapped by her own father, that punk of a son-in-law! Henry wanted to explode with rage. He'd worked so hard at founding The Congregation and building this compound. When he'd come out here from Illinois over twenty years ago, this had been a pathetic ranch with a tumbledown house and a couple of outbuildings. Now down the slight hill stood the four family dormitories, the Gathering

House where all the meals were taken in common, the Prayer Hall, and of course the long, low bakery where everyone worked producing the whole-grain, yeast-free sourdough bread that had become so popular in town and supported the entire Congregation.

And now that little shit of a son-in-law wanted to ruin it all!

He'd always known that Zeb had a bad attitude, that he'd been an unbeliever. He hadn't realized, though, how dangerous he really was. Nor had he ever imagined that he could cause such tribulation.

"Oh, Suzanne," he said, his back to his daughter, " 'The heart is deceitful above all things, and desperately wicked: who can know it?' Jeremiah chapter seventeen, verse nine."

"Daddy . . ." moaned the young blond woman huddled on the couch, her eyes red with tears. "When's my baby coming home?"

"Soon, precious. Real soon."

As God's Apostle on earth and the leader of The Congregation, he and his daughter lived in the only private house on the compound, this small white rambler, and Henry now crossed the living room, his fat, round face red with fury. Dropping himself on the sofa next to his daughter, he took her in his arms. Beautiful Suzanne. She was so gorgeous with her thick, curly hair, her perfect rosy complexion, those blue eyes and white teeth. How in the world could anyone do something like this to his wonderful baby doll?

Henry said, "I can't wait to personally beat the crap out of that juvenile delinquent husband of yours. I could kill him. I really could, and maybe I will, darling. Maybe I will. How dare he kidnap your baby!"

"I want my little girl!"

"I know, Suzanne, I know, this is just so ghastly."

As his daughter burst into another round of tears, Henry wrapped his big arms around her and pulled her deep into his chest. This poor child. Here she'd lost her own mother when she wasn't even ten, and now she'd had her young baby ripped away in the middle of the night.

"Dear Lord, I just knew you shouldn't have married that boy. I knew he was trouble, I surely did," he muttered. "Didn't I tell you that? Didn't I tell you he was going to be nothing but trouble?"

"Y-y-yes, Daddy."

"That's right, I did. And are you going to listen to me from now on?"

"Yes."

"And do just what I say?"

"Yes."

"Yes, what?"

"Yes, sir."

"That's my good girl."

He ran his hand through her hair, bent over, and kissed her on the forehead. He closed his eyes, felt sinful, for all he secretly wanted right now—as he always did in times of stress—was a cigarette, a strong one, nothing filtered, to take a long, deep drag on. But he forced the wicked desire from his mind, for he'd long ago given up such an unclean vice, and instead he clung to his daughter.

"Don't worry, precious. I'm gonna make everything all right. Just you wait. Your little baby's coming back before you know it. And when they drag that animal of a boy back here, he's gettin' a whipping he'll never forget. Not to worry, precious. Daddy's gonna take care of everything. Everything's gonna be all right."

# 6

As he came around the corner he accelerated too quickly, the rear of his sedan fishtailed out, and his pistol slid across the front seat. He quickly steered in the opposite direction, the car whipped to the other side, and his gun slid back against his hip. He then braked on the snowy street and came to a slick, slow stop. After taking a long, deep breath, he started over.

Paul wasn't used to such a consummate winter. And he wasn't used to driving on such slippery streets. A large, thick-chested man with dark hair and a bushy mustache, he carefully pressed down on the gas, testing the slickness of the road as if he were testing thin ice. As his car gained momentum he proceeded down the curving, sloping streets of Tangletown, the well-to-do neighborhood that straddled the hills along Minnehaha Creek in south Minneapolis. When he came to the bottom of a slope, he did just as he was told: pumped and pumped the brake. It worked too. Rather than sliding through the intersection, he glided to a complete halt at the stop sign, whereupon he let out a deep sigh. Thank God for miracles, large and small.

Rick and he had been by the house earlier this afternoon, so

Paul knew he was close. They'd driven by slowly, seen that delivery truck, which they both assumed could mean only one thing. And now that it was dark Paul had come back to check out the phone lines on this house. But the roads had gotten so bad that the trip, which had taken only twenty minutes this afternoon, was tonight taking almost an hour. So much snow. It was ridiculous, none of it melting but piling up, he thought, turning the windshield wipers up to high speed. On the other hand, the heavy snow might prove fortuitous, for his footprints around the house would quickly disappear.

In the glow of a streetlight he nudged aside the black pistol and lifted a pad on which Rick had scribbled the directions. Yes, a left here. Next a right across the creek itself, and then another left. From there it was only about a block. Easy, Paul told himself. All he had to do was manage to stay out of the snowbanks lining the road. Or the frozen creek, for that matter.

Paul turned the last corner and felt his car glide as freely as a hockey puck. His heart began to surge, but then the car sank into some deep snow and the treads of the tires bit down. Driving cautiously on, he wondered how the next hour would play out. At worst he'd only be able to scope things tonight. At best it would be simple, the phone lines would be right there, and he'd be able to install the device. He'd be done and gone within minutes.

His was the only car passing down the parkway that ran alongside Minnehaha Creek, and he drove slowly, his eyes as much on the road as on the large houses to the right. And there it was, covered in white, the red tile roof buried beneath snow and deep drifts crawling up the light stucco walls. The four arching windows that lined the front of the house had been lifeless this afternoon but were now all ablaze. A party, a group of neighbors gathered to while away the storm? As he drove past, however, he could see no one lingering in the windows. Only a single car on the street. So maybe just one guest.

At the first corner Paul turned right, found a spot neglected by the streetlight, and parked. He reached for his pistol, which he dropped into the large pocket of his coat, then from the backseat he took the small white device, identical to the one he'd installed on the house in Santa Fe. Next he removed his winter gloves, slipping on in their place a pair of skintight leather ones.

As Paul started down the alley, he was amazed by the snow falling on his head and shoulders. Sure it snowed back home, sometimes as heavily as this, but this was different, a winter that was absolute in its chill and purpose. He had a sense that this snow wasn't going to melt until March at the earliest.

A garage light suddenly flashed on, and he lifted a gloved hand as much to conceal his face as to shield his eyes from the glare. But no one appeared and there wasn't even a hint of movement. And after he passed, the light snapped off. Only a motion detector.

Her house was the third one down, the garage door painted a rust red to match the Spanish tiled roof. And as he neared, he scanned the ground. In the faint winter night light he searched for signs of tire tracks, could see none, and then behind the garage itself bent over and brushed aside some of the new snow. No indication that she'd gone out anytime recently. Edging up alongside the small structure, he peered into a small frost-covered window, saw a red car. Very good. So she was here.

The small plastic device in hand, he opened a gate and scanned the backyard, which lay under a mat of fresh, downy snow, not a footprint to be seen. His eyes trained on the back of the house, he pressed forward. He eyed the kitchen window and then, to the left, the side door. Next to that the small blue sign of an alarm company struggled to poke from the layer of snow. He doubted very much, however, that her alarm system would be on; it was too early, she had company. Checking the spotlight attached to the back of the house, he was relieved to see that, unlike the other one down the alley, it wouldn't be triggered by his movements.

A muted light flashed, and Paul flinched. Dear God, had someone snapped his picture? No, he realized, it was the flat, dark sky above crackling with bizarre brilliance. He stared up, saw nothing more, but then heard a deep, threatening roar. Snow thunder. And even as he recognized the strange phenomenon, the snow began to fall in a heavy squall, the flakes huge and thick. He trudged quickly across the yard, paused at the edge of the house, and peered up at the threatening sky. The wintry thunder had been an omen, a bad one.

He just had to be businesslike about this, he thought, his eyes searching the power lines until he fixed on the telephone cable. Right. It was a big thick line coming from the alley, drooping slightly until it reached the house at this rear corner. As his good luck would have it, the lines didn't enter the dwelling up at the attic level, but were instead attached to the stucco exterior and ran all the way down to the basement level, where they ended in a gray plastic box. Perfect. He'd be able to accomplish his goal.

It didn't take him long. Back in Chicago he'd installed hundreds if not thousands of burglar alarms for both homes and businesses. Which of course was why he was now in charge of security at The Congregation. So with expert hands, Paul snipped a couple of wires and within moments had the small white box attached to the wires. This would make things all the easier.

He was about to retreat to his car when he heard something else. A rumble, but this one rhythmic. Music. The stereo inside was blaring the songs of the unconverted. So was it a party after all? He checked the house next door, saw that a hedge of evergreens would keep his presence concealed, and slipped along the side of the house. He ducked beneath one window, spied through the next, and saw a gleaming wooden table. There was no one in the dining room, though, and he moved forward, drawn by the music. He remembered that tune, didn't he, from his days prior to his conversion? Sure. Diana Ross.

Approaching the next window, Paul hesitated. Light was flooding out. He peered in, saw no one. There was only one car on the street, but perhaps she'd invited a handful of neighbors over and they'd arrived on foot and were now dancing away the storm. If that was the case, though, where were they? He leaned forward, could see no one.

A figure whirled into view.

Paul quickly pulled back, pressed himself against the cold stucco wall. He waited a moment, leaned forward again. There was a man, fairly tall, rather overweight. Balding. And twirling. Perplexed, Paul bent low and moved to the other side of the window. Suddenly the man inside froze, planting his feet to the floor, and holding out the palm of his hand as Ross sang "Stop in the Name of Love." But the man was singing too. Or maybe he wasn't. His mouth was moving perfectly, his body now swaying as if he himself were performing the song. Was this all pretend? Was this grown man who was now wiggling his hips and holding out his hand so effeminately merely pretending to be a star?

It didn't make any sense. Trying to ascertain the situation, Paul moved further. The man appeared to be singing to someone. Surely it had to be the woman who lived here. But no, as the heavy snow fell upon Paul's head and shoulders, he pressed himself against the edge of the window. And it was then that he saw the man's audience: a tiny baby lying on the floor.

Of course it was Ribka, for he most definitely recognized the white cotton knit blanket in which she was wrapped. Sure, it was one of the blankets made at The Congregation for all the children born there. So what was Paul to do, stand out here in the freezing cold and watch this sodomite perform some Satanic dance in front of the child?

Just as he knew there was no time to seek Rick's approval, Paul knew that it was his Godly duty to get this ailing child back to The Congregation as soon as possible so she could be healed.

# 7

"Oh my God, Janice, did you see that?" asked Todd, leaning over the steering wheel of his Grand Cherokee and staring up at the dark sky in amazement. "That was it again—lightning."

Before she could reply, an earthquake-like rumble shook the air, the ground, the car. The stoplight had turned green, but neither Todd nor the car next to him moved. Passengers in both cars, like the patrons of the small pizzeria across the street who were pressed against the glass, stared up at the heavens.

"That was so cool," he said.

Bundled tightly in her wool coat, Janice blotted her eyes with the back of her gloved hands. "Thunder in winter—it's not right. Particularly January. Maybe in November or March, you know, at the beginning or end of winter, but not now. Not in January. It's gotten warmer, but it's still too cold for something like that."

"Maybe it's going to do it a third time," said Todd, still studying the sky.

"Come on, let's go. It scares me."

"But it's so great."

"Todd, I want to get home," she urged in a desperate voice that he knew only too well.

*"Todd, I'm going home tomorrow and then off to Europe,"*
*she said, locking the door of her room. "Who knows when*
*we'll see each other again. If ever."*

*"But aren't you worried?" he asked almost desperately. "I*
*mean, isn't it a bit dangerous?"*

*"No, it's all part of a cycle, and it's okay. For a few days*
*now I can't get pregnant. I'm not fertile."*

*He didn't quite understand it, this timing stuff. All he knew*
*was that on the way up here she'd said she wanted to do it, to*
*make love. It was her farewell present to him, to them. This*
*was what he wanted, wasn't it? Sure, he'd said, nodding, feel-*
*ing that as a guy he couldn't really respond otherwise and at*
*the same time trying desperately not to let her see his fear.*

*Now he watched slender Janice as she lit a candle and*
*turned off the overhead light. Next she thumbed through some*
*records, found a Carly Simon one, and put on the very same*
*song that they'd danced to downstairs. Then she was next to*
*him, kissing the side of his neck, rubbing his thigh. He reached*
*out, his movements awkward, stilted. Oh, shit. Would he be*
*able to do it? What if he couldn't even get hard?*

*"Todd, what is it? What's the matter?"*

*"I'm . . . I'm just nervous, that's all." Unable to stop*
*himself, he started shaking.*

*Ever gentle, Janice ran one hand down his back and asked,*
*"Are you cold or is it something else?"*

*If only he could tell her. This past week since Greg had died*
*had just been so horrible. He clenched his eyelids shut, felt his*
*eyes swell up. Oh, Jesus, was he going to start crying right*
*here, right now? No, don't. You . . . you can't. He just*
*wanted to tell her. Tell her everything that had happened that*
*night. How he'd been about—could she forgive him?—to do it*

*again with Pat. How he'd run downstairs and out back. How he'd looked up and . . .*

*"Todd?" asked Janice softly.*

*He had to say something, but all he could manage was a different truth, albeit a very revealing one, and with a nervous laugh he said, "I . . . I haven't done it before. I'm . . . I'm a virgin."*

*"Oh." She lifted his hand and kissed it. "You know, there's a lot going on in that thick skull of yours."*

*"No kidding." He tried to manage a grin. "What about you? Have you done it?"*

*"Actually I have," she said with a slight nod. "But you know what, I think we're an awful lot alike."*

*"What?"*

*"Nothing," she said as she reached for the top button of her blouse. "Listen, I don't care if we don't do it. Let's just get naked and get under the blankets. It's so cold outside."*

*And before Todd knew it, they had in fact stripped away their clothing and were lying naked in her bed, their warm bodies pressed close to each other. He was amazed at how smooth she felt, so soft and pure. He took it all in, the gentle sculpt of her back, her long thin arms.*

*"You're a nice guy, Todd," she volunteered.*

*Unable to say anything, he squeezed her tightly, pressing his firm chest against her soft one. If he was so nice why had he had sex with another guy and why hadn't he told the police just what he might or might not have seen that night Greg had died?*

He knew that tone, feared it, and he pressed on the gas. Glancing at her, he saw that her eyes were still misty with tears. What the hell was all this about? Janice had never been one to let something smolder.

"Come on, out with it," said Todd, wearing a puffy beige down jacket. "I haven't seen you this upset in years, if ever."

"Like I said, I'll tell you when we get home."

"But it's about the baby?"

She hesitated. "Yes, Todd, it's about the baby."

The thunder seemed to have ripped open the sky and the snow was now falling so thickly that he couldn't see even a half block ahead. There weren't that many cars out, mainly four-wheel-drive vehicles like Todd's, and everyone slowed to a near crawl. It still took a major storm to shut things down—last year a twelve-inch snowfall had only slowed things for a morning—and Todd wondered if this would be it, the storm of the year. He guessed that almost ten inches had fallen so far, so this would have to keep up all night to really affect things.

"Oh, shit," moaned Janice. "It's going to take forever to get home."

"We'll get there."

"We should never have gone out."

"Janice, you haven't been away from that baby in five days."

"Oh, I hope Jeff knows how to handle her."

"Of course he does. That old queen's great with kids. He's the perfect grandmother. I'll bet you dollars to doughnuts that he's cooing some lullaby in her ear even as we speak."

"I doubt it. He mentioned he had to rehearse a new piece for the drag show at the Gay Times," she said, referring to the huge bar downtown where Jeff performed. "He's probably got my stereo cranked so loud that Ribka can't even get to sleep."

"Dear God, Janice, just chill, would you? We'll get there." He eyed her. "You don't have a new lover, do you?"

"What?"

"You know, a girlfriend? Like a girlfriend with a baby that she happened to dump on you for a while?"

"Hardly."

"So what is this, a mid-life crisis?"

"Who knows." She scraped away some of the ice on the side window and stared out. "I mean, all of a sudden every-thing's coming into focus. For the first time I'm seeing everything I did wrong. And now I'm wondering what I've ever done right.''

"Yup, that's it—a full-blown mid-life crisis." Todd laughed. "Which means I'm going to have some company.''

When Michael died, Todd had realized for the first time that his own career ambitions weren't so much based on working toward a goal as they were on proving something. That's what had driven him in his television work—trying to show himself that everyone liked him even though he was gay.

He felt something on his thigh, looked down, saw Janice's gloved hand resting there. Placing his right hand on top of hers, he squeezed.

He said, "It's going to be okay.''

But for the immediate future at least, he was speaking too quickly. Just as he was approaching the intersection of Hennepin and West 28th Street, a small car appeared out of nowhere and ran the stoplight.

"Todd!'' screamed Janice.

"Oh, shit!''

Clutching the steering wheel, he furiously pumped the brakes. The Cherokee fishtailed on the slick road, and Todd steered to the left and then the right to compensate. But it was to little avail, and Todd watched his Cherokee close in on the other car as if in slow motion. It flashed through his mind: Mazda. He was going to smash directly into the driver's door of that little two-door Mazda. Reflexively Todd wrenched the steering wheel to the right.

"Hang on!'' he shouted to Janice.

His large vehicle swerved to the side, somehow missing the Mazda but in turn steering directly toward a parked car. Todd oversteered a second time, and then he found himself shooting onto the sidewalk and into a large snowbank, which his Cherokee hit with a deep, forceful thud.

# 8

Zeb had been waiting for something like this, a storm that would change everyone's pattern. Work here at the hospital had been too hectic to accomplish what he needed to, but all afternoon things had been slowing down, the talk about nothing other than the snow, which was getting deeper, deeper, deeper. There were fewer visitors as well, fewer deliveries, even fewer doctors and nurses. He'd guessed that would happen, but hadn't expected the dramatically lower number of patients being admitted today. He just hadn't thought about it, never realizing how a major storm could prevent so many people from becoming ill enough to go to the hospital. Then again, he was sure there'd be a compensating surge tomorrow or the next day when everyone was mobile again. And his boss would probably have him cleaning the main entrances all day long.

So if he was actually going to steal any of it, tonight was his best chance. Or so he hoped.

He'd never had to fend for himself like this, certainly not at The Congregation nor at his mother's, so he'd never known how complicated all this reality stuff could be. Those stupid zombies at The Congregation had taken care of everything—work, food, religious education, even clothing and that dumb-ass music. Before that he'd lived with his mom until he was eighteen, and she'd always seen to it that he ate well, had clean clothes, and studied. Yeah, that was her. Always grumbling at him, always pushing the books. Now he saw how dumb he'd been to leave her to join his father at The Congregation. Really dumb. For starters, if he were still living with his mom he wouldn't be in this mess. He'd probably just be going to college and dating. He'd just be normal.

Instead, a little over three years ago he'd come home from school and asked that one stupid question that had changed his entire life.

"Hey, Mom," he'd called from his room where he sat working on a biology report, "what blood type are you?"

"Uh . . ." she'd pondered from the kitchen, having no idea of the ramifications. "O. Yeah, that's what it is, O."

So that was what he'd written. He recorded his blood type, his mother's, and said his father's was unknown. And thought that was the end of it. But, no, two days later the biology teacher pulled out his report and told him in front of the entire class that Zeb and his mother couldn't have such radically different blood types and still be genetically related.

One of the kids next to him elbowed Zeb and asked, "Hey, moron, maybe you're an adopted extraterrestrial creature. Maybe we should call you Marty the Martian."

So when he'd come from school Zeb had tossed his backpack on the kitchen floor and said, "Gee, Mom, thanks for making me look like a complete idiot in front of the entire class. Either you don't know your own blood type or . . . or, I don't know, I'm adopted or something."

Which was how that delicate subject was finally and crudely opened. She just started crying, and Zeb stared at his mother wondering what in the hell was going on.

"I've just been so afraid of losing you," she sobbed over and over again. "I love you so much."

Of course she couldn't hold back the truth. Not any longer. Yes, she loved him more than anything in the entire world, yes, she'd give her own life for his, but, no, she hadn't given him life. And Zeb had listened to the woman he'd always thought to be his real mother explain that she had a congenital problem in her uterus and had had a hysterectomy when she was a teenager.

Zeb was too stunned to be angry, too shocked to cry, and he'd asked, "Does . . . does that mean Dad's not my real father either?"

Martha, who had refused to speak of Zeb's father ever since they'd fled The Congregation seven years earlier, tearfully disappeared into her bedroom.

Emerging several minutes later, she handed Zeb a good-size file, mumbling, "It's all in here."

Not sure how much he really wanted to know, Zeb hesitantly accepted the papers. Then it was his turn to disappear, and he went into his bedroom, where he stayed up most of the night. The following morning he and a friend skipped school and went in search of some dope, only the guy they bought the joints from wasn't some down-and-out dealer but an undercover cop. When the police made it clear that Zeb and his pal were going to be made an example of, Zeb declared them all fucking idiots. His mother. His teachers. The cops. And just as soon as he was released to his mother—his "fake" mother, he called her—he ran away in search of his real parents.

He pushed the wide dust mop up one side of the long corridor, then down the other. Up one side, down the other. Now that he was a father himself, now that he had fled The Congregation just like his own mother had, he saw how complicated it really was, this parenting stuff. He understood, too, just how far a parent would go, what you'd do for your own kid.

After the first two or three passes the floor was perfectly clean, yet still he continued, hoping no one would notice. When he reached the far end he paused and stood there, his broad, lean figure clothed in the blue janitorial uniform, his short dark hair covered by a hair cap. He glanced to his left, saw a nurse coming toward him, which in turn spurred him down the hall one more time. Within a few steps he passed a nurses' station, which was surprisingly empty—short of staff, were they?—and then a door that was marked with the initials M.S. What lay in the room beyond was the primary reason he'd taken the job at Edina Hospital here in one of Minneapolis's suburbs. Now if only he could get in.

As he passed yet again down the corridor he wondered when he'd be missed, when one of his bosses would wonder where he was. At best he had another fifteen minutes. Earlier he'd tried with no luck to locate a key. He knew they'd be closely guarded, but he hoped he might get his hands on one. After all, they'd given him a couple of passkeys already, and certainly that room needed to be cleaned at some point. But by whom? Perhaps he'd have to work here for a month or two before they trusted him. On the other hand, he didn't have that much time. The drugs he'd already stolen had been purely by chance, a few things he'd noticed on a passing cart and then swiped, but the drugs behind that locked door, well, they were the good ones, as expensive as hell.

"Nice and quiet in here tonight, isn't it?" said a pleasant voice.

Zeb looked up, saw a nurse with short red hair and a round face moving quickly toward him, and replied, "Yeah, it's kind of dead."

"Say now, you can't use a four-letter word like that in a hospital." She laughed, her teeth flashing brightly. "You must be new here. I haven't seen you before."

"I just started this week."

"Welcome aboard. My name's Brenda."

"I'm Zeb."

"Well, Zeb, there's gotta be a couple of miles of corridor in this joint, so I'm sure they're keeping you busy."

"Yeah."

Trying to look just that, he kept moving on, but stopped

suddenly when he saw her taking out her keys. Shit, he thought. This was his chance. She was unlocking that room. How the hell was he going to do this?

Suddenly the words were spilling too eagerly out of his mouth, as he said, "Hey, I'm supposed to clean in there. In . . . in that room."

She stopped at the door, eyed him. "Do you have a key? All the meds are in here, you know. No one gets in here without authorization and a key."

Zeb lifted out the two keys he'd been given. "I thought one of these was supposed to work."

"No offense," said Brenda, "but I doubt it. If you're new I don't think they'd just give you a key for this room."

"Oh, well . . . well, maybe I got the rooms mixed up."

"Yeah, probably," she said, unlocking the door and swinging it open. "But come on, you can take a couple of swipes in here with the mop. God knows the last time it was cleaned, probably months ago."

"Great. Thanks."

Pushing his large dust mop, Zeb swung around, going directly for the doorway and following both his good luck and her into the chamber. It was a small room, maybe eight by six, lined on either side with towering shelves of bottles and small packages, medicine all of it. While Zeb knew he'd hit the proverbial gold mine, he scanned the entire situation and realized immediately that getting in here was only the first battle. The stuff, he saw, was so valuable that every pill, every drop of medication, was stored in a locked case, the front of each a metal grille. Zeb pushed the broom to the end of the chamber, glanced side to side. Shit. What now? Behind him Brenda was opening one of the cases, reaching in, taking out a small bottle. And then, to his horror, he realized that she realized he was looking at her.

She grinned and said, "One of my patients is having a coughing fit. This codeine stuff ought to calm him down."

"Oh, right . . . right."

He plowed the dust mop forward, while out of the corner of his eye he watched as she shut and locked the cabinet door. He bent forward, pretended to pick at something on the floor. He moved forward a bit, used the dust mop to scrub at some imaginary spot. Glancing up, he saw Brenda standing by the door and staring at him.

"You're right," said Zeb, "this place hasn't been cleaned in months. It's filthy. I mean, look at all the dust."

She said nothing, merely grinned, her round face animated, her red hair thick and bouncy.

"You'd better get that medicine to your patient. Don't let me slow you down," he continued. "I'll just pull the door shut behind me."

"That's okay. I'll wait. You need a key to lock the door."

"Well," said Zeb, thinking as fast as he could, "just leave me your key. I'll lock up and bring it to you when I'm done."

"What are you trying to do, silly, get me fired?" She stared at him with a soft smile. "I don't mind waiting."

"But . . ."

"Say, do you want to get a cup of coffee?"

Oh, shit, thought Zeb. He hadn't stopped to think that this thirty-something woman might have her own agenda. She was kind of cute. But she was too old for him and . . . and . . . He saw her standing against the closed door. He felt the thick handle of the broom in his hand. The drugs were right there, everything he wanted ready for the taking. In his mind he saw himself ripping the keys from her, shoving her down, helping himself to exactly what he'd come for.

"No, I can't. Not tonight," he said, shaking his head and starting to push the mop again. "My shift's almost over and . . . and I gotta be someplace."

"Oh, well," said Brenda, still smiling, "maybe some other time."

"Sure."

Zeb then pushed his small pile of dust and dirt toward the

door, which Brenda held open. Stepping into the hallway, he turned to the right as she locked up behind him.

"Bye," called Brenda with a wink. "Don't work too hard."

"Don't worry, I won't."

He kept pushing his broom, working his way to the end of the corridor, then turning at the first corner. Crap, what was he supposed to do now? How was he going to do this? Tonight the place was so deserted that he'd been sure it was the perfect opportunity. Even the nurses' station was empty.

Across the hall he saw a pay phone. He'd almost called her before. And he wanted to again. He just hadn't expected to be, well, so lonely, and reaching into the pocket of his blue uniform, he felt a handful of quarters. He shrugged and leaned his dust mop against the wall, crossed to the phone, dialed the number, and deposited over a dollar in change. The line clicked, and then the phone on the other end started ringing. And ringing. Zeb clenched his eyes shut.

"Shit." Where could she be?

After he'd run away to his father and stayed at The Congregation, his contact with his mother had been sparse, not much more than a letter per year. When he'd started thinking about leaving the cult, though, she'd been the first and only person he'd told; knowing that they were always watching, always listening—there was a persistent rumor that the phones were tapped—Zeb had wisely snuck off the compound and called her from a pay phone. Yes, she said, run as fast and as far as you can. Don't come to Santa Fe, because they now knew where she lived. And they will look. Just run, she said, and if there is a God they won't find you.

He was about to hang up on the eighth ring when the phone was finally answered, and he said, "Mom?"

"Oh, my God, Zeb," replied Martha. "Where are you? Are you all right? How's the baby?"

"We're fine, Mom. We're in Minneapolis."

"I've been so worried."

"Really, we're okay," he insisted, not wanting to go into it all. "How about you? You don't sound so good."

"It's just been . . . well, things have been a little rough here."

"What's that mean? They haven't been there, have they?"

"Don't worry, I'm fine," said Martha, avoiding the answer. "Just be careful, okay?"

"But—"

"Zeb, I want to come up there."

"No, you don't need to."

"But you might need help. I want to be close."

"Aw, Mom," moaned Zeb, now wishing he'd never called her. "It's really cold up here and there's a ton of snow. There's a huge storm going on right now. You wouldn't like it."

"Zeb, I'm coming up."

"But I don't have enough room for you. My place is really small."

"Then I'll stay at a Holiday Inn or something. There has to be one of those downtown."

"Listen, Mom, we'll talk later. I'm at work."

"Zeb, I'm coming. I—"

"Mom, I love you. Gotta go. Bye."

He hung up and stood there shaking his head. Oh, brother. He leaned his head against the wall, banged it several times. Talk about dumb things, calling his mom. It would be just like her, too, to come up here. In fact, he'd be surprised if she didn't just show up.

What a frigging mess. He was flat broke and he thought this would have been the perfect time to slip into that room and steal some of the expensive stuff. He just hadn't been around hospitals enough, hadn't known, hadn't realized how tightly things would be controlled. Not only were all the drugs locked in one room, they were locked in cages in a locked room.

So how the hell was he going to get it? And if not tonight, then when?

He should just leave here. Just drop this stupid dust mop, go back to his locker, get back into his jeans, and take off. After all, all he really wanted was to see Ribka, his baby girl.

# 9

Paul wasn't quite sure what to make of the situation. He stood in the deep snow just outside the kitchen window and so far he hadn't been able to locate her, the woman who owned the house. Perhaps she was upstairs resting. Or bathing. Perhaps this man, the one who was dancing and singing out there in the living room, had come over just to watch the baby for a bit. Or maybe he'd come over to watch the child while she went out. Wait, no. Her car was in the garage, so she was here. Then again, maybe she had gone somewhere. Perhaps she was just at a neighbor's or someone had picked her up.

The unknown made him uneasy. The snow was making him cold. Unbelievable, he thought, looking at the light in the alley. The snow was coming down in thick sheets. This had to be a sign, he thought. Perhaps this was just like one of the great biblical sandstorms that had shielded God's worthy. Most certainly. And he was The Chosen, here to rescue the infant Ribka. Praise Jehovah, for it was He who had brought this storm, He who was laying down this snow like a protective cloak. Yes, Paul would take the child in his arms and flee, and his tracks would soon be buried by the huge flakes.

Filled with an inspired sense of purpose—by their fruits ye shall know them, he thought—he moved back around the corner of the house. He looked down at a solitary basement window and realized just how he was going to accomplish this, his heavenly duty. No front or back door for him. No, he thought, bending over and tapping the glass. He'd just have to suck in his gut.

Paul stroked his mustache with his right hand, looked around to be sure no one was watching. He backed around a bit, and then with one swift movement he mule-kicked a sharp hole in the storm window. Leaning over, he pulled aside as many shards as he could, then reached through and opened the latch. Tugging at the window, he felt it move. Excellent. His main concern had been that the windows were nailed shut. But they weren't, and once he had lifted the storm window he punched another hole in the inner window. Paul peered into the dark basement. A washing machine. Dryer. Bicycle. A pile of laundry on the floor.

On the edge of the window frame he saw a small rectangular device, a magnetic contact, part of a security system. He tensed, quickly pulled his pistol from his pocket. And waited. He forced himself to be patient. But nothing happened, no alarm crooned. Very good. So the system wasn't activated.

Now came the true test, he thought as he lowered himself to the ground. Whether or not he could actually fit through this small window might prove to be his biggest problem of the night.

# 10

Numb with shock, Todd stared at the front bumper of his Cherokee stuck deep in the snow. "Wow."

"That was close."

"No shit."

Janice said, "I can't believe you didn't smash into that car."

"Thank God there wasn't anyone up here on the sidewalk. I would've plowed right into them." Todd turned to Janice. "Are you sure you're all right? Not even a bruise?"

"Nothing." As the snow blew all around her, the shivering Janice moaned, "Just cold."

"I'll check things out. Why don't you get back in?"

"But . . ."

"Janice, the engine's still on and the heater's going full blast. You're cold and I'm not." Knowing exactly what was going through her head, Todd added, "Just let me take care of this."

"Okay, okay, you be the hunk."

"Right," he countered, "and you be the babe and get back in the car before you freeze."

As she went around the other side of the Cherokee and climbed in, Todd walked slowly around his vehicle, shocked at how close they'd come to a major accident. Somehow he'd avoided sliding into the other vehicle, and yet that stupid other car, the Mazda, hadn't even stopped. Perhaps the driver hadn't realized how close he'd come to being smashed.

Shaking his head, Todd examined the fenders. When he couldn't find a single nick, he bent over, studied the front tires. No apparent problems there, even though he'd flown over the curb at such a good clip. At worst he might need an alignment; at best he might only need a car wash.

Behind the steering wheel a few moments later, he plunged the stick shift into reverse and said to Janice, "Well, let's see if the Butchmobile will live up to its name."

He gave it some gas and the vehicle tugged at the snow that was gripping the front bumper. Todd released the gas pedal and pressed on the clutch, thereby letting the Cherokee roll forward, then he pressed down again on the accelerator and the car pulled backward. He continued this rocking for another few seconds, and then in a burst the four-wheel-drive vehicle was free. Much too quickly, the Jeep shot across the sidewalk and dropped its rear tires onto the street. Todd braked, checked for traffic, then backed onto the street.

"So far so good," he said as he put the car into first gear and drove off.

"Just get me home," said Janice, slumped against her door.

Todd drove through Uptown, a busy shopping district now deserted, and all the way south to 36th Street, where he turned left at the cemetery. Michael was in there, buried in the Gracewood plot Todd had bought, his body now sealed in the ground by the frozen earth. It was still hard to imagine that he was gone, that Todd would never speak to him again, never hear his laugh, never hold him in his arms. He saw Michael's image: his dark brown hair, his mustache, his cute face always eager with a smile. Would those four years of their relationship, albeit closeted, prove to be the best of Todd's life? Perhaps. A pity he hadn't realized and appreciated it at the time. And it was no wonder he'd been taking it slow with Rawlins; if it did get truly serious, Todd didn't want to make any of the same mistakes.

Todd drove in silence through the storm. Neither he nor Janice said another word as they continued through the snow and down the slick streets toward Minnehaha Creek. When they finally crossed the frozen stream and turned left, Janice's brightly lit house shone on the hill.

"As much as I love Jeff," began Janice, "I don't want to get into any of this with him. He's going to want to linger, but I don't want to talk about the baby until he's gone."

"Sure, whatever," replied Todd, parking behind Jeff's snow-covered car. "Don't worry, everything's going to be fine."

Todd stared up at the large, arching windows and glimpsed a figure whooshing across the living room. Oh, brother. What was Jeff up to? A bank teller by day, the drag queen in him erupted when the sun went down and the music came up. And then, by God, you had to look out for a 230-pound guy in spike heels who thought he was the all-in-one Judy-Barbra-Tina. So what was he up to tonight? Or rather, who?

Todd grabbed their boxed food from the rear seat and followed Janice over a snowbank and up her snowy front walk. By the time they reached the front door on the side of the house, they were both covered with downy flakes.

As she took out her key Janice peered in a side window. "Seems pretty quiet to me."

"Yeah, I don't hear any music. Maybe the baby's asleep."

"Wouldn't that be great." She unlocked the front door, stepped in, stomped her boots, and softly called, "Jeff?"

With a grin Todd said, "I feel like Ward and June coming home from the club."

Paying him no attention, Janice moved toward the living room and again called, "Jeff, we're home. Hello?"

There was no response, the house offering nothing except

silence. For a moment Todd wondered if something was wrong. A shot of fear dousing his heart, he followed Janice, passing from the entry hall, stepping down one stair and into the large living room. And there sat Jeff, the baby Ribka cradled in his arms.

"Shh!" he hissed. "She only just, just went to sleep."

Janice unbuttoned her wool coat, dropped it on a chair, and zeroed in on the baby. Hurrying across the living room as if she hadn't seen the child in months, she eased herself onto the couch next to Jeff and carefully lifted the baby from his arms.

"Hello, gorgeous," she whispered, cradling her. And then turning to Jeff, "Did you feed her? How about her diaper, did you change it?"

"Yes and yes." His voice hushed, Jeff added, "The baby Ribka was purr-fect. But why are you two home so early? I didn't expect you for at least another hour. Whatsamatta, you queers didn't have a fight, did you?"

"Of course not," said Todd as he set their food on a table. "The restaurant was just so crowded we couldn't talk."

"Oh, so does that mean you two have come home to gossip? About whom? I'm all ears."

Janice said, "Jeff—"

"Really, no problemo. I can stay the whole night. In fact, I'm going to have to. I've got rear-wheel drive and there's no way I'll be able to drive in all this snow." He mimicked his best Minnesota accent, his voice as nasal as possible. "Oh, for fun, a sleep-over."

Todd saw the look of despair on Janice's face. Yes, she needed to talk. But she wasn't going to divulge a thing while Jeff was here.

Todd slipped on his gloves again, saying, "Come on, Jeff. Time to take the baby-sitter home."

Jeff opened his mouth, was about to protest, then took a look at Janice and replied, "Okay, okay. I get it when I'm not wanted. But just remember, I want a full report later."

"You're a doll," said Janice.

"Of course I am." Then he puckered his lips and leaned toward Janice. "Kiss, kiss."

"Good night."

Todd buttoned up his coat and said to Janice, "I'll be back in a few minutes."

After all, Jeff lived less than a half mile away.

# 11

It was a cool, breezy night in Colorado, and Suzanne stood at the window of her darkened bedroom. Her father was out on the driveway, the hood of his car raised, his heavy body bent over the right front fender. Him and that car, his prized Cadillac, long and white and so big. Since he was the only person at The Congregation with a private car—there were a handful of other vehicles here on the compound, but they were all shared—she called it the Popemobile. But her daddy, God's very own Apostle on earth, sure as heck didn't like that, she thought with a devilish grin. Among other things on the compound there was to be no mention whatsoever of that false church and his unholiness.

Standing inside and in the dark, she watched her father work in the floodlights out front, first twisting the oil filter, next measuring some fluid. She wanted to be out there too, but he'd ordered her to stay inside in case the phone rang with news of the baby. The baby, the baby, the baby. Her father had been using those two words to shackle her to the house not only for the last week, but also the last thirteen months, ever since she'd first gotten pregnant. Eat this, don't eat that. Now rest, Suzanne. Rest and pray to Jehovah for a healthy child. Well, she was sick of it. Yes, she wanted news of Ribka, but how long was she supposed to stay cooped up in here before she started bouncing off the walls?

Still without turning on the lights, she dropped herself on the edge of her bed, stared up at the black ceiling. Her father had never trusted her, not really. Always keeping tabs on her, questioning her whereabouts, who she'd seen, what she'd done. Maybe if her mother were still alive things would be different; Suzanne cursed the day her mother had died of melanoma. Instead of a nice family, it was just she and her dad, and he was like the Gestapo, always watching her, getting furious—even jealous—if she attracted too much attention. She couldn't help it if all the guys liked her. Her dad said she attracted boys like a cat in heat. Well, maybe so. She was pretty, so what? And she had nice tits, full and round, or at least that's what all the guys said. The guys. She laughed. Her dad actually thought Zeb had been the first to crawl through her bedroom window. Oh, Daddy would be so, so angry about all the guys she'd known. Maybe one day when she wanted to make her father nice and mad she'd go ahead and tell him.

And then she started to cry.

Her round cheeks flushed red, her almondy eyes crinkled up. She wanted Zeb. She wanted Ribka with her dark curls. She wanted them both to come back and take her away too. How could Zeb have done it, gone and left her like this? Sure, both of their fathers had made them get married, but . . . but why hadn't he at least told her that he was going to run away? Didn't he know she would've fled The Congregation too? It was just so . . . so incredibly boring here.

She wiped the few tears from her cheeks, sat up, and glanced outside again. Her father was still out there, still monkeying with his stupid car. It doesn't make any difference, she thought. None of it does. And she stood up, left her room, crossed the hall, and entered her father's room. She didn't need to turn on the lights here either, for she knew just where he kept it, placed there after the government's attacks on others. Crossing to the far side of the bed, she opened up his bedside table, pulled open the drawer, and there lay his gun, a heavy, silvery thing. She studied it in the faint light, reached for it once, then retracted her hands. She stood quite still for a moment and realized that, no, for once she was going to do what she wanted instead of what Daddy or God the Son or God the Father said. Or The Congregation. This was her decision. Or maybe it wasn't, she thought with an impish grin as she sat down on the edge of her father's bed. Sure, she was just going to put her faith to a little test and see what God had in store for her.

Her hands quite calm, she lifted the pistol and a small box of bullets from the drawer, arranging them all on the bedspread beside her. Never keep a gun loaded, that's what her daddy always said, so she just had to find out how you opened this thing, the barrel. She pushed at a couple of levers, and finally it opened, the barrel flopping to the side. She held it up toward the window, peered through the chambers, and sure enough saw a series of holes in the dim light. Not loaded. So her daddy was a man of his words.

Now for the test of faith.

She opened up the small box of bullets and ran her fingertips over the smooth tips. Okay, okay, she thought, if there was a God, if He was watching over her, then everything would be all right. It would mean that He had a plan after all. Simple. She brushed aside her hair with one hand, then selected one bullet. Just one. Suzanne studied it, rolled it between her fingers. A bullet of truth, she thought, that's what it was. No, a piercing bullet of faith.

Her hands working quickly, she picked up the pistol, slipped in the bullet, closed the gun, and then spun the barrel, which rolled with a gentle clicking sound. God the Father, God the Son, and God's Apostle on earth. She spun it three times. Next she held the pistol up to her right temple, pressing the cool barrel right against her skin.

"Is there a plan?" she asked aloud, her eyes peering heavenward. "If so, am I part of it?"

Her body rigid with tension, she pulled the trigger, which clicked with a sharp, hollow sound. Nothing else happened however. There was no shattering explosion. Suzanne sat there on the edge of the bed, surprised, almost disappointed. She was alive. So what did that mean? She was tempted to pull the trigger again, to see how much she could truly prod fate. Realizing she shouldn't press the matter, however, she stood up. She had her answer: The gun hadn't fired, she was alive, so there must be a plan for her life, she must have to live for some unknown reason. But, she thought, biting her bottom lip, she did have one more question.

Carrying the pistol carefully in her right hand, she left her father's bedroom, crossed the hall, and returned to her own room. With the lights still off she went up to the window. Her father was still out there, bent over that big white Cadillac and poking around at the engine. She cracked the window and lifted the gun up to the slender opening. So He had a plan for her, but what about her father? Crouching down, she took aim as best she could, for the only gun she'd ever fired was the BB gun at the county fair, the one and only county fair her father had allowed her to go to several years ago. She considered spinning the barrel yet again, then thought otherwise, for she'd already spun it three times and certainly the fate of this household had already been decided.

Just aim and squeeze. Right. That's how you're supposed to do it. She squinted, trained the barrel on her daddy. And gently, gently pulled. To her surprise, once again nothing happened, only a sharp click. So He had a plan for him too.

With a shrug, Suzanne closed the window and returned the gun to her father's bedside table.

# 12

Cradling Ribka in her arms as she sat on the couch, Janice was just starting to doze off when she heard an odd noise, a thunk of sorts from somewhere within the house. At once her eyes popped open, and she glanced toward the entry hall, half-expecting to see Todd returning. Had he gotten stuck? Had the storm proved too much for his four-wheel-drive vehicle?

But no, there was no one, and the silence hung in the house like an invisible fog.

Must have been the snow, she thought, glancing out the large front windows. Must have been a sheet of snow sliding off the roof and onto the bushes. Or an icicle must have crashed down.

When Ribka started to squirm in her arms, Janice said, "Sweetheart, I think you're hungry, aren't you?"

As if she understood, the baby smiled back up, her mouth opening in a big, toothless grin.

"Oh, yes, you're so pretty. And so funny, aren't you?" Janice lifted one teeny hand to her lips and kissed it loudly. "Wouldn't you like a bit more to eat? Would that help you sleep a little better?"

Dear God, thought Janice, staring down into this little bundle. She'd never known such pure happiness. She'd never imagined she could be, well, so gaga over a baby. If the guys at the law office could only see her now!

Scooting to the edge of the couch, she held the baby in her left arm, grabbed a clean white cloth, then pushed herself to her feet. She didn't ever want to put her down, to lose her. Never. Baby Ribka. Janice started for the kitchen, cooing and rocking the child. Whispering. Who knew how or why or, for that matter, how long. But the baby was here and Janice was going to cherish every instant.

"Yes, you're here and you're all mine," she whispered, kissing the infant yet again. "You're mine, mine, mine."

It definitely seemed a miracle that this baby had found her way into Janice's arms. Janice just prayed to God it didn't portend a tragedy. How many days now—five?—and not a word from Zeb. When she wasn't thinking about the baby's health, when she wasn't filled with unspeakable joy at the sight of her very own granddaughter, then Janice's heart was aching with worry. And she had every right to worry. Sure, Zeb had an entire life that she didn't know about, including, of course, parents and aunts and uncles, but damn it all, he'd come into Janice's life and left this child on deposit. So what was going on with him? Dear God, it certainly sounded like drugs. Or had he borrowed a bunch of money from some gang or whatever and then gambled it all away at one of the casinos? In her law practice she'd seen every kind of tragedy, and she knew all too well it could be something like that. Why else would he fear for the child's safety and hide her at Janice's house?

Not to mention the baby's mother.

Janice didn't even know if Zeb was married or how to find Ribka's own mother. Worried about that one, in the middle of the night Janice had rolled over, fearful that Zeb had done something like kidnapping Ribka.

Hugging the baby and admiring her dark curls, Janice

passed from the living room and toward the kitchen. As she was moving through the entry hall her eye was caught by a blinking red light on the panel of her security system. Broken again. That was all she needed. A couple of months ago she'd had some painters in and something had happened. The stupid alarm was going off every twelve hours, its digitized voice calling out morning and night, "Sensor Five dysfunction, warning. Sensor Five dysfunction, warning." So what had happened now? Had Jeff been playing with the alarm or had someone broken into her garage, which was also wired? Janice punched in her security code, then the OFF button.

The digital voice called, "Security system off."

Yet the red trouble light was still blinking. Wondering if the front door wasn't shut securely, she opened it and then closed it, twisting the bolt shut as was her custom. Still the light flashed. Rolling her eyes, Janice walked away, not knowing what the hell it meant but certain of only one thing: get the baby some food. Ribka was starting to squirm and grow cranky. Janice would deal with the security system later.

Her kitchen was a big, bright space, the cabinets a pure white, the countertops a deep forest green. About three years ago she'd gutted the old kitchen, combining a back hall and opening up the whole thing. Expensive, but worth it. Now, just past the door to the basement she had an eating area in one corner, a small color TV on a bookshelf, and even a couple of stools at a counter. As she crossed into the space she rocked the baby and easily imagined the room filled with bright toys, balls, and one of those jumping things hanging from a door frame. She had tons of space here, more than she could ever use. When Zeb surfaced again maybe she could convince him to move in.

From the refrigerator Janice took a prepared bottle of formula, unscrewed the lid, and added three drops from the small vial Zeb had given her. She was about to place the bottle in the microwave when she thought she heard something from the front of the house.

"Todd, is that you? We're in the kitchen!"

She waited a moment, and when there was no response Janice stepped to the edge of the kitchen, the baby cradled in one arm, the bottle clutched in one hand. She peered down the dark hallway toward the front door, saw no one.

The anxiety clear in her voice, she called out, "Todd?"

Wait a minute, that couldn't be him. The front door—hadn't she just locked it? Of course. And seeing that the entry was completely deserted and the front door shut tight, a flutter of worry began to stir in her stomach. Had the blinking light of her security system been trying to tell her something after all?

She saw that the hall closet door was ajar. Oh God, she thought. Three or four times over the last year the neighbor's cat had snuck into her house and started spraying, and she was going to have a fit if it was Max in the closet ruining her boots and coats. Without hesitation, Janice hurried forward and yanked open the door. Something shot out at her, and Janice dropped the baby bottle, clutched Ribka in both arms, and screamed as she was struck on the shoulder.

A broom.

Oh, shit. Janice caught her breath, glanced down, and realized what a nerve case she really was. Just a broom, which now lay on the floor next to a creamy white puddle of formula. A few feet away Janice spotted the lid to the baby bottle and was about to bend over and reach for it when Ribka's mouth opened in a terrified shriek.

"It's okay," soothed Janice. "I'm sorry, Ribka. I scared you, didn't I? It's okay. Everything's fine."

She held her tightly, kissed her on her smooth, round cheek, and turned toward the kitchen. She'd mop up the mess later, for now she just had to fix Ribka another bottle. And quick. Hurrying back into the bright white space, however, she stopped immediately. The basement door was wide open.

"Todd? Jeff?" Her heart started charging. "Hey, you guys, don't fool around like this."

Before she could ponder another thought, a complete

stranger stepped out from behind one of the cabinets, and Janice jumped a second time.

Trying to make her voice as strong as possible, she demanded, "Who the hell are you and . . . and what are you doing in my house?"

"I've come to save the baby," said the mustached man.

"Are you crazy? Get out of here! Get out of here right this minute!"

It flashed through her mind: Rush to the phone, call 911. Run to the security system, hit the panic button. Before she could even flinch, however, the man raised his right arm and trained a pistol directly on her. In response Janice Gray clutched her granddaughter tightly against her chest.

Her voice tougher and deeper than it had ever been, she threatened, "You're going to have to kill me first."

# 13

"You know, it's been nice getting to know you these past few months," said Jeff as they approached his house.

"Thanks," replied Todd.

"No, I mean it. I never understood why Michael cared so much for you. I just didn't get it. I mean, you seemed so uptight about being a homo."

"Trust me, I was. Michael was very patient."

"Michael was a saint."

Todd pressed on the brake, began to pull over in the snow, and said, "Yeah, I really miss him."

"And Rawlins is a doll too," Jeff continued. "Or, *mon Dieu,* maybe you call him Tiger?"

"Maybe."

"He's a bit more complicated than Michael, but he's still fab." Batting his eyes and queening it up, Jeff said, "Oh, I just love a man in uniform, don't you?"

"He may be a cop, but I haven't seen him in a uniform yet. I think most detectives wear street clothes."

"Oh, I'm sure he's got a nice blue police outfit hanging

somewhere. You should just get down on your knees and be-e-e-g.''

"Okay, Jeff, I get the idea," replied Todd, rolling his eyes.

"Can you believe it, I've known him since he had his very first uniform. He was a Cub Scout. And then a Boy Scout too." Jeff shook his head. "He was such a little firecracker. Who would've guessed all three of us would turn out queer, Michael, Rawlins, me. Well, I guess I was the obvious one; French poodles like me always were. And I use the past tense because I no longer have the hair to poof up!" he said with another laugh as he ran his hand over his balding scalp.

"Life's certainly turned out to be different than *Father Knows Best,* hasn't it?"

"No kidding. Did I ever tell you that I'm pretty sure my dad was gay? He was a sweetheart . . . and very unhappy. I guess he really didn't have much of an option back then, but instead of coming out he drank himself into the grave. I mean literally—he got real drunk one night and drove sixty miles per hour right into an oak tree."

"It's a long road."

"Lordy, ain't that the truth."

Todd pulled up to Jeff's small house just off 46th and Lyndale, a quaint one-story bungalow with a large chimney right at the front and a steep roof now getting buried under a mantle of snow. His former home, a huge Victorian in an unsavory part of town, having burned nearly to the ground, Jeff had moved here about a month ago.

"How are you settling in?" asked Todd.

"The best thing about getting burned out is you don't have any boxes to move," he said and then started cackling. "And I kind of like this new place. It's tiny in comparison to the old house, but it's mine. No family ghosts. Besides, I get to buy all new furniture with the insurance money. I've been at Dayton's looking at couches on almost all of my lunch breaks."

While Jeff and he had certainly become friends since Mi-

chael's death, they hadn't ever talked much beyond the super-
ficial. So was this to be the time? Could Janice wait?

As if he were reading Todd's mind, Jeff said, "I always
invite my taxi drivers in for a drink. Care for a quick one?
Janice is so wrapped up in that baby I'm sure she won't miss
you."

Todd looked at the car clock. He thought about the take-out
food waiting to be eaten. He recalled Janice's downcast mood.
What was with her anyway?

"You know, thanks anyway, but I've got to get back."

"Whatsamatta, big boy, ain't I your kinda guy?" pressed
Jeff, batting his lashes.

"That's not the point, Jeff."

There'd been a time, however, when a queen like Jeff would
have been too threatening for Todd, when his swishy hips and
fey wrist would have twisted Todd's insides with the
homophobic question: If I'm gay, do I have to act like that?
And only once Todd had realized that he himself didn't have
to wear high heels did the full rainbow of sexuality come into
focus.

"Oh, okay. Good night, gorgeous," said Jeff, leaning over
with pursed lips.

Todd felt a big smack of a kiss on his cheek, which he
returned with a large hug. He then waited as Jeff trudged
through the snow and up to his front door. Only when Jeff
stepped halfway in and turned and blew Todd a kiss did Todd
put his car in gear and start off.

He pulled a U-turn, plowing through the ever-deepening
snow. There seemed to be fewer and fewer cars on the road;
glancing down a side street he saw a couple of people skiing
down the middle of the street. He didn't know how long he
and Janice would end up talking, but perhaps he'd wind up
spending the night at her place, which could be kind of fun. In
fact, he should probably just plan on it. After all, Janice most
likely wouldn't be able to get around in her car tomorrow, so
she'd probably want him to get some supplies—formula,

diapers, whatever. And again came the gnawing question: Whose kid was it anyway and what had Janice gotten herself involved in?

Just up ahead he saw a young woman pushing the rear of a car as the driver tried to steer out of a parking space. Todd slowed, watched as the car rocked back and forth but failed to make it onto the main part of the street. Following Minnesota winter etiquette, Todd stopped and climbed out.

"You want an extra hand?"

"Oh, that'd be great. The tires are just stuck in a rut," said the girl who was pushing. "If you can believe it, my friend and I are trying to make it down to First Avenue to hear a band."

"Do you think you can make it?"

"Yeah, well, if we do we're going to park in one of the city ramps and leave the car there overnight. We'll take a cab back." She brushed aside a long strand of red hair. "Say, aren't you that TV guy?"

"I was."

"Wow, that was really terrible, what happened to you and everything. Sorry."

"Thanks."

The driver gave the car a long, gentle thrust of gas, the tires spun, and Todd and the girl leaned into the rear of the car and pushed. At first it seemed as if the car wouldn't budge, but then it began to inch forward. In a quick blip the tires popped out of the rut and the car surged forward and into the street.

"Keep going, don't stop!" shouted the young woman who'd been pushing. She ran after the car, then turned back to Todd and shouted, "Thanks!"

"You bet," called Todd.

He got back in his Cherokee, watched as the other car fishtailed down the street, and wondered if they were even going to make it to the next block. When he pressed on the gas and plowed into a snowdrift, he wondered about himself as well. Driving slowly, though, he headed toward Minnehaha Creek and made it back to Janice's in about ten minutes. He pulled in behind Jeff's car, shut off the engine, then bounded through the deepening snow up to the front door of the large Spanish-style house.

When he found the front door locked, he knocked and called, "Hi, it's me. I'm back. Oh, June!"

But there was no reply, no movement of any kind from within. Presuming Janice had taken the baby up to bed, he wondered why she hadn't left the door open. Glancing around at the thick flakes that were falling as steady as ever, he knew he couldn't stay out here forever.

He pushed the doorbell. "Janice?"

Still nothing, no reply. Shit. How long was she going to be tied up with the kid? Or perhaps she was down in the basement, throwing in a load of laundry or something like that.

Todd pressed the bell again. Knocked too. If worse came to worst, he supposed, he could go next door and phone her from there. Perhaps she was upstairs and simply couldn't hear. He waited what seemed like forever, and just when it looked as if he would have to go to the neighbors', he heard some rustling. Then the lock.

"Hurry up, Janice, I'm freezing to death!" he called.

The door slowly eased back several inches. Todd dusted the snow from his shoulders, his head, then peered into the house and saw no one inside. He stomped his feet and started to step in.

"Janice?"

Todd pushed on the front door, which swung half open. And there she was, pressed flat against the wall of the entry hall, the baby in her arms, but her face looking tortured, a steady stream of tears running down her cheeks.

"What is it? What's the matter?" Todd demanded.

She glanced to her left, looked behind the door. Todd pressed on the front door, swung it completely open.

"Jesus!" he shouted.

A large man holding a gun emerged. Holy shit, it flashed

through Todd's mind that someone had broken in, Janice was being ripped off, this was a robbery. At the sight of the pistol aimed at his chest, Todd flinched, took a half step back. Immediately the gun was raised higher, and Todd froze.

"What the hell's going on?" demanded Todd.

Her voice quivering, Janice said, "I . . . I don't know."

From his work on the CrimeEye team at Channel 7, Todd knew you weren't supposed to fight these things, that if you were held up you were supposed to just cave in and give them all your valuables. Yet when he quickly appraised the situation everything changed, all the stories he'd heard vanished. This wasn't about stereos or jewelry or cash. No, this guy was too well-dressed, too professional-looking. Todd glanced at him, then at Janice, and noted the way she was clutching the mysterious child. Oh, shit, thought Todd. That's what this is about, isn't it?

So when the intruder, who was still standing partly behind the door, silently waved Todd to move toward Janice, Todd knew he had to act. With his right shoulder Todd plowed into the open door, which sent it hurling against the intruder like a solid wall. At the same time Todd ducked and swung as hard as he could with his left hand, punching the guy in his right side, directly in the kidneys.

"Oh, God!" shouted Janice, clutching the baby and turning away to shield her.

Bent over, Todd assumed the very worst, expected a blast. He kept diving forward, swung at the intruder again.

"Janice, run! Get out of here!"

Then it came. Not a gunshot, but a powerful blow. Todd felt it on his shoulder, this powerful explosion of pain. The guy had hit him with the butt of the pistol, the thick metal smashing into him. He stumbled, and next he both felt and heard it on the side of his head, a huge thunk that reverberated through his body. Oh, shit, he realized. I'm falling. Todd opened his eyes. Saw alternately a flash of white, a burst of black. Crap.

He threw out his hands, tried to catch himself as he tumbled onto the tile floor.

"Todd!" yelled Janice.

Oh, Christ. There was nothing he could do. He'd lost, that was already more than clear, and he felt a powerful blow on his left side. The bastard was kicking him, hammering him with his foot. The air rushed out of him, and Todd collapsed, tumbling into a quiet black world.

# 14

With the baby swaddled in several blankets, including the pure white one, Paul pulled shut the front door of the house. He hadn't expected any of that, not only the woman's resolve and strength, but the guy. Where in the world had he come from? Dear Jehovah in heaven, he muttered to himself as he scurried through the snow and down the front steps, he'd been listening from his hiding place in the basement as the two men left. Paul hadn't been able to make out much of their conversation, but he had clearly heard the woman say good night. And then the two men departed, firmly shutting the door behind them. Just to make sure they were really gone, Paul had waited a good ten minutes. Once he was positive the woman was alone he'd waited even more, hoping she would go to bed, which would have made things incredibly easy. When it was clear that wasn't going to happen anytime soon, he'd snuck upstairs.

Oh, brother. Nearly everything had been screwed up, the opportunity almost ruined. Trudging through the snow, his heart still pounding, Paul glanced back at the house and saw the lights glaring in the large arched windows. Praise heaven, he muttered to himself. In spite of everything the baby was rescued, everything was okay. He had succeeded. Now they'd be able to get Ribka back to her mother and the people who truly loved her.

As the snow poured down, the baby started squirming and fussing. Was she hungry? Her diaper dirty? He had no idea. All he knew was that he had to get this little thing to Rick, and then it would be his problem. He only hoped that Rick had thought ahead, that he had the supplies he needed to care for the infant. Thinking of the situation, he realized they shouldn't fly back, not two adult men and one little infant. If the police were looking for them they'd be too conspicuous at the airport. They'd either have to rent a car and drive back to Colorado or fly Suzanne out here and have her take the baby back. That would suit me best, Paul thought, for he really had no desire to do a cross-country trip with some kid screaming in the backseat.

The snow was now so deep that there was no discerning the sidewalk from these front yards or, for that matter, the street itself. Driving was going to be awful, especially the side streets. But if he could just get out of this neighborhood with its hilly roads and return to the highway, then he was sure he could make it back to the hotel. By morning this was going to be easily knee-deep. Perhaps that would work in their favor. Maybe it would hamper any search for the child. Then again, this woman and her friend wouldn't dare come after the kid, would they?

When he came to a street sign he turned right. There was his car, still the lone vehicle on the street.

"Just a couple of minutes, little one," he said to the child in his arms. "I'll get you in the car and I'll get the heat on. Just hang on. You're going to be okay. You're going back to your mom. Jehovah is watching over you, little angel. We all love you and everything's going to be fine. You're safe now."

He trudged up the road, carefully holding the baby girl in his left arm, and then took out his key and unlocked the passenger door. As he opened the car, snow dusted and blew inward, covering the front seat with a film of light snow. He reached in, brushed off the seat, and then quickly opened his briefcase and dumped the contents on the floor. Next he placed the hard-sided case on the passenger seat. It wasn't much, but it was the best he could do for a makeshift car seat.

"Yes, it's okay. Everything's fine. Don't worry."

But as he laid her down, some flakes fell from his head and onto the baby's face, and Ribka started to shriek.

"Quiet, little one. It's okay. I'm taking you home to your mother."

As he pulled the blankets up and around her in the open briefcase, she started to cry even louder. Oh, brother, between the kid and the roads this was going to be no joy-ride back to the hotel. He shut the car door, brushed off the side windows, and turned to go around to the driver's side. Just as he started, however, he saw a black figure move against the white landscape of snow. He flinched, plunged his hand into his pocket for the pistol. But it was too late. Before he could even raise a hand in defense, he was struck in the side of the head by a huge board. Everything seemed to explode, and as he collapsed into the snowbank he got one clear glimpse of the young kid, the devil-possessed one, who'd started this all.

# 15

---

Todd woke shivering with cold. What the hell had happened? When he heard her long, deep sob he forced his eyes completely open, scanned the floor, but saw no one. Where was she? With his right arm he pushed himself up, and a shock of pain zipped through his body. Holy shit, he hurt like hell, his head, his shoulder, his side. In a very unpleasant flash he remembered it all, returning and finding the intruder. Was he gone?

First he looked down the hall and into the kitchen, saw nothing. Then he rolled over. The front door was shut but the intruder wasn't about, at least he didn't appear to be. And there was Janice, at the bottom of the step that led to the living room, her arms and hands wrapped around her ankles.

"Janice?"

She was curled into a tight ball. Shaking. Todd looked at the back of her, saw that she was trembling ever so lightly.

"Are . . . are you all right?"

In reply she threw her head back, opened her mouth, and this long, awful shriek exploded out of her mouth. Todd scrambled across the floor toward her. Oh, dear Lord. He remembered the gun—had she been shot? Knifed? He scanned everywhere, but saw no blood pooling from her body.

"I'm here!"

He ignored all the pain that was spearing his own body, wrapped his arm around her. Her body was tight and rigid, as if everything in her life had been shrunk to one horrendous moment.

"Janice!" he shouted.

She opened her mouth again and another wretched cry shot out. Todd clutched her, tried to comfort her. Checking her body, he saw no wounds, no evidence that she'd been beaten.

"Oh, shit!" he exclaimed.

Her wrists were bound to her ankles by thick tape, forcing her into a pathetic and immobile ball. He started grabbing at the tape, ripping it away, and it was then, of course, that he realized what was missing. His eyes darted around the living room, he saw a toy ball dropped by a chair, a rattle on the couch.

"Jesus Christ, where's the baby?"

Janice's face was clenched into an hysterical mass, tears soaking her cheeks, her hair. She opened her mouth, but only a mass of garbled noise and saliva emerged. As quickly as he could he tore the last of the tape from her, leaving her wrists a deep, painful red.

"Janice, what happened?" he demanded. "Where's Ribka?"

Unable to speak, she pointed to something on the floor. It was a piece of paper, a note, the handwriting neat and the words direct. Todd grabbed it.

Dear Ms. Gray:

We're sorry for taking the child in this manner, but it's imperative, of course, that she be returned to her natural mother. Do not report this to the police nor pursue this matter in any way at all. If you do so we will be forced to prosecute Zeb for kidnapping across state boundaries. This is exactly what he did and we have ample evidence to prove it. To press this sad situation will only result in pain for all involved and certain imprisonment for the boy. Do not worry, the baby will be in the best possible loving care. Jehovah is watching her and she'll be safe.

A Concerned Group

There was too much that Todd didn't understand. Obviously the intruder hadn't come for Janice's color television or her jewelry. He'd come for the mysterious infant. But . . . but . . . Todd reread the note, for there was plenty that didn't make sense.

Todd rose to his feet and ran across the living room. "How long was I out? When did he leave?"

"Fi-five minutes. Something . . . something like that," she muttered, struggling to get up. "Maybe more. I . . . I don't know, I'm not—"

"Which way? Out the front?"

"Y-yes."

He peered out the window, searched the street. There were only two cars parked out front, Jeff's and his, but perhaps there was still time. Perhaps they could still catch the guy. The snow was so thick, the roads so terrible. He couldn't have gone very far. Turning around he saw Janice pushing herself to her feet and starting for the door.

"Did he say anything?" demanded Todd, hurrying after her.

"No!"

"Was the baby okay? Did he hurt her?"

"I . . . I don't know!"

Todd was right behind Janice as she hurled open the door. A blast of wind and snow hit them both and they hurried outside, Todd still in his winter parka and boots, Janice wearing nothing warmer than a light sweater, her feet covered by nothing more than a pair of loafers. Looking at the snow-covered walk, Todd recognized his own partially buried tracks, then saw another set leading down to the street.

"Those are his!" said Todd.

They hurried through the nearly knee-deep snow, following the tracks across Janice's front yard to some short steps and down onto the sidewalk. Shielding his eyes from the falling snow, Todd checked the street, but saw no sign of tire tracks. Had there been no accomplice, no one waiting to whisk them away? Apparently not, for instead the footprints clearly turned right and continued up the block.

As a huge gust of wind came up, Todd clutched Janice's hand and they followed the prints like a pair of bloodhounds. Moving as rapidly as they could in the deep snow, they moved toward the corner, where a streetlight illuminated the prints turning again to the right. Now hurrying up a small hill, Todd could tell that Ribka's abductor had veered off the sidewalk.

"His car must have been parked here!" said Todd, pointing to the tire marks in the deep snow.

"Oh, my God!"

Frantic with worry, Janice broke away and scrambled through the snow, over the deep bank along the edge of the road, then into the middle of the road itself. Slipping, nearly falling several times, she raced up the street, only to stop and look desperately around. Rushing after her, Todd saw that the tire tracks blended with those of at least three other cars.

Todd turned around, trudged back to the place where the car had obviously been parked. Perhaps there were other footprints, which would indicate how many people were involved in the abduction. And Todd did indeed find a second set of prints. But they were odd, disjointed, a scramble of tracks that made no sense. What the hell had been going on? Were there not two but three or four people involved in this? Then, seeing a spray of red dots, he froze.

Janice was quickly running toward him. "What? What is it, what did you find?"

He bent into the snow, hoping that he was mistaken, that it

wasn't what it appeared to be. Yet it was far too obvious to be anything else, and he realized, his body filling with dread, it was clearly quite fresh.

"Blood," he muttered.

Janice rushed through the snow to Todd's side and stood there, staring down at the scarlet drops. She bit her knuckle, started to sob. Todd rose, wrapped his arm around her waist.

"It might not be from the baby," he said. "She might be all right. It could be his, after all." Feeling her tremble with cold and fear, he pulled her closer. "Maybe he cut himself when we were struggling. Maybe I gave him a bloody nose, something like that."

He looked up the street, through the sheets of thick snow. Somewhere in the back of his mind Todd had believed the guy would still be here, that his car would be stuck or something. But clearly that wasn't the case.

"Shit," he muttered as he shook his head, realizing there was nothing they could do, not right there in the middle of that snowy street anyway. "Come on, we've got to get you back to the house before you freeze to death."

"But—!"

"We've got to call the police."

She stood motionless in the snow, wouldn't budge, her chin trembling from cold and fear, and meekly said, "Don't you understand?"

Todd's gut tightened. "Understand?"

"The . . . the baby."

He brushed some snow off his face and said, "What do you mean?"

"I've just screwed up everything," she muttered, standing there as if she were in the middle of her living room instead of the middle of a raging winter storm.

Taking her by the arm, he said, "Janice, we've got to get you inside. Come on, we'll call—"

"You don't understand!" she shouted, ripping away from

him and pushing toward a snowbank. "That baby's my . . . my granddaughter!"

The wind gusted around Todd, the frigid air nipped at him. He turned, looked at the corner streetlight, saw the snow still falling in heavy sheets.

"Your . . . your what?"

"I had a child, Todd. A boy. Ribka is my son's daughter."

The storm vanished around him, his feet not cold, his brow not chilled with flakes. She said she'd slept with other guys, didn't she? After they'd dated in college there were others, she claimed, perhaps a whole bunch. So what if she hadn't been the consummate dyke? It was only natural to be out there exploring the world, testing the waters, discovering what she really wanted. What the hell, he himself had sought a beautiful, intelligent woman and gotten married.

"I . . . I can't believe this," Janice said, turning away, strolling through the snow. "I've just done everything wrong, made such stupid mistakes."

Todd flashed back to that night at Northwestern right before Christmas break. Just how connected was he to all this?

*They'd been in bed for, what, maybe two Carly Simon songs when Todd felt it, the stirring. Oh, shit, it was working. It was happening. He was getting hard. As he lay next to Janice in her room in the sorority, all the trials of the last week vanished and he felt suddenly and unbelievably happy. This was what was supposed to happen, how things were supposed to go, wasn't it?*

*He started kissing her, tasting her lips, her sweetness, as never before, and before he knew it he was on top of her. He stared into her eyes, kissed her chin, her breasts, nibbling gently on one nipple, then the other. It was all rather instinctual, really. He was on top, she was opening herself to him. And then his penis was inside her, moving smoothly, warmly, easily. So this, he thought, is what it feels like: nice. At first he merely drank it in, savoring every second, but then as the*

*intensity built so did his purpose. Unbelievable, he thought.
He was actually in bed with a woman. They were fucking.
He'd actually been able to get an erection, and now he was
inside her and everything was going fine, even great.*

*So, he thought with a grin upon his face as he worked
himself in and out of her and toward that ultimate goal, this
could mean only one thing, couldn't it: that he wasn't gay
after all.*

He remembered the stress, the pleasure, the joy and relief that
it worked, he could do it, could screw a woman. And he also
remembered that the next semester Janice had disappeared,
supposedly on a semester-long program in Europe, after which
she'd come back claiming she was a dyke.

Suddenly he was shaking, not from the cold and the snow
that was all around him, but from within. Something was coming into perspective, a truth was forcing itself to the surface.

With the storm blustering all around him, in a hushed voice
Todd said, "So . . . you have a son." And then he pushed
himself to ask, "Tell me, Janice, is he *our* son?"

"Todd, I've just done everything wrong."

"Well, is he?"

"I've got so much to explain."

"Janice!"

"It's so complicated."

"Damn it all, Janice!"

"Todd, I've got to talk to him. It's not so—"

"Tell me, Janice, is he my son, too, or not?"

She stood in the middle of the street, the snow up to her
knees and covering and clinging to her hair, her shoulders. She
started to say something, then clamped her eyes shut. Wrapping her arms around her body, she squeezed herself tightly.
Or was Todd wrong, was she not trying to hold something in
but squeeze it out?

Her voice strained, Janice finally said, "Todd, I'm sorry. I should have told you a long time ago. I . . . I wanted to, but . . . but . . ." She shook her head. "The truth is, I . . . I don't know."

# 16

Fully clothed, Rick sat on his hotel bed, the pillows cushioned against the wooden headboard for support, his Bible cracked open. Staring down at the pages before him, he saw passages and entire verses that he'd underlined, as well as his own comments and interpretations that he'd written in the margins. But tonight he hadn't been able to read a word in over thirty minutes. Instead of visualizing the miracles of Jehovah, in his mind's eye Rick was visualizing all the horrendous possibilities.

Where in the name of heaven was Paul and what could possibly be taking him so long?

Maybe they'd done this all wrong. Maybe, Rick wondered, he shouldn't have allowed Paul to go off on his own. Paul was supposed to just check out the house and, if he thought it safe, do his little business with the telephone lines. All that shouldn't take so very long, yet here Paul had been gone for almost four hours. Four hours! Rick shook his head. He should have called by now if there were any problems. If Paul got to the house and thought the situation was different—if he detected that the child wasn't there, if he spotted Zeb himself, if the authorities were around—Paul was supposed to slip away and call Rick immediately. But he hadn't phoned, which led Rick to only one possible conclusion: There'd been trouble. Rick knew it, they should have equipped Paul with a cellular phone, which would have allowed him to call Rick at even the hint of a problem. Always security-conscious, however, Paul wouldn't allow it; wireless phones weren't secure, he insisted, a conversation could be tapped far too easily.

Dear Jehovah, he prayed, please don't let the police be involved. That would only complicate things to a horrendous degree, not only for his granddaughter but also for The Congregation. What if the local police or the FBI stepped in and began to investigate things? The publicity would be awful, lawyers would come out of the woodwork, the issue would probably go to court. Little Ribka could easily be taken from all of them and placed in a foster home, which would be the worst possible thing for his family.

Or was Paul simply detained by the roads?

Oh, Lord. It was the lesser of two evils, but Paul could easily be in some ditch. Or he could easily have been sideswiped on these slippery roads and taken to a hospital.

Rick slammed shut his Bible, jumped off the bed, and went to the window. Pulling aside the curtain, he peered into the parking lot. A blanket of white covered all the cars, antennas poking out here and there. No movement. Glancing at the lampposts, he saw thick clouds of snow billowing in the light. Pressing closer to the window, he saw the highway. The traffic was much lighter than before, the cars progressing slowly. But they were moving. And there were two plows, huge orange trucks that were clearing and salting the roads. Maybe there was hope yet that Paul would return safely.

His stomach growled, for on top of everything he was famished. He hadn't eaten since lunch; he should've gone down to the restaurant when Paul first left. An hour after that Rick should've ordered room service. Now, though, Rick couldn't do either. He certainly couldn't leave the room, not even for a minute. And he most definitely didn't want to tie up the phone. What if Paul called? What if he had but one quarter?

"Lord watch over them," he muttered, turning away from the window.

He walked across the room, running his hand along the top of the dresser, then up and across the television set. He couldn't live up here in this northern city. It wasn't just the snow. Nor the cold. It was the lack of faith. An hour ago he'd turned on the TV, but hadn't been able to find even a single minister. That was a sign, of course, of just how lost these souls were up on this northern prairie—they were so blind to their woes that they weren't even reaching out—but there wasn't much Rick could do about it. God's true church was prophesied to be small and persecuted. And The Congregation was just that, small, with slightly over twenty families and not even a hundred members total, and ever fearful as well that government forces would descend upon them and wipe them out. So not only did The Congregation not have the millions and millions of dollars it would take to start something like one of those cable Bible shows, such aggressive proselytizing wasn't part of their mission. No, the destiny of The Congregation was to be small and inward, focused solely on Jehovah and His true mission for them.

Rick walked into the bathroom, flicked a switch, and recoiled from the blinding light. Then he stood there, staring at himself. Gray pants. White shirt untucked, the top three buttons opened. The red-and-blue-striped tie long gone. And the face. He stared at himself. Martha was right. He looked awful. So tired. His hair had started to gray just three years ago, and already his sideburns were a bright white. And the top? Well, never mind about that. His front hairline had receded several inches. Actually, it was pretty thin all the way back.

Okay, so he didn't look the greatest. Martha was right; no wonder some people assumed he was over fifty. Of course, the extra weight didn't help either. He pinched himself at the waist. There was a good twenty-five pounds extra there. Hard to believe, he thought, staring at himself. Somewhere inside this figure was the skinny kid with the eager smile. But enough of that. As written in Proverbs 31, favor is deceitful, and beauty is vain.

Then again, he thought, hitting the light switch and plunging the bathroom into darkness, those long gone, frivolous days were the stupid days. He'd wasted so much time, did such heinous things, until he'd found the Lord our Father, and now he had so much to work for, so much to accomplish. If he was looking older it was because he was pushing himself, reaching, striving. The power of Jehovah, the word of God the Son, his family, The Congregation: These were his duties. He was a leader, a valued one at that. All of which was more than the vanity of Martha. She'd been so weak, so fragile. No wonder she'd fled. No spine, no vision. No devotion. He, on the other hand, was strong, determined. With the word of God the Father and the work of God the Son, he had been saved. Yes, he had to be focused.

He looked directly at himself in the mirror and muttered, " 'A double minded man is unstable in all his ways,' James chapter one, verse eight."

Heading back to the bed and his Bible, Rick glanced at his watch. This was absolutely ghastly. Where in the world was Paul?

Seating himself, he cracked open his Bible and shook his head. This couldn't be happening. His stomach hurt, but it was worry that was eating him now, not hunger. Was Paul stuck in the snow? Stuck in jail?

A heavy hand pounded on the door.

In response, Rick spun around and called, "Paul?"

He leapt off the bed and charged across the room. As he started to twist the lock, he suddenly stopped. The authorities?

"Paul, is that you?"

"Yeah," came the mumbled reply.

Rick ripped open the door, only to find the heavy figure slumped against the doorjamb, one hand pressed to his ear.

Snow was melting on his head, his shoulders, and Rick grabbed Paul by the arm.

"My God in heaven, what happened?" he demanded, and then looked up and down the hallway. "No one followed you here, did they?"

Paul shook his head and then lowered his hand, exposing a broad, raw gash over his ear and across his cheek. His hair was twisted and matted with dark blood, and he tried to take a step but stumbled.

"What happened?" exclaimed Rick, steadying the other man. "Was it the car? Were you in an accident?"

"No."

As quickly as he could, Rick slammed shut the door, bolted it tightly, and demanded, "Did something happen at the house?"

Paul started to talk, but his words dissolved into a mumbled mess. Rick led him to the bed, where he seated him. Studying the injured man, Rick appraised the bleeding, swollen cuts, then hurried into the bathroom and turned on the hot water in the sink. Grabbing one of the white hotel towels, he soaked it, wrung it out, and returned to Paul.

Rick begged, "Tell me nothing's happened to Ribka. Tell me our little baby is okay."

"I . . . I . . ."

"Is she okay?"

"I think so."

"What do you mean, you think so? Did you see her? Did you see my little Ribka?"

Paul took the towel, pressed it against the side of his head, and nodded.

"She's not hurt? She's all right?"

Paul's head slowly went up and down again.

"Then where is she? What happened?"

The heavyset man lifted the towel from his head and studied the brilliant scarlet stain left by his wound. "Oh, crap. I hate getting hit like that. I should've known better."

"Hit? Hit? Tell me what happened!" demanded Rick.

"I went in."

"The house?"

"Through the basement. And . . . and I had her."

"Ribka?"

Nodding, he held the damp towel to his head and winced in pain. "But there was kind of . . ."

"Kind of what?"

"Kind of a problem inside—some other guy. First it was just her, the woman, but then this other guy came along and . . ." He shrugged. "But . . . but I got her. I had the baby, had her right in my arms. And then I was all the way to my car. I was just putting her in when . . . when . . . shit, no one's ever done anything like this to me! No one's ever . . . ever dared!"

"Someone attacked you?"

"What are you, a rocket scientist?" Paul closed his eyes and moaned in pain. "Shit, the roads are so bad I didn't think I was going to make it back here. It took me an hour and a half!"

Rick's rage was soaring, and he grabbed Paul by the shoulders, shook him, and shouted, "What happened? Who did this to you?"

"Your . . . your son, the bastard. He jumped me and took the baby," snapped Paul, glaring up at Rick. "I'm gonna kill him."

# 17

Zeb pulled into the employee parking lot behind the hospital and drove to a far corner. Turning off his car, he bowed his head forward, resting it on the steering wheel. What a horrible drive that had been. Thank God little Ribka and he had gotten away. But what the hell was going on? Why was Paul here? And how the hell had he found out where Ribka had been hidden? Zeb had been so sure, had felt so clever. He'd thought no one would have guessed that he'd run all the way to Minneapolis. He'd been so smugly confident that no one would find his baby girl at his own birth mother's house. That was supposed to be the very last place anyone would look; after all, he'd met Janice only once and he'd had no ongoing contact with her. So how the hell had they known to look there?

Oh, crap, he thought. It could have been her. Janice could have called someone—his mother, his father?—and told them she had the baby. Maybe that was Zeb's mistake. He'd thought and hoped this Janice Gray, the woman who'd given him birth, was someone he could trust. Or maybe she'd just panicked and called one of them. No, he thought, she was a lawyer, she wasn't dumb, she wouldn't panic. So what the hell had she done, who the hell did she think she was, giving up his own baby girl like that?

And was Paul the only member of The Congregation who'd come looking for him? There could be an entire posse of those lunatics after him, including his own father. He hoped at least that Suzanne's dad hadn't come too. When Suzanne had first found out she was pregnant, that fart of a father had locked her in her room, then come after Zeb, dragging him into a barn behind the bakery and hurling him against a wall. Who knew what would have happened if Zeb's own father and several others hadn't come running. As it turned out, he'd gotten married. Suzanne and he were barely given the chance to wash up before they were wed in the presence of The Elders and the entire Congregation. Some day-old carrot cake had served as their wedding cake.

And it was all because of what they'd been taught.

From living with his mother and attending public school in Santa Fe, Zeb knew he should have used a rubber. Some kind of protection anyway. But, no, God was their protection. They needed nothing else. Or so went the teaching of The Congregation. And Suzanne had agreed that fateful night, for He had always been watching over her. After all, she hadn't gotten pregnant yet, and how many guys had she already done it with?

Well, at least he had this little angel, he thought, staring over at his baby girl, who was bundled in a car seat. Maybe God had been watching over them and this was the best possible thing that could have happened to him. He was a dad and she was an angel. Never mind how horrendously complicated his life had become, at least they were out of there, hundreds of miles from The Congregation. Looking at his daughter, Zeb had never thought he'd care so much for a kid, never realized that being a dad would mean so much to him. But it did, and that's why he'd taken her and run away. All of his parents, both his birth and adoptive ones, had screwed up their lives, and his as well. He wasn't going to ruin hers, though, not little

Ribka's. He was going to be there for her always. That was why he'd taken her in the middle of the night and fled The Congregation.

So now what? He had to get out of Minneapolis as quickly as possible. If they knew the baby had been at Janice's, then did they also know about the small room he'd rented by Powderhorn Park? He couldn't conceivably see how, but they might, and he wondered if he dared return there even simply to gather his clothes. Perhaps, but he certainly couldn't stay for any length of time. No, he was going to have to load up Ribka and his few things and they were going to have to hit the road. But where would they go? Someplace south, for sure, where there wasn't cold and snow like this, but how would they get by? He was flat broke, with less than fifty bucks to his name; everything he'd earned at the bakery had gone into the general funds of The Congregation. If only he'd been thinking ahead he would have stolen some of their money. At least he had one of their cars, he thought with a grin. One of their baby seats too. But . . . but where were they going to spend the night tonight?

As he mulled over the options the baby woke up.

"Hello, sweetie," he said gently, leaning over his daughter. "Yeah, it's me, Dad. Remember? Sure you do. Everything's going to be all right. I'm here and we're together again."

Together and getting cold. They couldn't stay out here. Within minutes the cold would overtake them. Zeb had to take Ribka into the hospital and then . . . then . . . Well, if there was a God, then He'd figure it out. With no money Zeb had no choice. How was he going to get those keys?

One thing was for certain, Zeb knew he had to be more careful than ever. He couldn't stay long at the hospital, because if The Congregation knew the baby was at Janice's, then maybe they knew about his working here at the hospital as well. But how? Could they have planted some sort of tracing device on his car?

As he unstrapped his baby daughter from her car seat, he

wondered if they'd gone down to Santa Fe, if they'd hurt his mom. And what about his birth mother, Janice? She might have contacted them, but would she just have handed over the kid like that? Now that he thought about it, Zeb doubted it, for he'd seen with his own eyes how crazy she was over Ribka. Janice had no way of knowing how dangerous The Congregation was; maybe she had contacted them, but maybe they'd come and stolen away Ribka. If so, might they have hurt Janice? Gripped with worry and confusion, Zeb wondered if he shouldn't call the cops, tell them there was an emergency at Janice's. Perhaps he should just call 911 and get them to check it out.

With the baby bundled up and Zeb himself zipped up in his large nylon coat, he opened the car door and scurried through the blasting snow. Once he'd traversed the nearly empty employee lot, he passed through the side doors and entered the hospital, finding the place more deserted than ever. A lone woman sat at the reception counter, not a single soul was in the waiting area, and no one was strolling the usually busy halls. There almost always was a guard down here, but now even he was gone. As if it were the middle of the night, a number of the lights were off. So, thought Zeb, proceeding directly to the elevator, his daughter in his arms, the hospital was down to a skeleton staff. Maybe it would be easier now after all, maybe this was the time he'd been waiting for.

Zeb boarded the lift and rode it up to the third floor. Stepping into the hall, he found it completely deserted. No patients, no nurses, no one from maintenance. Standing there, he peeled away the blankets covering Ribka, then unzipped his coat. If anyone questioned his presence what was he going to say, that he was going to visit someone? No, better to claim he'd just gotten off work and that he'd forgotten something, say, his wallet.

He proceeded down the hall, his now-wet shoes smacking the linoleum and the baby beginning to squirm in his arms. Passing by several rooms, he peered in the open doors, saw one patient sleeping, another reading, yet another watching television, and he was amazed all over again that just about anyone could walk in here like this. Turning a corner, he eyed the nurses' station, saw it still darkened and empty. Then he saw the door labeled M.S. There were stacks of expensive drugs in there, but how the hell was he going to get in?

Ribka began to fuss more, and Zeb lifted her up, kissed her on the cheek, then settled her in his left arm. She was hungry and he had no food, but that was the next problem. First things first.

He tried the door, twisting the handle and finding it solidly locked. He pushed harder yet. No way in hell was the door going to budge by force alone. Zeb next checked the halls, which still stretched empty and silent, and then hurried over to the nurses' station. He grabbed at the main drawer, found it, too, locked, as were the file cabinets on either side. The overhead cabinets, a door to a back room, the cabinet beneath a sink. Crap, thought Zeb. Everything, all of it locked tight. A key to the medical supply room might or might not be lying around in one of these drawers, but he couldn't get into any of them, nor could he find anything with which to force the door. The countertops were completely clear, no letter openers, no pens, nothing long and hard and rigid.

Giving up on that, he carefully held the baby and reached into the pocket of his jacket and took out his wallet. He had a few dollars, a driver's license, and a credit card his mother had given him years ago, which he'd kept even though she canceled it once he'd stayed on with The Congregation. Could it be so simple a lock that a credit card might work on it? With nothing to lose he crossed the hall, bending over and examining the lock on the medical supply room.

"Come on, Ribka," he whispered to his child, "work some magic for us, okay, little girl?"

He slipped the credit card into the space between the door and the lock and hit a solid piece of metal. Sliding the credit card upward, he hit something else, pressed, but nothing moved. No, he realized, this was a reinforced lock, there was no way in hell this was going to work, no way. . . .

Suddenly there was a figure standing nearby, saying, "Zeb?"

Startled, he dropped the credit card, felt himself tumbling to the side, and clutched his daughter. Above him stood a woman in a white uniform.

"What are you doing?" demanded Brenda, the nurse whom he'd met not more than three hours earlier.

"I . . . I . . ."

"You were trying to break in there, weren't you? What are you after, drugs?" When he started to get up, she quickly backed away. "That's what it is, isn't it? That's what you were after before too, right? You didn't want to clean in there, you wanted to steal something. God, I'm going to call security!"

"Wait!" he shouted as she turned away. "Wait, Brenda, I can explain!"

"Like hell you can."

"Brenda!"

His plea was so desperate that she hesitated and looked back at him.

"You don't understand," he called after her. "This . . . this is my daughter. She's sick. She's sick and she needs medicine and I don't have any money."

# 18

"You saw the note, Todd," said Janice flatly, now seated on her living room couch, a blanket draped over her shoulders, both hands clutching a mug of steaming coffee. "We weren't supposed to call the police."

"I didn't call the cops. I called Rawlins, that's all."

"He is the police."

"No, he's my boyfriend. And your friend too, for that matter. He's family, Janice."

"I just want to do what they say. I . . . I don't want anyone to get hurt. I don't want to complicate things."

"It's too late for that," said Todd as he began to pace in front of the four arching windows of her living room. "What do you call these bruises on my side or those marks on your wrists?"

"Todd—the baby. I . . . I just don't want anything to happen to her, I don't know what I'll—"

"What the hell are you saying? She's already been kidnapped." He shook his head, trying to make sense of this all. "Or maybe I should say she's been rekidnapped. I don't get any of this."

"I just hope she's okay, that he hasn't already hurt her."

Reminded of the blood they'd found in the snow, he said, "Me too."

Todd looked out one of the windows, but saw nothing. Rawlins was on his way, but who knew how long it'd take in this storm. And who knew what the hell they'd do after he got here. Touching the painful bruises on his side, Todd glanced anxiously about the living room with its tall, beamed ceiling. He shuffled across the light brown carpeting, stopped near an overstuffed chair. What a mess. Why the hell had she kept this from him?

"Janice, I can't believe you didn't tell me about any of this," he said, unable to hide the anger in his voice. "I mean—"

"That's what I wanted to talk about tonight."

"Well, I wish you'd told me earlier, like sometime within the last decade or two." He shook his head, clenched the back of his head with his right hand. "We're talking about something that happened—what was it—over twenty years ago."

"It's just so complicated."

"Obviously."

"But Todd—"

"Janice, I might not only have fathered your kid, but I'm also one of your best friends, aren't I?"

"Of course you are, but . . . but I couldn't tell you back then. I couldn't tell anyone. You just don't understand."

"No, I guess I don't."

"Please," she said, pulling the blanket tight around her and closing her eyes, "I can't talk about it now."

"You can't talk about it *now*? *Now?* You secretly had a child when we were in college and you never told me that I might be his father—and you don't want to fucking talk about it? And now that kid's daughter has been kidnapped, and what, we're supposed to sit around a fire and do a crossword puzzle or something? Gee, doesn't that sound nice and fun?" He slapped his forehead with his right hand. "What's happened to you, Janice? Are you crazy? Have you lost your mind?''

''Todd—''

''Here I thought you were so open and honest, the epitome of self-awareness and integrity,'' he said, raising his hands, ''but you're nothing more than . . . than the original closet case, are you?''

''Stop it!'' she demanded, her eyes brimming with tears.

''Why, is there something else? Don't tell me you've got more skeletons in there? Twins maybe? Or perhaps I begot triplets? And if I am the chief, just tell me, how big is my tribe?''

''Shut up!'' she shouted.

''Oh, you mean I'm supposed to just forget that I might have reproduced and my genes are out there running around?''

''Oh, Todd,'' she sobbed. ''Please, not now. We'll talk about it later—I'll tell you everything. I want to, I need to, but I just can't get into it right now.'' A Kleenex to her eyes, she glanced toward the front windows. ''If anything happens to that child I'll kill myself.''

Todd turned around, felt a stab of pain in his side, and stared outside into the dark night. Yes, the baby.

''Of course,'' he muttered.

Janice's granddaughter was out there. His granddaughter as well? He shook his head, for it was a loop and a twist he just couldn't make, couldn't comprehend. A few hours ago he'd been thinking he was glad he didn't have kids, and now he might not only have a son but a granddaughter as well. It was possible, wasn't it? Of course, and he shook his head, for he was just so confused. None of this made any sense.

''You didn't really go to Europe, did you?'' he asked.

She looked up, her eyes red and swollen. ''What?''

''Back in college. What was it, our junior year? You were supposed to have gone to France to study. Aix-en-Provence—something like that. And then Greece too, wasn't it? But you never went, did you? You didn't even leave the country, did you?''

''No.''

''You took off that semester to have a baby.''

She nodded. ''Right.''

''When did you have him?''

''August. He was a few weeks early.''

''And then you gave him up for adoption?''

She stared at her lap. ''Yes.''

''You gave him up, and then by fall you were back in school as if nothing had happened. You came back all smiles, telling everyone that you'd been off gallivanting around Europe for seven or eight months. Oh, and that you were first and foremost a dyke.''

She sat there in silence, his words like daggers of guilt and shame cutting at her, slicing, ripping, tearing. Todd watched her, saw those long-concealed events all finally boil to the surface and burn across her face.

Her voice barely audible, she said, ''You . . . you don't have any idea what I was going through, how hard it was, how awful.''

He turned away, walked across the room, and stopped next to a bookcase. That period of his life was coming into true focus. It was as if he'd finally found the correct pair of glasses to look back through time and he was finally seeing it clearly, able to make sense of what had happened and why.

''We dated that fall before you left. We started going out in September, and we were little boyfriend and girlfriend for a while there. It was pretty fun too.''

''Todd, that was so long ago.''

But he couldn't stop himself. ''We made it almost all the way to Christmas break, of course. You remember, don't you? There was the Christmas party at your sorority. And then we slipped upstairs and did it. Screwed, if you know what I mean. Fucked.''

''Todd, stop it, would you? You're being a real asshole.''

"I went up to your room. It was right before Christmas break, just a day or two. I still think of that night every time I hear Carly Simon. God, I was so scared. And . . . and then we crawled into bed and it just sort of happened. After that we hardly saw each other."

"Right," she agreed sadly.

The question popped out of his mouth. "So if I'm not the father of your kid, who is?"

"Oh, shit, Todd."

"Were you seeing someone else?"

"God, that sounds so suburban, so middle-class."

"Well, I want to know."

"Forget it."

"But you were screwing around on me, weren't you?"

"I can't believe this conversation—a queen and a dyke talking about cheating on each other!"

"Janice, we were dating at the time. I really liked you. I—"

Suddenly she was on her feet, her fury erupting seemingly out of nowhere, and her finger pointing at him. "How dare you!"

"How dare I what?"

"Todd, you asshole, how dare you talk to me about cheating! For your information I went out West right after I left Northwestern, and I did have sex with some guy a couple of days after we did," she said. "But would you please stop pretending to be the pure one?"

Oh, Christ, he thought, turning away. She knows.

"God, when it comes right down to it, you're just another fucking guy with his own fucking double standards. It must be testosterone. You get a dose of that stuff and you think you can put your dick anywhere you want and it doesn't matter, there aren't any consequences." She shook her head. "You were screwing around too, and don't tell me you weren't!"

He hesitated and then muttered, "So you know about—"

"Pat?" she said with great emphasis as she glared at Todd. "Sure I do. I know that you two guys had sex a few times while we were dating. Which explains a lot, namely why you were scared to screw me.''

''Shit . . .''

Todd turned away, shaking his head in shame. He tried to say something, but his mouth was so dry he couldn't speak. He cleared his throat. ''I'm sorry, Janice. I . . . I . . .''

''Oh, so you have a complicated story too?''

''Yeah, but—''

''Nice and sordid, but you don't want to talk about it tonight, right?'' she taunted.

''Janice, please.''

''Please, what? Please let me have my own double standards? Please let me be a hypocrite? Or what?''

He couldn't do this. He couldn't fight this battle.

''Who . . .'' he began, his voice faint, ''who told you?''

''Who do you think? Pat.''

''What?'' gasped Todd, suddenly looking up at her. ''When?''

''Let's just say I knew by that Christmas.''

All this time, all these years, the secret had been burning within Todd like a smoldering fire. That little bastard. Todd had kept up his part of the bargain. He hadn't told a soul. And here Pat had gone and told Janice. Janice of all people! He clenched his fists, felt his shame boil into anger, and wanted to strike out, hit something. Pat was such a shit. Todd had been such a fool. He should never have had sex with him, and by all means he should never have let Pat tell him what to do later on.

The frustration, the anger, just popped. Todd pulled his leg back, looked for something, anything, and then as hard as he could kicked a side table, causing a lamp and a handful of magazines to crash to the floor.

''Todd!'' screamed Janice.

But her plea went unheard. Instead, Todd kicked the table two and three more times until one of the legs cracked, and then he started kicking the magazines, sending them flapping across the room like insane birds.

"Goddamn it all!" he shouted as loudly as he could.

"Stop it, Todd! Just stop it!"

His face seething, he turned to her, saw the tears streaming down her cheeks. So how much had Pat actually told her? Not simply that they'd had sex, but everything? Half of him wanted Janice to know the entire truth about that night Greg had died, half of him was terrified that she already did.

# 19

The doorbell was ringing. Janice was slumped on the couch, sobbing. Todd was seated on the floor leaning against a wall, his face buried in his hands. And the doorbell was ringing.

Todd raised his head, wiped the tears from his own eyes. Glancing around, he saw the broken leg of the side table, the scattered magazines. Crap. When was he going to get ahold of his temper?

Yes, the doorbell. There it was again.

With the pain from his bruises cutting into his side, Todd pushed himself up from the floor. He paused, picked up one torn magazine that sprawled like a dead pigeon on the floor, laid it carefully on a chair. This was unbelievable, all of it.

His voice hoarse, barely audible, he said, "Janice, I . . ."

But he didn't know what to say, and in any case it didn't make any difference. She didn't want to hear. Seated on the couch, she pulled the blanket up even higher, covering her face, and wouldn't even look at him. Who could blame her?

As the doorbell rang again, Todd shuffled to the entry hall. Opening the front door, he found Rawlins standing there, his compact body shivering, his head and leather jacket covered with snow.

"Shit, it's really coming down," Rawlins said, entering and stomping his boots. "Sorry it took me so long to get over here—we haven't had a storm like this in a few years." He glanced back to the kitchen. "Where is she?"

"In the living room."

"How is she?"

"Not good."

Rawlins studied Todd. "Man, you don't look so good either."

"I'm not." He shook his head. "This is really a mess. Come on, there's a lot to tell you."

Todd led Rawlins down to the living room, where they found Janice still slumped on the couch.

"Hi," she said, wiping her eyes and looking only at Rawlins. "Thanks for coming."

"Of course, but, Janice, what the hell's going on?" began Rawlins in his usual direct way. "Let me get this straight. That kid, that baby you've had for the past week, she's your granddaughter?"

Janice nodded.

"It's a tad more complicated—I'll tell you later," added Todd, wondering what Rawlins would think. "About an hour ago someone broke in, tied up Janice, knocked me out, and took her."

"Oh, Jesus, a kidnapping."

Janice looked away. Then she reached down to the coffee table and took the note.

"I don't know what to say," began Janice. "Read this. We're not supposed to contact the police. I'm just afraid of what they'll do if . . . if . . ."

Rawlins said firmly, "Relax. They won't know."

"Janice," added Todd, placing his hand on Rawlins's shoulder, "you've got to tell him everything."

Obviously angry with him, she glared at Todd and

shrugged. She motioned for Rawlins to sit down, and then slowly, hesitantly, she began with the facts. She'd had a kid between her junior and senior years in college, she explained, her voice flat, almost defeated, and she'd not heard nor seen anything of the child until three years ago when he'd simply shown up at her law office one day. Eventually, she told Rawlins everything, excluding one simple thing: the identity of the father.

"I left a letter with his mother," she said. "I asked her to give it to Zeb if he ever inquired about me. Well, three years ago he did inquire, he did get my letter, and after that he decided to come up and meet me."

"Just out of the blue?" asked Rawlins.

"Totally."

Janice continued to explain that there'd been nothing after that, not a word or a call or anything, until just a few days ago when he'd phoned and told her they had to meet, that night if possible.

"So I meet him in the parking lot of the Rainbow Foods store last Monday. It's real cold, and he gets in my car and says hello. And in his arms, wrapped in his parka, is this kid, little Ribka."

"You didn't know about her?" asked Rawlins.

"Are you kidding? Not at all."

"What did he do then?" Todd ventured.

She explained how Zeb had said he was worried about the child, how they were coming after him, how he was worried about his own safety.

Rawlins pressed, "Who? Who's this 'they'?"

"I don't know." Janice shook her head. "It just all happened so quickly. He was in my car, then he was pushing the kid into my arms, and then he was jumping out. It all happened about that quickly. But . . ."

"But?"

"Well, when he was here the first time he told me that his parents were divorced—apparently when he was ten or eleven his mother took him and ran away from his father. Something about his dad being in some religious cult. Then when he was here the first time, he told me he was going back to live with his dad for a while."

"So maybe he stayed for a few years and then he had to run away too."

"That's what I've been thinking," added Janice. "Maybe there was no way to get away from them but to run. And he took his daughter just like his mom took him, and now they're after him. It's either that or drugs, because I know he got into some trouble in high school for smoking pot."

Todd gently asked, "Did he say anything about what he was going to do? Where he was going?"

"No, not really."

"You don't have any way of getting in touch with him?"

"No. He didn't say a thing about his plans." She stopped, tripped on something in her memory. "Wait a minute. He said something about a job interview, that he'd just had one."

"Here, in town?" interjected Todd.

"I think so."

"Good. Then it sounds as if he wasn't planning on going far. He probably wanted to be close to the kid."

"Did he say where he interviewed?" asked Rawlins.

"Uh. Oh, crap, what did he say?"

"At a factory, a business downtown, an insurance agency, anything like that?" suggested Todd.

She looked at him. "A hospital, that's what he said." Her eyes opened wide. "A hospital in Edina."

Todd smiled slightly. "There's only one hospital out there, right?"

"As far as I know." Rawlins started to get up. "Let's just hope he was offered the job and that he in fact took it."

"What, you're not going to go out there, are you?" demanded Janice.

"Of course," replied Rawlins.

Todd said, "How else are we going to find him?"

"But the note, the letter. We're not supposed to—"

"Don't worry," interjected Todd, looking squarely at her. "I'm going to make sure nothing happens to that baby."

"We're not going to do anything stupid," added Rawlins. "You'll see, we'll just try to find him and then you can ask him some questions."

"What?" she protested. "You're not expecting me to go out there too, are you?"

Rawlins glanced at Todd, then back at Janice. "Well, it would be helpful. You could identify him at least."

"No." Janice was vigorously shaking her head. "I'm not going. I've . . . I've got to stay here by the phone."

Todd knew there would be no changing her mind, no way to talk her into going out to the hospital, at least not tonight. Yet neither he nor Rawlins had any idea what this Zeb looked like.

His voice full of trepidation, Todd asked, "You don't have a picture of him, do you?"

She nodded, wiped her nose, shed the blanket from her shoulders, and got up. After crossing the room, Janice took a color picture of a young man from her wallet.

"It was taken a few years ago," she explained. "He gave it to me when he first came up here, when we first met. He's older now, more mature-looking, and his hair is short, but . . . but . . ."

Todd crossed to her, pulled the photo from her hands. It looked like a high school picture, a handsome boy poised in front of a blue background. Long brown hair, nice smile. Todd searched the face, tried to see a hint of his own reflection.

Rawlins came up behind Todd, studied the picture, and volunteered, "Wow, cute kid."

"Yeah, well don't get any ideas, you're much too old for him," snapped Todd as he placed the photo in his shirt pocket. "Come on, let's go."

"Call me," implored Janice. "Tell me if you find him."

Todd stared at her, wondered how deeply Janice and he

were actually connected. Then he went over and kissed her on the cheek.

"I'm sorry," he said.

She shrugged, pulled back a bit, and said, "You scared me."

"Yeah, well, I'm an ass."

"Just let me know as soon as you find out anything."

As they headed for the door Rawlins said, "If anyone calls, take notes. Write down exactly what they said, when they called—everything. Do you have call waiting?"

"No."

"Then if any friends phone, just tell them you can't talk. And don't make any calls either. You want to make sure to keep the line open."

"Don't worry, I won't tie up the phone. And I'm sure as hell not going anywhere either," stated Janice. "Just be careful. Be nice to Zeb too. In spite of whatever he's done, he's a good kid."

# 20

From the windows of her living room, Janice watched Todd and Rawlins trudge through the snowy night and down to the street. She wondered if Todd had guessed, if he even suspected, but as far as she could tell he hadn't. The entire truth was just so bizarre that it probably wouldn't occur to him. She wondered what he'd do if he ever did find out. God, she was so tired of this secret, exhausted from working so hard to conceal it for so very long.

They didn't take Rawlins's silver sedan, which was relatively free of snow, but instead brushed off Todd's Cherokee, Rawlins wiping the rear window with his gloved hand and Todd scraping nearly a half foot from the windshield and hood. She wanted them to be gone, to be on their way at once, for there was something she had to do. Oh, Lord, how had this gotten so incredibly screwed up?

It seemed to take forever, but finally the two of them climbed into the large four-wheel-drive vehicle. The headlights burst on, and Janice stared after them as the Cherokee began to plow forward and slowly make its way into the middle of the street. As Todd drove on, Janice pressed closer to the window, watching in the light of a street lamp as he turned right at the first corner and at last disappeared into the wintry storm.

Thank God they were gone, she thought, quickly turning away from the window. There was something she had to do, a call she had to make, right this very second.

Not wasting a moment, she hurried across her living room to the staircase. Taking the stairs two at a time, she climbed to the second floor, then passed through the upstairs hall. She had the address somewhere. The phone number too. But where? Damn it all, where?

Turning into the first room, she entered her study, a small room with beige walls and dark brown blinds on the windows. She went to her desk, a long white laminate table with stacks of papers and bills on one side, her black cordless phone with the short rubber antenna on the other. She yanked open the single drawer. Six months ago she'd gotten one of those electronic organizers, into which she'd entered all her addresses. Except one. She didn't know why. She remembered staring at the address and name, remembered that of all the numbers she had, this was the one she didn't want to lose. After all, what if she dropped the electronic organizer and it broke? What if she sat down next to a large magnet; might that not make it go haywire? Almost every other address could be replaced, either through friends or from her Rolodex at work. But not this one. Which was one of the primary reasons she'd kept her old worn address book.

But if she'd been so blasted careful about keeping the little book, then why the hell couldn't she remember where she'd put it? Shit. This was all too typical of her, of the disorganized manner in which she kept things, and she swept aside pencils and pens, paper clips and stamps, her stapler, as well as the cordless phone. But no worn and cracked little black leather book. What the hell had she done with that stupid thing?

Janice stopped, put her hand to her forehead. Wait a minute, she told herself. Where did she put things that didn't have a file or a place of their own? Of course. From the bookshelf she took a large blue bowl overflowing with everything from the extra garage door opener to a broken calculator she was sure was repairable to, finally, the book. She put the bowl on the middle of her paper-strewn desk, snatched out the little black book, and started thumbing through it.

And sure enough, there it was, Pat's telephone number.

Not hesitating a moment, she knocked an entire stack of papers onto the floor as she reached for the cordless phone. Without even thinking what she was going to say, she punched in the numbers. Only as it started to ring did she wonder if indeed Pat still lived in the same place, if in fact she'd be able to reach him. How many years had it been? They'd spoken by phone a couple of times since then, but she hadn't seen him since that year Zeb was born. Oh, God, if Todd thought he had some explaining to do, wait until he heard about this. And, yes, she realized. She had to tell him. She couldn't hold it back anymore. This final aspect of the truth was eating at her.

*After Greg died in that horrible accident, she knew what they were saying, all of them, about Pat. That was why she was nice to him. Heck, it was almost Christmas, you were supposed to be nice to others.*

*So they had coffee at a little restaurant in downtown Evanston.*

*"I can't wait to get to France—and I can't believe I have to wait until the end of January." Seated in a cold, plastic chair, Janice brushed aside her long, straight hair. "I'm supposed to go to my parents' in Phoenix over Christmas, but I'm sure as hell not looking forward to it. It's just so boring down there."*

*Pat's face suddenly brightened, and he reached out and grabbed Janice by the hand. "I know, let's take a road trip! I've got a car; we can just take off and get the hell out of here. We can do whatever we want! Hey, I even have friends in Colorado we could stay with!"*

*That was how they eventually ended up in bed, Janice and Pat.*

*The trip was a lark, a way to escape their foreboding lives. Now, two days out from Northwestern, they were in some dumpy motel room with only one sagging double bed. And no TV. That was all they could afford. It was freezing too; Phoenix, not to mention the south of France, was beginning to sound better and better. To make matters still worse, Pat had bought a bottle of tequila, of which he'd drunk half, and they were lying on the bed together—Janice in her flannel nightgown and heavy socks, Pat in a T-shirt and jeans—because there weren't even any chairs in the room.*

*Actually, she knew why she'd been nice to Pat. Of course she had an ulterior motive: She needed to talk to someone. Someone safe, nonjudgmental. Someone in the same boat. She wanted to tell him about herself, that she liked women. Or that maybe she did. She didn't know, wasn't sure what she felt. Was he confused like that?*

*Finally she asked the question that she hoped would lead to the larger conversation, the big picture. "So, Pat, are you gay?"*

*Suddenly his drunken breath was in her face and his hand was on her breast. "What do you think?"*

*She grabbed him by the wrist. "Pat . . ."*

*"Well, do you?"*

*"I just want to talk. I thought it would be good. Actually, I don't care what you are."*

*"Well, I'm not," he said, twisting his hand free and then grabbing at her nightgown and rubbing her left tit. "I'm really not."*

*"Pat, stop it."*

*"Why?"*

*"Come on, cut it out."*

*"But . . ." And then he was raising himself up, crawling on top of her. "You know, you're really sexy."*

*She started pushing him away. "Pat, don't."*

*"Why? Don't you think I can do it with a woman?"* He kissed her on the neck, his lips all sloppy and wet. *"I . . . I . . ."*

*"Frankly, I don't care if you can do it with a tree."*

*"Well, maybe I can't manage that one."* He giggled and reached down to her crotch, then started pulling up her night-gown. *"But you, on the other hand, are unbelievable."*

*"Don't!"*

*"Just try and stop me."*

*"Pat!"*

*"Yeah, you want it, don't you."*

*"Get the fuck off me!"*

*"Yeah, fuck . . . fuck . . ."*

Janice started bucking and twisting, the fear coursing through her as he hiked her gown up over her knees, up her thighs. Shit, this couldn't be happening. Pat was supposed to be like her, he was supposed to be safe. And just as she realized how drunk he was, she realized how much stronger he was than her.

*"Stop or I'm going to scream!"*

He lunged for the tequila bottle, and then Janice felt a shower of burning booze as he dumped the bottle all over her face. She clenched her eyes shut, started to shout, but then he poured the rest of the booze into her mouth, at least a quarter bottle.

*"Drink up, little girl!"* he laughed.

She gasped for air, inhaled, and her body screamed as the tequila whooshed into her lungs like liquid fire. Christ, she couldn't breathe! She couldn't make a sound! Please, Lord, she begged, don't let me die here!

He slapped her once, twice. Maybe more. And when she opened her eyes she saw that he'd ripped off his own jeans and his dick was hard and arched.

*"I'm going to fuck you, Janice,"* he said, his voice deep and slurred. *"You know why? You know why I'm going to fuck you? Because my cock goes everywhere. Just last week your*

*boyfriend, your Todd, was sucking on this cock—that's right, don't look so shocked, he's the faggot, not me. My cock was in his mouth, and now I'm going to put it right in your pussy."*

*It was as if he'd taken an electrical cord and shocked her. Todd? Todd and Pat together? She just lay there, the tequila still burning within her body, Pat's words searing her mind. And he did it. He fucked her. In the end, Janice was just so freaked out that she lay there as passive as a pillow.*

*When he was done, she crawled out from underneath him and stumbled into the bathroom, where she locked the door. She curled up in the bathtub and cried, and then in the middle of the night she got up, snuck out into the room where Pat was snoring. She took all his money, all of his credit cards, and walked across town to the bus station, where she caught a Greyhound at 5:03 A.M. She arrived in Phoenix two days later.*

When an answering machine picked up after the fourth ring and announced that she'd reached a particular business office, she recognized the deep voice. Okay, she said to herself, don't be afraid. It's okay. Just sound strong, sound calm. Standing up and starting to pace in the small room, Janice told herself to be brief, to the point.

When the signal came for her to leave a message, Janice put one hand to her forehead, closed her eyes, and said, "Hi, this is Janice Gray calling for Pat. Please tell him there's a problem and that we need to talk."

She left her phone number, then hung up. Clutching the cordless phone against her breast and wishing it to ring that very instant with a return call, she headed down to the kitchen, where she heated a mug of water in the microwave. When it was hot she dropped in a tea bag and sat down at her small breakfast table, the marble one with the black iron base.

Now all she had to do was wait.

# 21

―――

"I can't believe it," said Rawlins once Todd had finished telling him the brunt of the story.

"*You* can't? What about me?" Todd hung tightly on to the steering wheel as he drove south on the whitened Xerxes Avenue. "It's just too weird, finding out in a matter of a few seconds not only that I might have a son—in his twenties, no less—but a granddaughter too."

"It's a strange world."

"No shit."

A huge gust of wind and snow belted the car, which caused the entire vehicle to heave to the side. Todd steered back to the right, and he had no idea whether he should be elated or heartbroken. Then again, if Janice didn't even know, how could he?

He heard some chuckling to the side, glanced over, saw Rawlins leaning against the car door, a gloved hand to his mouth.

Todd demanded, "What the hell are you laughing about?"

"I don't know if I would've started dating you if I'd known you were a grandfather."

"Very funny."

"Gramps—that's what I'm going to start calling you."

"Why do I suddenly feel very old?"

"Responsibility does that to a person."

Not quite five minutes later Todd turned off Xerxes Avenue and proceeded to the rear of Edina Hospital, where he parked in a three-story ramp. Both of them pulled up their collars and then ran through the snow and wind to the hospital entrance. Once inside, the electric doors closed behind them, sealing out the storm, and the two of them brushed themselves off, stomped their feet, and glanced about. Not a soul was to be seen. Even the guard's desk was vacant, a desk lamp on, but no one sitting there.

"God, this place is like a morgue," said Todd, checking out the halls and empty waiting areas. "Now what?"

Rawlins shrugged. "As my Russian grandmother used to say, 'Your tongue will lead you to Moscow.'"

"Meaning?"

"We start asking questions and supposedly we'll find out how to get there."

"Well, I highly doubt the personnel department is going to be open at this time of night."

"No, but there's a receptionist right over there. Where's the picture of the young hunk?"

"Don't talk about him like that," said Todd.

He reached inside his coat, pulled the photograph from his shirt pocket, and stood there staring at it. Okay, so the kid was good-looking. Supposedly bright and pleasant too. But then, as Todd studied the high school picture of the kid that might or might not be his son, he had a terrible realization. Had he known for sure at the time that Janice was pregnant with his kid, he wouldn't have encouraged her to do as she did, to put Zeb up for adoption. Rather, he would have encouraged her, been very persistent, and somehow, he was sure, persuaded her, to have an abortion.

Suddenly the photograph was yanked out of his hands.

"Hey, Todd, come on," called Rawlins, pulling Todd back to the moment. "Let's see if anyone recognizes the kid."

It was warm back here in the hospital laundry room. And it was safe. Settled deep in bags of sheets as if they were nothing more than a hill of beanbags, Zeb cradled his baby in his arms and started to doze off. Ribka had the medication she needed, she'd just eaten a full bottle of formula, she even had a clean diaper, which was more, much more than he'd ever hoped for tonight. And, of course, they had a warm place to sleep, all thanks to Brenda, the nurse, who'd fortunately understood his dilemma, or at least as much as he'd been able to explain. Then again, how could you describe The Congregation and have it make sense to anyone who hadn't been there, living on the compound, working in the bakery?

Fuck, fuck, fuck, he thought to himself with a grin, for it felt so incredibly great just to think it let alone say it.

Whispering so as not to wake the baby, he said, *"Fuuuuuuckkkk."*

Those morons at The Congregation would only say "Ghastly" or "Worldly." Worldly? What the hell did that mean? How stupid. He was so sick of their Bible babble, so sick of them creeping into every part of his life, demanding that he think one way, their way, and always looking at him suspiciously because, after all, he was a "fringer," someone who wasn't really one of them.

He felt old, not only because here he was, his own baby asleep in his arms, but because everything was beginning to make sense. He finally understood why his mother had left The Congregation over ten years ago. After her closest friend in the group, Louise, had died of skin cancer, Zeb's own mother had lost her faith completely. It had been treatable, Zeb's mom had explained that night as she stuffed him in one of the cars and drove to the Colorado Springs bus depot. Louise didn't die because of a lack of faith. She hadn't given over to Satan, she didn't have the mark of the beast. Plus she'd even been rebaptized when she'd joined The Congregation, making that a nonissue. No, none of those had been a problem. Louise believed, Louise trusted, Louise stood on The Promises. And yet she'd died, even as The Elders had gathered and placed a drop of blessed oil upon her forehead. She'd died not for lack of faith, but because of the ignorance of The Congregation.

"People get skin cancer all the time," Zeb's mom had sobbed as they rode the bus that morning. "You just go to the doctor and have it treated. Louise spotted it real early. She could have just had it frozen off. Zap—that's it."

Instead, all the prayers in the world, all the faith in the world hadn't been able to save Louise, and she had died a slow, painful death. Funny, thought Zeb, Louise was the mother of Zeb's wife, Suzanne, the one he'd screwed and been forced to marry. In spite of all the pain Suzanne had experienced over her mother's death, however, she still hadn't wanted to take her own baby to a doctor. The Elders and her father had prevailed, placing a drop of oil on the baby's forehead, and then telling Suzanne and Zeb to pray to God the Father and God the Son. When the child failed to improve, The Elders had asserted that it was their fault, Suzanne and Zeb's. They just didn't have enough faith. They just had to pray more, believe more.

Well, bullshit. Who cared if Suzanne's own father was head of The Congregation, there was no way in hell that bastard was God's Apostle on earth. Hell no. He was Satan. Zeb's baby girl just had a chronic, low-grade infection in her middle ear. That was why she was so cranky and crabby.

"You should have brought her in sooner, because from the looks of it this has been going on for a while," said the doctor Zeb had taken her to right after they'd fled The Congregation. "What that means is that we're going to be fairly aggressive with one particular antibiotic. It's rather expensive, but we want this to clear up as soon as possible."

Zeb had wanted to tell Suzanne about his plans to take

Ribka to a doctor, he'd thought about asking her to run away with him, but he just couldn't tell what she'd think, say, or do. Supposedly they were married, but he really didn't know her—not what she really wanted anyway. So rather than jeopardize the baby's safety and health—The Elders would have locked Zeb up in the bakery basement if they'd found out he was planning to kidnap the baby—Zeb had kept his plans a secret, encouraged only by his mother in Santa Fe.

He'd done the right thing too. He'd known that when he was less than a mile away from the compound; he was positive as soon as he'd taken Ribka to the doctor. Maybe sometime soon he'd call Suzanne and apologize, but little Ribka was more important than anything, and he hugged her gently, kissed the top of her head. She was getting her medication, the infection was clearing up, and she was fine, just fine, sleeping peacefully, eating well. What a relief. Yes, there was a God. Or there probably was. But it certainly wasn't theirs.

There was just one more problem. After tonight where were they going to sleep?

Okay, so now he couldn't go back to Janice's, and he doubted he could go back to that tiny rat hole of an apartment he'd rented. Brother Paul, that King Kong of a jerk, was in Minneapolis, and if there were other members of The Congregation here, sooner or later they'd find him. Which meant, Zeb realized, that he was going to have to take off, leave Minneapolis completely. Maybe the storm would slow things down, give him a little extra time so he could at least collect his first paycheck from the hospital. Maybe Brenda might even know of a place where he could crash for a while. Sure, he hardly knew her, but she was nice, she probably would help. Just look at what she'd done for him tonight. Not only had she been the one to steal the medicine, she'd also suggested that Zeb and Ribka sleep in the laundry room so they wouldn't have to go back out in the winter storm.

Someone knocked on the door and Zeb immediately stiffened. Two taps, a pause, three taps. Good, all was safe. It was her, Brenda, and he couldn't help but wonder why she'd come back so soon. Dinner? She'd said she was going to try to scrounge up something for him. Maybe she had, and maybe she'd even brought something for herself and he would have some company.

When the door opened, he looked up with a smile and said softly, "Hi, I was just thinking about you."

She quickly slipped in, pulled the door shut, locked it, and turned to him with a worried expression creasing her brow. Oh, God, he thought. He feared what was up. The Congregation was just that conniving.

"Don't tell me they're here already?" he said.

"I don't know if it's them, those guys from that cult or whatever, but there are two guys upstairs looking for you," said Brenda, obviously concerned, even scared. "They came up on the third floor and asked some of the nurses if we'd seen you tonight."

"Oh, no. This is bad, really bad."

"Yeah, and they even had a picture they were showing around. They asked if I knew you, but I lied. One of the other nurses, though, well, she said she thought she'd seen you around earlier this evening."

"Shit." Zeb clenched his forehead with one hand. "I can't stay here. I gotta go, I gotta get out of here."

"No, I think you'll be okay," countered Brenda. "I just wanted to come down and tell you so you'd stay in here, so you wouldn't go out in the hall."

"No, you don't know them. They won't give up until they'll find me. They're like bloodhounds. And if they're this close, they're going to search the whole building."

"Zeb, I—"

"What if Ribka wakes up and she starts crying? What if one of them is right out in the hall?" Zeb started pushing himself out of the nest of laundry bags. "I gotta get out of here right now."

"But—"

"Brenda, they'll beat the shit out of me if they catch me. And . . . they'll take her, little Ribka. That's what they want, what they came for. They'll probably kill me, but they'll take her."

"What about the police, maybe you should go to them?"

"Yeah, right, and be arrested for kidnapping?"

"But she's your daughter," pleaded Brenda, "and she would've gotten sicker if you hadn't gotten her away from them."

"Trust me, I've thought of every angle."

"So where are you going to go?"

"I don't know. I don't think I can go back to my apartment. If they're all the way out here at the hospital, then for sure they've already been there. I just don't get how they could've found me so quickly."

"Well," said Brenda, glancing around, "there's always my place. I guess that'd be okay. I'm here all night, but I don't think my roommate would mind. There's no way they could find you there."

He looked up at her. "Not if I get out of here without being seen."

"Relax," said Rawlins as the two of them rode the elevator down. "It wasn't so hard finding him."

"What are you talking about?" countered Todd with a distinct frown. "We haven't found him yet."

"Well, at least we know for sure that he works here. Don't worry, we'll find him tomorrow. First thing in the morning we'll come out and talk to the personnel department. They'll have an address for him."

"What if it's a P.O. box or something?"

"Then we'll just have to wait until he shows up for work. If he was here earlier tonight, then he works a late shift and he'll probably be here tomorrow afternoon. You'll see."

The elevator doors opened on the ground floor and Todd started out, unable to hide his frustration. Sure, they needed to find Zeb to tell him that the baby had been taken and see if he could help locate the child. But most of all Todd wanted to see Zeb, meet him face to face, look into his eyes.

They headed to the left, down the long quiet hall and toward the front doors. Realizing how sore he was from the scuffle at Janice's, Todd felt himself moving slower and slower.

"You look exhausted," said Rawlins, placing a reassuring hand on Todd's shoulder. "Let's get you home so you can rest."

Todd nodded and managed a smile, for this was what he liked about Rawlins, not simply his ability to read Todd, but the ease with which he offered comfort. Comfort that Todd not only found easy to accept, but for the first time in his life, easy to return.

"Thanks, but I can't go home," said Todd. "We should head back to Janice's. I'm sure she's a wreck."

"So let's spend the night there—she's got plenty of room."

"Okay."

They proceeded down the hall in silence, passing a closed gift shop, another hallway, the lone receptionist sitting behind the counter. Farther down they came to the hospital guard, a lanky older man, who had just returned and was now seated at his small desk.

"Good night, gentlemen," he said, looking up from a fishing magazine. "Now drive safely. It's pretty nasty out there."

"Good night," replied Todd.

They paused before the revolving door, zipped up their jackets, slipped on their gloves.

"Ready?" asked Todd.

"Yeah, ready to go to Florida," griped Rawlins.

Todd went first, and as soon as the automatic doors slid open and he'd exited the building, he was slapped by stinging snow. He looked up at a tall streetlight and saw not only how heavily the snow was still falling but the nearly horizontal angle at which it was blowing. Great, the wind had picked up and the conditions worsened to near blizzard. Clenching his jacket collar around his neck and squinting his eyes, Todd thought this was unbelievable, things were going from bad to worse. Stepping into snow well above his boot, Todd led the way, trudging quickly through the deep white stuff and toward the parking ramp.

"Hey!" called a voice through the wind. "Hey, you two!"

They paused, looked back, and saw the tall guard poking his head out and waving at them.

"Hey!" he called again. "Come back here!"

"Maybe this is our lucky break," said Todd to Rawlins.

They turned around, running through the snow, their heads bowed. Rushing inside, Todd and Rawlins found the guard gesturing with his hands, unable to hide his excitement.

"That kid you were looking for, he's here. Now, right now. One of the nurses just called the front desk, and she said she just saw him."

"Where?" demanded Todd.

"Right here on the ground floor, straight back this way!" The guard turned quickly and said, "Come on!"

The woman at the front desk leaned over the counter and added, "The nurse said he's got a baby!"

"What?" snapped Todd.

"A baby—she said he's got one all wrapped up. Is that his? Does he have a baby? Dear Lord, he didn't take one from the maternity ward, did he? That's all we need, trouble like that."

"Oh, shit," Todd muttered as he glanced at Rawlins.

Both Todd and Rawlins hurried after the guard, rushing past the elevator and turning right at the next corridor, which was long and dimly lit. The guard then turned left, hurried up a ramp, through some large, swinging double doors, and into another part of the building.

"She saw him back here in the annex," he said.

He led them past the X-ray department, past a lab, through another set of doors, and back toward the commissary. Rounding a corner, they came upon a nurse, a woman with short brown hair and one of the people that Todd and Rawlins had shown the picture to upstairs.

"One of my patients was hungry, so I came down to get something for her to eat. And there he was, the kid you showed me in the picture, the one who works here. I mean, I'd seen him earlier tonight, but just now he was coming out of a room—with a baby. He saw me, I tried to say something, but then he got real scared and took off."

"When?" demanded Todd.

"Just a couple of minutes ago."

"Where'd he go?" asked Rawlins.

Pointing down the hall to a door, she said, "He went out the back."

Todd and Rawlins took off, racing down the hall, hurling the door open, and bursting outside once again. Todd quickly looked from side to side, took note of a parked truck with a thick layer of snow covering its windshield and hood. Straight ahead on the edge of a small parking area sat a brown Dumpster. And there, leading off to the right and through a line of drifting snow, was a set of tracks.

"This way!" shouted Todd.

Bracing themselves against the weather, they followed the prints around the corner of the brick building. From there, the broken trail of snow led across an open area and past the parking ramp itself. Their heads bowed against the wind, they finally reached a well-lit parking lot. At most there were twenty or thirty cars parked about and buried in the blowing snow, yet there was no immediate sign of Zeb or anyone else.

"Either he was parked out here in the employee lot," speculated Rawlins as he surveyed the area, "or someone was out here waiting for him."

In which case, Todd realized, Zeb could already be gone. Shielding his eyes, Todd glanced around, unable to make any sense of this.

"I don't get it," said Todd, totally perplexed. "If he's got a kid, whose is it? I mean, it couldn't be his own, could it?

Ribka was taken from Janice's not even two hours ago. And I was there, I fought with the guy who took her. Zeb was nowhere around. He couldn't have her, could he? If Zeb nabbed a kid from the maternity ward or something like that, however, then this is going to get really complicated.''

Rawlins was focused on the tracks, and as they reached the first row of cars the prints plunged through a pile of snow, then disappeared in a barren, windswept area. Right behind him, Todd searched to the left, then to the right. Some fifteen feet away he saw the tracks pass again between two parked cars.

''Over here!''

Even as he spoke he saw the taillights of a small car, one parked on the far side of the lot, suddenly burn red. In an instant both Todd and Rawlins were running through the snow. It had to be Zeb. Just as quickly, though, it seemed that Zeb saw them, for the car's tires started desperately spinning in the snow. Just let him be stuck, prayed Todd, who felt as if he were running through deep sand. But why would Zeb be trying to get away? What had he done?

Even though Zeb had obviously floored the gas, the vehicle barely moved, and the tires screamed a high pitch. Then the little beat-up car started fishtailing, swinging from side to side. As fast as he could Todd tore through the snow. But neither he nor Rawlins was fast enough, for the vehicle was gaining speed and circling around.

''He's headed for the gate!'' shouted Rawlins.

There was only one way out, an exit that was blocked by a wooden gate swung down into position, and Todd and Rawlins swerved around, tried to cut Zeb off. By then, however, the little car was going even faster, and in a desperate moment it went shooting past Todd. Right at that instant Todd's eyes locked on those of the terrified driver, a young man behind a frosty glass window who might or might not be Todd's son. Todd hung on to the image of those dark eyes, then slowed to a stop when he realized it was useless. His breath huffing out of his body in great clouds, he watched as the small car went swerving across the snowy parking lot, then smashed right through the wooden entry gate, blasting it to bits, and disappeared into the blizzardy night.

# 22

Oh, man.

Zeb's heart was racing. Little Ribka, barely strapped into the car seat next to him, was screaming and flailing her arms. It couldn't have been any closer—another minute and those guys would have caught him. As he sped much too quickly along a small road behind the hospital, he checked his rearview mirror, but couldn't see anything, for his rear window was covered with frost and snow. Cranking down his window, snow tumbled inward and freezing air blasted him as he brushed off the sideview mirror. As far as he could tell, though, there was no one following him. But Zeb didn't slow down. He couldn't tell who they were, but he was sure they were from The Congregation, which meant they wouldn't give up. No way.

"It's okay, Ribka. Everything's fine," he said, touching his daughter with a gloved hand. "They didn't catch us."

At least not yet. Luckily they had a place to go, so on to Brenda's, for she'd given him her address. She'd even called her roommate to say that Zeb and the baby were coming, get out some clean sheets. He pulled out a small piece of paper from his coat pocket, glanced at the map she'd drawn in pencil. Okay. Just go up here, turn right on France, cross over Highway 62, and head back toward 50th Street, then another right and head all the way down to Nicollet, then turn and go another block. Fifteen minutes, at most twenty or twenty-five in this weather, and his daughter and he would be safely and warmly hidden away. Now, if only the roads were passable.

He took a deep breath, switched the windshield wipers on high. God, that had been too close. Steering around a drift, he reached France, a broad, well-lit street that led in one direction to Southdale, the rejuvenated grandmother of all malls, and in the other direction back toward the city. Zeb glanced to the left, saw only a big orange plow with a flashing blue light, but no car speeding from the other side of the hospital. After he turned and slowly made his way over the highway, he was relieved all over again. So far so good. Way back behind him only one car was creeping along through the snow.

Driving up France, which had recently been plowed and sanded, Zeb reached over and placed a hand on Ribka, rocking her slightly, hushing her. Within a few seconds she began to quiet, lulled as much by the car ride as by her father. But Zeb couldn't relax. Okay, he thought, tonight was taken care of. Maybe the next few nights as well if Brenda was as generous as he hoped she might be. But then what? Oh, brother, just how in the hell were they going to survive? Should he call Suzanne and plead with her to call off the guys from The Congregation? No, she'd never be able to talk her dad out of pursuing him. His word was second only to God's, and he'd always ordered her around. What was it that gas bag was always saying anyway? "A man is the head of a woman as Christ is the head of the Church."

Which meant the decision wasn't Suzanne's at all. It was her dad's, the one and only self-proclaimed God's Apostle on earth. Shit. So there would be no reasoning. Zeb recalled being cornered by Harry in that barn after he'd found out his baby girl was pregnant. Okay, okay, so that way was out; there could be no rational discourse with Harry or anyone else from The Congregation. Maybe, though, Zeb could arrange a secret meeting with Janice. Maybe Zeb could explain why he'd taken Ribka in the first place and convince Janice how dangerous it would be for him and his daughter to return to The Congregation. Perhaps she'd give him some money. Maybe even a credit card. Or couldn't she do something as a lawyer to protect him and Ribka? Hey, he wondered, maybe she could arrange something like one of those witness-protection programs he'd seen in some movie before he'd rejoined The Congregation. Then again, he hadn't seen a movie—worldliness!—since he'd been at The Congregation, so maybe they weren't doing that kind of thing anymore.

He was somewhere around 54th Street when a small patch of frost on his rear window melted away and he could see the road behind him. Staring into the mirror, he saw a pair of headlights approaching quickly from behind, and suddenly he felt like a tiny animal about to be pounced upon by an eagle.

"Oh, no," he muttered.

He couldn't tell if it was a car or a truck or even a cop, but whoever it was was driving unusually fast and gaining on him, the lights growing brighter by the moment. What had The Congregation done, bugged Zeb's car? How else were they able to follow him like this?

Zeb saw a street sign and automatically turned right. He just couldn't continue along like this, out in the open, so easily seen, and he steered the car from the plowed surface of France Avenue onto a small street where the snow was at least a foot deep. All at once Zeb felt the car slide to the left of the side road. He spun the steering wheel, gave the car gas—wasn't that what you were supposed to do on a slippery surface?—but the vehicle did just the opposite of what he wanted. Struggling to maintain control, Zeb spun the wheel the other way, felt the car slowing. No, this couldn't happen. He couldn't get stuck so late on such a snowy night. He had a child to take care of. Eyeing a pair of tire tracks in the middle of the road, he stomped the gas pedal all the way to the floor and tried as desperately as he could to maneuver his auto to the packed-down snow. Using all his strength, he steered right, then left, next right again in an attempt to maintain control of the fishtailing car as it made its haphazard way down the street.

"Crap!" he shouted.

The car was rapidly sliding toward a parked sedan. He braked. What were you supposed to do, pump the brakes? Zeb had never seen snow like this, let alone driven in it, and as he turned way to the left the car oozed to the side, missing the parked snow-covered car by inches. Oh, God. He slid past an alley, and now Zeb's own car was nearly sideways. He frantically straightened the wheel, found himself sliding through the intersection of the next street. As quickly as he could, he turned the wheel again. Nothing. He pumped the brakes. Virtually nothing. Shit, this was like an amusement-park ride.

Finally, with a gentle thump, the car came to a stop.

Zeb looked around, realized he was over to one side of the intersection, right next to a stop sign. Okay, just give it a little gas. He pressed down, tried to sense even the slightest movement, but heard only the tired groan of the engine. With more firmness, he leaned on the accelerator. The car didn't budge an inch.

Shit.

No doubt about it, he was stuck and he wasn't going anywhere, at least not tonight. Forcing the door open and climbing out, he looked back toward France Avenue for any sign of those guys. There was no one turning this way, though, so maybe there wasn't anyone tailing him. That was a relief, but now what?

"Do you live near here?"

Zeb flinched, spun around, and looked over the top of his car. Through the falling snow he saw a man in a tan down parka and a dark blue wool cap, who was standing on the sidewalk, snow shovel in hand.

"What?" replied Zeb.

"I hope you live close by, because I don't think you're going anywhere tonight." The man, tall and slim with bright cheeks, pushed his wire-framed glasses up his nose, grinned and shrugged. "You just sort of have to accept that winter's bigger than all of us."

The snow already thick on his head and shoulders, Zeb didn't know what to say, let alone do. "Yeah, I guess so."

Ever fearful, he turned and glanced through the storm toward France. Still no one. But now, looking at his car, he could see what the stranger with the snow shovel was talking about, for the automobile was buried all around, the snow reaching up and over the front headlights as well as the rear bumper. At the back of the car the exhaust was steaming upward through a crack in the snow like a smoldering volcano. Even if he dug for a couple of hours, Zeb realized, he probably wouldn't be able to get himself out.

To complicate things just a bit more, Ribka let out a huge wail.

"I'm here, I'm here!" called Zeb softly, diving headfirst into the open door and awkwardly seating himself behind the wheel.

First he turned off the ignition, pocketing the keys, and then he reached across to his daughter, whose face was red and puckered. Bundled in her white blanket, she was halfway through a scream and almost didn't appear to be breathing until a clump of snow fell from Zeb's head onto her cheek. All at once she tore into a loud, piercing shriek. Unbuckling her from her car seat, Zeb lifted her into his arms, held her, cooed to her, patted her on the back. Her crying, however, only seemed to grow more panicky.

"I'm here, it's okay!" desperately pleaded Zeb.

What was wrong with her, what did she want? Was she cold? Did she want food? A clean diaper? He patted and bounced her, yet she cried louder, in turn causing Zeb to grow more desperate with each moment. Oh, God in heaven, this wasn't supposed to be like this. He wasn't supposed to be stuck out in some blizzard, and his baby daughter wasn't supposed to be so miserable. Was this Zeb's punishment? Was God punishing him for taking his daughter and leaving The Congregation by hurting Ribka?

"You need to get your baby inside," called a voice through the half-open driver's door.

Zeb flinched, hung on to Ribka, and looked up to see the stranger, the guy in the down coat. "What?"

"It's too cold to stay out here with a baby. You need to get her someplace warm. Do you live nearby?"

"No," said Zeb, shaking his head slightly and looking pathetically desperate. "I was on my way to Fiftieth and Nicollet."

"You'll never make it, not tonight anyway. Why don't you get your things and come with me?"

"Well . . ."

"It's okay. My name's Mark. I'm the minister at this church. I've got plenty of room."

Zeb looked out his frosty windshield, and saw what he hadn't seen before, a small stucco and wooden church occupying the corner. He shifted Ribka in his arms, kissed her forehead. What choice did he have? It was either sit out here and freeze or accept this stranger's offer.

"Thanks. I'm Zeb." Over the baby's wailing, he added, "And this is my daughter, Ribka."

"Come on, let's get you out of this storm."

Not wasting a moment, Zeb reached down to the floor in front of the passenger seat and gathered her bottle, the medication, a couple of diapers. There wasn't much, only the things that Brenda had given him at the hospital.

"Here, let me help you," said Mark, reaching in and taking the loose items. "It was a good thing I was out here trying to get a jump on the shoveling, which, I must add, has been quite the losing battle."

Pressing his screaming baby close to his chest and trying to shield her from the weather, Zeb climbed out of the car and waded through the snow and around the back of his car. He followed Mark through the gusting snow, over a snowbank, onto the partially shoveled but now drifting sidewalk, and not up to the wooden church, but to a small beige house immediately next door.

"This is the parish house," explained Mark, holding open the porch door and ushering in Zeb.

As Ribka cried on and on, they stepped into a small entry at one side of the living room and Zeb looked around, saw two couches, lots of chairs, a black upright piano. His gut clutched. He recognized the signs, the accoutrements of a church. They'd had a room not unlike this at The Congregation, where people had gathered for prayer and song. At once he worried what he was falling into and made a mental note that in no way could he mention The Congregation. The last thing he wanted was for this minister to rat on him. For the night, though, at least they'd be warm. He had no other choice.

"Crisis averted, Ribka," he said, kissing the baby who continued to cry.

The minister shed his down coat and wool cap, revealing a thin man with red cheeks, a warm smile, gold wire-rim glasses, and thinning blond hair. Immediately he reached for the baby.

"Here, let me hold her while you take your coat off." Mark looked down at the baby in surprise. "She's quite young, isn't she?"

"A little over four months."

"It's okay, everything's fine, little girl," he said, rocking her gently and then looking up at Zeb. "And what, asks the fatherly minister reproachfully, were you doing out with a child this young in a storm this bad?"

Zeb looked down and replied, "She's sick. I had to go to the hospital to get her some medication."

"Well, if there's a good reason I suppose that's it. But where, I might ask, is the mother?"

"She's . . . she's . . ." Well, he thought, it really wasn't a lie. "Um, she's at her father's."

"Oh, so you're being the consummate dad. Bravo." The baby started to howl louder than ever, and Mark said, "A lot of good I'm doing."

"I think she just needs to eat." Zeb lifted a can of formula out of the pocket of his parka. "Can I heat this up?"

"Absolutely, but why don't you let me do that?" he said, handing the baby to Zeb. "There's a tape recorder and a lullaby tape over on the shelf there. It's a great tape, one of our members brought it over. It's got the voices of babies cooing, and it works like a charm; someone used it just last week."

As Mark disappeared into the kitchen, Zeb, cradling the baby in one arm, fumbled to get the tape into the small machine. Even when he succeeded in getting the tape going, however, Ribka cried on and on, her sobs becoming more desperate, more intense. Nothing quieted her at all until a couple of frantic minutes later Mark reappeared with the warmed formula, which he handed to Zeb. Bottle in hand, Zeb then sat down in a rocking chair and started feeding his daughter. And within moments all was blessedly quiet.

"Finally," said Zeb, looking up at Mark.

"Yes, indeed, that's better."

As Zeb fed Ribka, the minister called his neighbor, a young mother, who brought over a portable crib and some baby blankets, which they set up in the ground-floor guest room. The double bed for Zeb was already made, and just over an hour after getting so horribly stuck, Zeb found himself bidding good night to first the neighbor and then Mark.

"Thank you very much," Zeb said as he stood in the doorway to his room. "I don't know what we would've done without your help."

"Certainly." Mark hesitated. "Pardon my asking, but isn't there anyone you'd like to call just to tell them you're okay?"

"Uh . . . such as?"

"The baby's mother, who might also be your—"

"Wife. My wife." Zeb rubbed his chin, for after being at The Congregation for three years he'd come to dislike these kind of inquisitions. "Sure, I should call her, but she's at her dad's. And . . . and that's out of town."

Mark studied him a moment. "You're not in any kind of trouble, are you?"

"Oh, no. Not at all."

"Anything you want to talk about?"

"No, not really."

"Well, if I may be so bold, you should probably call your wife and just check in. Perhaps she's heard about the storm."

"But it's long distance."

"That's okay. The church will never know," he said with a wink. "Just don't make it too long. You're a stranger, but I'm good on character calls, and I know I can trust you on that one. Just use the phone in your room. I'll be upstairs. Holler up if you need anything. Hope your daughter sleeps through the night."

"Yeah, me too." Zeb nodded. "Thanks again."

"Wait a minute." Mark ducked back into the living room and returned with the small tape recorder. "Here, the lullaby tape is still in there. You can give it a try if she wakes up in the night."

"Okay, but I hope she sleeps. I'm exhausted."

Zeb retreated into the small blue room, dropping both the tape recorder and himself on the edge of his bed. A brass lamp shone on the bedside table, and he stared down at his daughter. What a mess. At least, though, she was all right. Tonight she was crying simply because she was hungry, which hadn't been the case at all before he'd left Colorado. Then Ribka had been sick, shrieking and shrieking in pain, and nothing, not milk and particularly not that stupid anointed oil of The Elders—it really wasn't anything more than cooking oil, and not even olive oil at that—had been able to soothe her.

So tonight was okay, they were inside and warm. But he should at least call Brenda at the hospital and let her know he wouldn't be making it tonight. He couldn't even do that, however, because of all things Zeb didn't know Brenda's last name. And he couldn't call Brenda's roommate to let her know what had happened either, because he didn't have Brenda's home phone number.

This was so confusing, so hard. Maybe he shouldn't have left The Congregation. At least there all he had to do was get up at four in the morning and show up at the bakery and knead, knead, knead. All the decisions were made, all the meals cooked. All the day care provided. Now here he was out on his own, twenty-one years old, a single dad without a job or good education. Seated on the bed, his head slumped forward into both his hands, he wondered if he could do it, take care of himself as well as his baby. He'd been so worried about Ribka's health before leaving The Congregation that he hadn't even stopped to think how incredibly hard this would be, life in the big world. He wondered if his mom was just going to show up in Minneapolis as she'd threatened. He wouldn't put it past her, and that might not be so bad. He could use the help.

He felt as if he were at the bottom of a dark well, and before he could even think to stop himself his hand was reaching for the phone, an old rotary model that sat on the wooden bedside table. He hadn't called there that often, really, but he knew the number, which flowed from his head and down his hand.

Seconds later it was ringing and the old bastard himself picked it up, his gruff voice saying, "Praise Jehovah."

"Suzanne." He added, "Please."

The surprise was evident in Harry's voice. "Is that you, Zeb?"

At first Zeb didn't say anything. He couldn't. His whole stomach tightened. No, he never wanted to see him again.

"Let me speak to Suzanne."

"It is you, isn't it? Come back to us, Zeb. You and little Ribka are part of our family. I love you, we all do, and we want what's best for you." Harry paused and added, "Son, you must resist Satan, because Satan is wily. He's tricky, he is, and once he has you he'll hurt you, I guarantee, and ruin everything you love, including that beautiful baby of yours."

A voice in the background started shouting, "Is that him? Is that him? Give me the phone!"

"Suzanne, just stop it!"

"No, I want to talk to Zeb!"

"Suzanne, I—"

"Give me the phone!"

Zeb sat upright, listening long distance as father and daughter battled over the phone, and it brought it all back to him, the life there, the constraints. The rigidity, not to mention how sick the baby had been. Yes, he'd done the right thing by leaving.

Huffing, her voice finally came on the line. "Zeb? Zeb, is that you?"

"Hi."

Hearing her voice, he didn't know what he felt. Or maybe he did. Maybe the lack of feeling was all that he needed to know about their relationship.

"How's my baby?" she demanded. "Is she all right?"

"She's fine now. I got her some medicine and she's all better."

"How's her crying?"

"She's not crying anymore, Suzanne. I mean, she cries sometimes, but she's not crying because she's sick anymore. She's all better."

"You gotta bring her back, Zeb. I miss her. I miss you. You gotta come home to us."

"I'm sorry, I just can't."

"But, Zeb—"

"Suzanne, no. She'd have died unless she got medication."

"You've been blinded! You've been swallowed up! You've been associating with non-Christians!" She started sobbing. "Zeb, it's not too late. Come home! You can become a believer again!"

But it was too late, far too late, for Ribka's pained crying had long ago caused him to lose faith, at least their faith anyway. He started shaking his head too, for he realized that she'd never be able to understand and that he'd been right in not telling Suzanne of his plan to escape The Congregation. He couldn't imagine her coping anywhere else but under the confines of The Congregation and the heavy command of her father.

"Don't worry, Ribka's okay. She'll be fine," said Zeb. "I'd give my life for her."

With that he dropped the phone in the cradle and gave a great big sigh of relief. Sure, he realized, he'd been meaning to call home to let Suzanne know the baby was all right, but he'd called specifically tonight in a moment of despair and self-doubt. A moment that was gone. Thank God he'd left. Praise Jesus and all that stuff that he'd had the brains to escape.

Leaning over the edge of the portable crib, Zeb whispered, "Don't worry, Ribka, everything's going to be okay. We'll see what tomorrow brings."

Wave after wave of sobs shook Suzanne. Seated on the couch, she pulled her legs up, pressing her knees against her chest, then wrapping her arms around her shins so that she was this little ball of misery. Oh, God, she thought silently as the tears spilled out of her. She wanted Ribka. She wanted Zeb. She wanted to be anywhere but here.

"Hush, little girl," said her father, sitting down next to her and putting one of his big arms around her. "Everything's going to be okay."

"But . . . but . . ."

She stared at that old fat face of his, saw that syrupy smile, felt him pulling her into his embrace. Gross. Of all the fathers on the earth, why was she stuck with him? Why? And why out here on the compound, the most boring place in the entire universe? She wanted to be with Zeb and her baby in some nice little suburb with a TV and movies and restaurants, restaurants with table service. They could still go to church. They could work for Christians, visit with Christians. They could lead godly lives. Oh, she wanted a car that she could just hop into and go anywhere. A car with a radio, no less!

"Don't you see, pumpkin?" continued her father with a huge, sly grin on his face. "We've got Zeb now. We're going to get your baby back and we're going to make that husband of yours pay for the sins he has committed."

A huge sob billowed up but then stopped, and Suzanne wiped her eyes. What was her daddy talking about now?

"Satan may be wily, but I'm more clever, I must say." He held up a piece of paper with a name and number scribbled on it and proclaimed, "Zeb's right here at this man's house."

"Wh-what are you talking about?"

"Don't you see? Zeb's at this guy's house, this Mark . . . Mark Olson, and this is the phone number. You see, Zeb called here and that little contraption over there," he said, pointing to small box by the phone, "identified the name and number of the phone he was calling from. That means we've found him. Tomorrow morning we'll have Paul and Rick head right over there and then you'll have your baby back!"

# 23

Almost two hours after they'd left, Todd and Rawlins pulled up again in front of Janice's snow-covered house. Parking his four-wheel-drive Cherokee behind both Jeff's and Rawlins's buried cars, Todd shut off the engine and let out a deep sigh.

"I can't believe he got away like that. If only we'd been a few minutes earlier."

"Don't worry," said Rawlins, giving Todd a reassuring pat on the thigh. "This'll all get worked out."

Shaking his head in frustration, Todd pulled up his collar, and then they climbed out, dashing through the snow and clambering up the front steps of Janice's walk. When they reached the front door Todd twisted the doorknob, pushed, and was surprised to find the front door open.

Stepping into the entry, Todd hesitated, looked around, and then called, "Janice?"

Both Todd and Rawlins stomped their feet and took off their jackets, which they tossed on a hall chair. When there was no response Todd glanced at Rawlins and then looked around anxiously.

"Janice, where are you?"

A moment later she softly replied, "Out here."

Followed by Rawlins, Todd ducked into the living room and found Janice staring out the front windows, her shoulders covered by a small lap blanket.

"Any luck?" she asked without turning away from the window.

"Kind of. He does in fact work at the Edina Hospital."

"Oh?"

"He took a job as a janitor just a couple of days ago."

"I see."

"And he was there tonight."

"Really?"

Todd hesitated, then asked, "Janice, are you all right?"

She bent her head, shook it, and looked at them. "No, I'm a wreck actually."

"Of course."

Todd crossed the large room and dropped himself on the couch. Rubbing his face, he wished he could offer some bit of hope. But there was none, was there?

"We saw him from a distance," said Todd, his frustration all too evident. "But it was like he was afraid or something. Or he was doing something wrong. We couldn't catch up with him, and then he got in his car and took off."

"Oh, God."

"Janice," stated Rawlins, "he had a baby with him."

"What?" she demanded, seeming interested for the first time. "It wasn't Ribka, was it?"

"I don't know. We couldn't tell."

"Well, it couldn't have been, it just couldn't have been."

Todd said, "Janice, if Zeb's mixed up in something we need to know."

"Of course, but what? I don't know anything more than I've already told you." Putting her hand to her forehead, she wandered across the room. "I just wish he'd call."

Rawlins said, "First thing tomorrow we'll go out and get his address from the personnel department. After that we'll try to find him and hopefully have a little chat. Then maybe we'll be able to get some answers.''

"Sure . . .''

As perplexed as he was concerned, Todd watched Janice as her eyes darted down to the floor. He understood her being upset. Who wouldn't be? But what else was going through her head?

"Janice,'' asked Todd, "is there anything else?''

"No.''

"Did anyone call while we were gone? You didn't speak to anyone, did you?''

"No,'' she replied faintly, her head bowed.

"The phone didn't ring at all?''

"What is this, an inquisition? I said no,'' she snapped as she turned and started to leave the room. "I'm sorry. I . . . I just can't handle this. It's too much.'' She rubbed her forehead. "Listen, I checked things out in the basement and that guy broke in through a window. I got out a board and some nails and plastic, but I couldn't quite reach the hole. Would you mind covering it up?''

"Sure,'' repied Todd.

"Thanks. I don't know if I'll sleep, but I've got to go to bed.''

"Yeah, okay.''

But it wasn't okay.

So, thought Todd, glancing at the side table with the leg he'd busted, on top of everything else was Janice simply still mad at him? Had his bad temper caused her to lose trust in him, or could there be something else eating at her?

"Janice, Rawlins and I want to stay here tonight,'' called Todd after her. "You know, in case anything comes up.''

"Sure . . . sure.'' Her back to them, Janice paused at the edge of the room. "I think there are already sheets on the bed in the guest room. If the phone rings, though, let me answer it. Oh, brother, I'm not supposed to contact the police, and here I'm having a sleep-over with a cop.''

"Don't worry," said Rawlins.

Janice said nothing, only shook her head.

Todd called, "Good night."

She didn't reply, and Todd sat there, listening as she slowly made her way into the entry and then up the stairs. He didn't get it, her withdrawing like this. It wasn't like her. He'd known her for almost twenty-five years, and the only times she'd pulled away from him and their friendship were when there was something she was withholding. Or avoiding. When she was angry at him—and she'd been royally pissed at him three or four times—she didn't hold back. He thought back on that school year following her supposed trip to Europe. Janice had been so cold toward him that she'd been outright rude, often not even responding to his greeting when they'd pass in the hallways. For years after that Todd had assumed her behavior was due to her coming out gay, that Todd, as her last boyfriend, represented some sort of threat; he'd always wondered how her actions toward him might have been different back then if she'd known the truth of Todd's own sexuality. But now all was perfectly clear, he understood. She'd turned away from Todd their senior year, not because she was a lesbian, but because she hadn't known how or what to tell him about the child she'd so recently given birth to, the boy who might be his.

Unable to stem a growing sense of paranoia, Todd quickly went over to the phone, which sat on a low wooden table at the far end of Janice's living room sofa. It was a slim phone, the buttons mounted right in the handset, but instead of dialing a number, Todd searched for one particular button, which he found at the very bottom.

"What are you doing?" asked Rawlins, following him.

"Being weird."

It did seem a strange thing to do, thought Todd, yet this method of checking on someone's story wasn't his idea. A year ago when he and his crew at Channel 7 had been taping the anatomy of a murder investigation, he'd seen a detective do the very same thing. And it had worked, had proven to be a key piece of evidence, for it had proven that the suspect at least had tried to contact the victim. So Todd now hit the redial button on Janice's phone and listened as the memory beeped through seven digits. A number started to ring.

When, he wondered, had Janice last called anyone on this particular phone—days ago, or perhaps while Rawlins and he were out?

Someone picked up on the other end and a voice said, "Uptown Pizza."

Todd hung up without saying anything. In the last day or two Janice had apparently been here at the house with the baby and hadn't had the energy to cook. Or something like that, so she'd had a pizza delivered instead. Not yet satisfied, though, Todd hurried out of the living room, passing through the entry and back toward the bright kitchen.

"What the hell's with you?" asked Rawlins, tagging after him.

Over his shoulder, Todd whispered, "I just want to see if she called anyone tonight."

He went directly for the wall phone, a large model with a speaker. Picking up the receiver, he hit the redial button on this phone. Again seven numbers were automatically dialed, and then a sleepy voice answered.

"This . . . this better be good, girlfriend."

Todd recognized Jeff's voice, but didn't say anything, instead hanging up at once. Okay, he thought, turning around and leaning against the counter, so maybe she called Jeff prior to his coming over to baby-sit. That would make sense.

"So?" demanded Rawlins, standing next to the large white refrigerator.

"The first number was a pizza parlor, the second was Jeff's." Todd shrugged, recognizing that there was no way he could now check it out. "But she's a lawyer, which means there's at least another phone or two upstairs. If she did in fact call anyone while we were gone, maybe she used one of them up there."

Rawlins calmly looked across the kitchen, and nodding with his head, said, "Well, Perry Mason, what about that one?"

Todd turned around and looked at the small marble breakfast table. There was a basket of fruit, this morning's paper, and a cordless phone, a black one with a stubby rubber antenna. Hurrying across the room, he snatched up the telephone and quickly studied the handset. He hit the ON button, heard a dial tone, and then pressed redial. Watching as one after the other of the tiny LED lights flashed beneath a number, he realized the first number dialed was "one."

"The last number Janice called on this phone was long distance."

"Doesn't this constitute spying—and on a friend no less?"

"Never mind, just grab a pencil!" he ordered Rawlins. "Over there, there's one on the counter. Write this down!"

Todd called it out, all eleven numbers, and then listened as the phone began to ring. In the last day or two Janice might have placed a catalog order with Lands' End or some other mail-order company; perhaps she'd bought something for the baby. Or she might have called a friend who lived out of state, in which case Todd would be disturbing someone yet again. Instead, though, he reached an answering machine, and the man's voice on the other end was deep and clear. By the second or third word Todd's stomach clutched. Was it the way he said "hello," the letter *H* pronounced long and slow? Whatever it was, Todd knew that voice, didn't he?

*This couldn't be happening. A blow job? Now? Was Pat crazy? Had he flipped? Todd stared as Pat unzipped his jeans in that dingy basement at Northwestern, and all Todd wanted to do was hit him. His frustration ran smack into his fear, boiled into anger.*

*And yet . . .*

*God, if anyone knew. If Pat told anyone, that would be the end. He'd do it too. Pat would tell. Tell everyone. Todd looked into his hooded eyes, saw Pat's sly grin, and Todd realized this was a part of Pat he'd never seen before. God, wasn't there anything Todd could do?*

*Desperate to change the course of events, Todd blurted, "That cigarette—it dropped right in front of me before Greg fell."*

*Pat stopped tugging out his shirt, said, "Forget it, man. Like I told you, just fucking forget it. Whatever you saw must have just blown off a windowsill or something."*

*"It was a cigarette. One end was glowing, it was still lit."*

*"So someone threw it out a window."*

*"Maybe, but I keep trying to remember what I saw and—"*

*"Fuck it, Todd, you didn't see anything," snapped Pat, his frustration more than evident.*

*"But I think I did. When I left your room I thought I heard someone else in Greg's room. And then when I went outside I think I saw someone else out there on the fire escape with Greg."*

*"Bullshit."*

*"What about you, Pat?" asked Todd, eyeing him suspiciously.*

*Todd couldn't let go of the idea of the other guy, the one at the frat house Pat had also screwed. Could Pat be protecting him?*

*"Are you sure you didn't see anything?"*

*"I told you, no. And I was right there. I couldn't get my window open, which is when I yelled at you for help, thank you very much, Mr. Chicken."*

*"Sorry . . ."*

*"Yeah, well, then I had to lock my door to keep those other jerks out. And then I went back to the window."*

*"So maybe someone crawled out Greg's window when you went to the door. Maybe that's when someone crawled out and pushed him."*

*"No, I'm telling you, Greg slipped and fell over the rail."*

*Shit, nothing was making sense anymore. Was Todd merely imagining things? He recalled looking up there, at first thinking a second person was on the fire escape, then realizing Greg was dangling from the railing.*

*"You must have seen Greg's shadow," suggested Pat. "There's a big light out in that courtyard, and you must have seen Greg's shadow against the building."*

*"Yeah. Yeah, maybe."*

*"Man, if you tell the police about what you might have, maybe, could have seen, well, then, do you know what kind of fucking trouble we're going to fucking be in, both you and me? We'd be fucked. Totally fucked. Everything would come out about where you'd been, where I'd been, and what we'd been doing. It'd probably be in the school newpaper, man, and everyone in the world would know that we'd been having sex. And let me tell you, it's not fun having everyone call you a faggot." Pat glanced around the dark basement, pushed his jeans down to his thighs, pulled down his white underwear. "Enough with all that crap, Todd. Forget it. Don't ever talk about it again and everything will be fine. Now get down on your knees. I need to relax. I need a release."*

"Oh, God."

"What? Who was it?" demanded Rawlins.

Having listened to the entire message, albeit short and concise, Todd hung up the phone. Of course that was Pat. Even after all these years there was no doubt in Todd's mind. He could never forget that voice, and he tensed, bristled with the bitter memories.

But it didn't make any sense. Janice had . . . had contacted him?

"Todd," pressed Rawlins, "who did Janice call?"

"An old friend, if you could call him that." Shaking his head, Todd went to the kitchen window and stared into the snow-filled backyard. "You know, I think the reasons I was in the closet for so long are a lot more complex than I ever realized.''

''What the hell are you talking about?''

''I'm not sure, exactly, but I think I've been carrying more secrets than I've been willing to admit.''

# 24

After Todd and Rawlins patched the basement window, they went to bed. Todd, however, barely slept. Of all the forks he'd come to in his life, the choice of direction he'd made that night at the frat house when Greg had tumbled to his death was the one he regretted most. Then again, he thought, naked in bed next to Rawlins, what could he have done differently? Talking openly to the police, telling them where he'd been, what had happened, and everything that he thought he'd seen, no matter how speculative, was what he should have done, even though that would have been tantamount to outing himself. It would have been the right thing, but he'd been so young. So stupid. So afraid. Never mind that outing himself back then would have altered the entire course of his life— would he have gone into broadcast journalism, could he have ever gotten a job in the late seventies as an openly gay reporter, would he have been more active sexually, would he have contracted AIDS and be dead by now?

Oh, shit. Would that he could do it over, that night, those events. Wide awake, he lay beneath the comforter in Janice's guest room spooning Rawlins—his chest against Rawlins's back and his left arm wrapped snugly around Rawlins's muscular stomach. How many therapists had he seen over the years as he struggled at first to deny his homosexuality, then later to accept it? Four, he thought, including the first one, the one he'd seen during college who'd used electric-shock aversion therapy.

"What the shock does," the shrink had explained, "is replace any positive feelings you might have toward other men with negative ones."

So Todd, young and wanting so desperately to reject his past and be straight, had done it. He'd crawled up on that table, let the therapist brush his right arm with salt water to make a good connection, let the guy attach the electrodes. Then Todd had closed his eyes and conjured up men, handsome, naked, butch guys. He'd filled his mind's eye with sensual fantasies of his encounters, and when he felt his erection pressing against his jeans, he'd nodded. Then: Zap! A current of hate shot through his body all the way to his heart, overshadowing any desire with a barbed-wirelike cut of pain.

Now lying in the dark, Todd looked blankly at the ceiling. A dozen sessions. A dozen searing shocks. Nothing, however, burned him as badly nor repressed him as much as the incident at the fraternity.

So what had Todd actually seen? Had he witnessed a murder and had his silence prevented the real story from surfacing? And why, why, why had Janice called Pat tonight of all nights, and why in the hell hadn't she told Todd?

Consumed by these thoughts and aching with pain where he'd been struck, he tossed until almost three, when sleep finally began to pull him under. Then at seven thirty the phone began ringing. Beneath the warm down comforter, Todd and Rawlins began to move and stretch. And then Todd quickly silenced Rawlins.

"Don't move," he said, suddenly awake.

Todd zeroed in on the voice as Janice answered the call. It was a short conversation, the words unclear to Todd, and as soon as she hung up Todd jumped naked out of bed, cracked open the door, and called down the hall.

"Janice, who was that? Anything about the baby?"

"No."

He couldn't rein in his curiosity, and he pressed, "So who was it?"

It was a moment or two before Janice replied, "My secretary from work, okay? She was just asking if I really needed her at the office today on account of the snow. I told her, for your info, to take the day off."

"Oh."

"So do I have your permission to make another call, Todd? I need to talk to one of the other attorneys about a court case. You don't have a problem with that, do you?"

"No, of course not," replied Todd, a tad sheepish.

Todd shut the door, then walked stiffly to the small guest bath off the other corner of the room. He turned on the shower and felt a blast of cold water. As he waited for it to warm up he leaned his head out the door.

His voice low, he said, "Rawlins, don't say anything about me checking the phones last night, okay?"

"What?" he asked, looking up from the depths of his pillow, his eyes barely open.

"I want to wait for her to tell me about Pat."

Rawlins groaned and dropped his head. "Whatever you say, boss man, but don't you think that's only going to cause trouble?"

"Yeah, probably, but I think it's the only ammunition I'm going to get, and I want to save it for when I really need some firing power."

Janice thought they would never leave for the hospital. She made a pot of coffee, some toast, then showered and dressed, staying up in her bedroom as long as possible so she wouldn't have to face Todd and his questions. At least he believed her stories about the phone calls.

Sometime during the night the storm had finally stopped, leaving the Twin Cities under a mantle of fifteen inches of snow, which today was glistening in the now cloudless sky. Finally, just after eight thirty, Janice came downstairs and bid them goodby, and Todd and Rawlins clambered out the front of the snow-laden house and down to the Cherokee. Once they had brushed and scraped off his vehicle, Todd rocked and blasted his way out of his parking space and into the single lane that been opened by the pass of a plow.

Janice watched them from the front windows of her house. She had no idea how long they'd be gone or if they'd be back within the half hour—who knew if the personnel department at Edina Hospital would even be open today. This being Minnesota, however, chances were that someone would show up at work and Todd and Rawlins would be able to secure Zeb's home address. But if they came back before she did, she'd deal with it then. She'd just say something like she walked to the grocery. Right, she told herself, and then made a mental note to buy a half-gallon of milk and something else. Soup. A can of chicken soup. Perfect. Who'd doubt a story like that? And before she even put on her coat and boots she hurried into the kitchen, grabbed a pad of paper, and scribbled, "Walked to the store. Back soon." Purposely not putting a time on it, she propped the note up in the center of the counter where they couldn't miss it. She next darted to the front hall closet.

The plows might have cleared some of the main streets, but they wouldn't get to the alleys for hours, perhaps not until nightfall. Without even checking Janice knew there was no way she'd be able to extradite her car from the garage, at least not this morning and probably not until this afternoon at the earliest. That was why she'd suggested they meet at the small restaurant up on Lyndale; she could walk, and he'd be able to use the highway and major thoroughfares to get there.

Amazing, she thought. They hadn't seen each other for over two decades. It was just too much to comprehend, and the last thing she grabbed were her sunglasses, for there was nothing brighter than a sunny winter day in Minnesota, particularly after a snowfall. Dressed in her Sorrel boots and long wool coat, she headed out and was greeted by the distant sound of shovels, snowblowers, and from one house the blaring music of U2. The temperature was all the way up to twenty-five, and evidently some neighbor thought it was spring and had thrown open his windows.

Not sure what to expect of this meeting, she tromped along the parkway and up to Lyndale, which was already pretty well cleared, and turned left. The restaurant was up just a block or two, past the theater and a newly opened coffee shop. Reaching her destination, a small family diner that had been around for years, Janice stomped her feet. Oh, shit, what was Pat going to look like after all this time? Still as skinny? Still as young-looking?

She took a deep breath, pulled open the door, and stepped in, her sunglasses perched high on her nose. She looked down the long counter, where every stool was occupied by locals who were eager to talk about the storm, but didn't see anyone that was obviously him. Her head then turned to the opposite wall and the row of red vinyl booths, all of which were also taken by weather gossips. Lifting off her glasses, she saw a couple of guys at the first booth, three women at the next, an older couple after that, and  . . .

A man at the fourth booth stopped drinking his coffee, looked at her, and started to rise. Dear God. His hairline had receded and his hair, particularly his sideburns, had grayed. No longer was he the kid with the lean swimmer's body, but a middle-aged man clearly out of shape. Or was that not him?

Janice wasn't even aware that she was moving through the room, but then she was there, not four feet from this man who was staring at her, and she was hesitantly saying, "Pat?"

"You look wonderful, Janice."

Suddenly they were embracing.

"Did you have any trouble getting here?" she asked.

"No, not really. The hotel parking lot was plowed first thing this morning, and the highways are pretty good too."

She pulled away, stared at him, and said, "I guess I shouldn't be surprised that you're here, but I still can't believe it."

"I would have called last night but I didn't get your message until this morning."

No, she really couldn't believe it was him. The last time she'd seen him he'd been lanky and young.

Janice shed her coat, tossing it into the booth, then sat down. "My God, it's really you, Pat."

"Now, there's a name I haven't heard in twenty years." He grinned as he sat down.

She smiled nervously. "What do you mean?"

"No one's called me Pat since I formally joined The Congregation."

"Really? What, do you go by a religious name now? Or Patrick? Is that what people call you?"

"No, actually just Rick." He glanced down at his cup of coffee. "I don't know, somehow Pat sounded a little too . . . too . . ."

Staring at him, she realized that everything had changed and nothing had. After that tumultuous December, including how the guys at the frat house had branded him queer as well as his assault on her in that motel, he'd done everything to steer his life away from the hate and rejection, the confusion and misery. Everything including altering both his speech and dress from a less flamboyant to a more conservative manner. And turning his life toward a way—a profoundly religious way—that precluded homosexuality or even the mere thought of it.

She finished his thought, guessing, "A little too feminine?"

He laughed. "Yes, if you want to put it that way, perhaps. After all that nonsense at Northwestern and how crazy it made me, I just wanted to clear my head. And my life."

"I see. No confusion."

"Nope, none of that."

"Really?"

"Yes, I'm still with the church, which has been a blessing and a godsend."

"But not with Martha?"

He looked at her, obviously pleased that she'd broached the subject. "Ah, so you have seen Zeb?"

"I'm sure you know that he was here three years ago. He told me back then that you two were divorced."

"But you've seen him more recently?"

"Come on, Pat. No games, all right? I know that's why you're here in Minneapolis."

"Of course." He took a sip of coffee. "And how about you? Ever get married or are . . . are you still—"

"A dyke? You bet. I had a partner, but . . . um, she died of breast cancer a few years back."

"You know your way of life is against Scripture, that it's against the will of God, but I'm still sorry."

"Am I supposed to say thank you?"

Rick looked down at his coffee. "And how's Todd?"

"Actually, he's doing well."

"I don't read the big papers much—we try to stay clear of the media, you see—but I did see something in one of the journals. Sounded terrible, that murder and everything."

"It was horrible, but Todd has come out of it changed." She was hoping the subject would make him uncomfortable, and she could clearly see it was. "For the first time in his life his private self and his public self are one and the same. No more pretending."

"Oh."

They fell awfully silent. Janice sipped her coffee, stared at him. Maybe she shouldn't have come. Already she wondered whose best interest Pat had in mind: his own, Zeb's, or quite possibly his church's.

Almost cheerfully, Rick said, "So what are we going to do about that son of mine?"

Janice took a deep breath and turned away. "Pat, I can't believe you—"

"Rick," he corrected.

*She made it down to her parents' by Christmas and was supposed to stay there until the end of January, when she was scheduled to leave for France. When she started feeling tired and not so great a few weeks later, she hoped it might be her mother's fruitcake, but the nausea went on and on. Then she missed her period. She was never late. Never. The very next day Pat called out of the blue, begging her forgiveness. When she told him about her predicament, he told her to come up to Colorado, he'd buy the bus ticket, he'd take care of things. Janice thought she understood what he meant. What other choice was there but abortion? France was just a week away. Her life would be ruined. She had to get rid of it, the baby.*

*But they said no.*

*The place where Pat was living wasn't a communal house full of hippies dedicated to dope and rock 'n' roll. It was an old ranch house full of Christians, many of them dropouts from Northwestern who'd dedicated their lives to God.*

*"An abortion is murder," Pat told her that night. "You have to keep the baby. And we'll keep you. Don't worry, you can stay here. We had a meeting about this and we decided. We'll care for you and we'll feed you until the baby is born."*

*"What?" she replied.*

*"Janice, the child's mine too."*

*"But . . . but you don't understand. It might not be."*

*"What?" Pat snapped.*

*"You don't understand, it could be—"*

*"Just stop it, Janice, you're just tired, your hormones are all upset. Of course the child's mine. That's why God brought you here. And I won't let you do it. I won't let you kill it."*

*Though she could have escaped, Janice didn't know where to go, what to do, for she certainly couldn't go home to her*

*parents. So she told her parents that the Europe program had*
*fallen through, and she stayed in Colorado.*

*When Janice's baby was born that August, almost a month*
*early as best as Janice could figure it, she delivered her boy in*
*a bedroom right at the commune. And by then she knew adop-*
*tion was the only choice. That would be best for the baby.*

*They called this child—the first born into their new tribe—*
*Zebulun, and they called themselves The Congregation.*

It had indeed been a horrendous year, that one so long ago,
and Janice now looked firmly at Rick and said, "He's my
child as well—I won't ever deny that again. I'm his birth
mother. I carried that child inside me. I was the one who gave
life to Zeb. And let me remind you that the identity of his
father was never—"

"Oh, Janice, please, let's not get into that."

"Why?"

"Well, there's no question in my mind. Not only did I raise
him, I know him completely. Zeb's my boy, I'm quite sure of
it."

"Then you must know something I don't."

"After all these years, watching him grow and learn and
become a man, maybe I do. Why else did God bring you back
to Colorado?"

Janice looked right at him. "You've never told him, have
you?"

"Told him what?"

"That he might not be your son, for Christ's sake."

"Of course not. First of all, there's no way to prove it."

"A blood test would clear it up."

"Janice, you don't understand."

"But it would. You're not afraid, are you?"

"My word, no, but I'd never do that." He smiled at her
smugly. "You see, my church, The Congregation, is quite firm
in its principles, in what we believe."

A voice interrupted, asking, "Coffee for you too?"

Janice looked up at the waitress, an older woman with red hair and a blue uniform, who had a poured cup already in hand.

"Say now, you ready to order?" asked the waitress as she set the coffee in front of Janice. "Can I interest you in the pancake special? It's two buttermilk cakes with—"

"We're not quite ready," interjected Janice.

"Okay, you just let me know when."

Once the waitress was gone Rick continued, saying, "At The Congregation we don't see doctors or believe in any of that nonsense."

"What?"

"Don't you understand? A blood test is quite out of the question."

"You're kidding."

"Of course I'm not. Our spiritual and physical business is with the Lord and the Lord only."

"How convenient—a direct line to God, just what I've always dreamed of." Janice poured a small spot of cream into her coffee, stirred it, took a sip, and asked, "So just what have you told Zeb? He knows, of course, that you and Martha adopted him. Or at least he found out when he was eighteen because that's when Martha gave him my letter."

Rick said, "He understands all of that. I told him a long time ago."

"You did?"

"Yes, I told him everything—that I fell in love with a young woman and that we had sex and she got pregnant. And I told him that his birth mother refused to marry me, which was the case."

"Oh, and let me guess, you told him you raped me too?"

"Janice, please. Maybe I was a little too aggressive—and I've apologized to you and the Lord for that—but we were in bed together and we'd been drinking."

"You'd been drinking, not me—"

"Listen, I don't want to argue. I simply told him you refused to marry me," interrupted Rick, "and that you ran away right after he was born."

"You . . . you told him I abandoned him?"

"Janice, please, you did leave."

"I . . . I left because . . ." No, she wasn't going to give him the righteous satisfaction, she wasn't going to tell him she left because she was a lesbian. "Besides, you and Martha were married by then. You were married by a judge so that you could legally adopt him. We had it all done officially."

"We had to, of course, be married outside of our church. Otherwise, even though I'm his father, you could have come back and claimed him."

Janice leaned forward, placing her elbows on the Formica tabletop and her face in her hands. A piece of her heart was breaking, she was sure of it. Zeb had grown up believing that she had recklessly left him, when in fact it had been the most difficult, most tortuous decision of her life, one that continued to plague her. A sob welled up inside her. She'd wanted only what was best for him, and she'd thought that she, the young dyke, couldn't offer what Pat and Martha promised: a normal family. She'd wanted only the best for him, but instead she'd done the absolute worst, leaving him not simply in the care of this closeted Patrick, but there, right in the eye of a religious cult.

"Oh, God," she moaned as the tears rushed to her eyes. "I . . . I was such a fool."

Rick reached across the table and touched her arm. "No, you weren't, my dear. You were just confused."

Janice recoiled at his touch and glared at him. "I was, and you still are."

Taking a paper napkin from a holder, she wiped her eyes. "Zeb left because of the baby, didn't he? I mean, he took the baby and left because she was sick and you wouldn't take her to see a doctor. She needed medicine, didn't she, and you wouldn't let Zeb get any, would you?"

"Zeb has transgressed. We're still praying for him. We're

still hopeful that he'll see the truth and return. The child's health problems are not with her own body but with Zeb's lack of faith.''

"Fuck you, you asshole," said Janice calmly, reaching to the side for her gloves. "Zeb did a very courageous thing. I'm proud of him. A long time ago I was hoping we could be friends, Pat. Back when we were in college I was hoping that I could learn something from you—namely, about being gay—which was why I agreed to drive out West with you. But you know what?"

"Janice, please," said Rick, trying to quiet her.

"I feel sorry for you." She started to scoot her way out of the booth. "I don't know what I was expecting by meeting you today. No, maybe I do. Maybe I was thinking that you'd have Zeb's best interest in mind, but obviously I was wrong."

"Janice—"

"Goodby, Pat. Oh, and you know what, I forgot to tell you that you look like shit. Something has been eating away at you all these years—your sexuality perhaps?—and believe me, it shows that there's no peace inside you."

"Janice, wait." This time he grabbed her arm and didn't let go. "This is serious. Maybe you don't know, but Zeb is married."

On the edge of the booth, Janice yanked her arm free. No, she didn't know. She had hoped he was. But until now she hadn't known for sure. And she now tried her best to show no reaction.

"So?" she replied.

"So do you know who his father-in-law is?"

"Maybe . . . maybe I don't."

"The Apostle. The Chosen One." He paused and leaned toward her. "Janice, he's the head of The Congregation."

"My, isn't that unfortunate."

"You're right there," said Rick. "It's really unfortunate, because he's sent one of his, how do you say, most persuasive and strongest followers out here to retrieve the baby. He's strong. And, I must say, he's quite zealous in his duties.''

Janice knew very well about whom he was talking. "I'm presuming you're referring to the same jerk who broke into my home, assaulted me, and kidnapped Ribka last night."

"Janice, please, you put things in such dramatic terms."

"You were in on it too, weren't you?"

"I don't know what you're talking about."

"Of course you do. Where were you, waiting in the car, something like that? Too much of a sissy even to come right to my front door?"

"No, I can honestly say that I had nothing to do with it, that I was back at my hotel. Unfortunately, however, I have to also tell you that neither this fellow nor I now has the child. That's the sad truth."

"What?" she nearly shouted.

Janice studied Pat, whose face was flat and nearly void of expression. And as much as she didn't want to, she believed him. So, she realized, if they didn't have the baby then somehow Zeb did. Or at least she hoped to God he did.

"I don't quite understand what's going on," said Janice, steeling herself and trying her lawyerly best not to show her fear. "But let me tell you, if you or this thug of yours so much as lays a finger on my son or my granddaughter, I'm going to have a whole squad of dykes on bikes and a platoon of leather fags hunt you both down and beat the shit out of you. Am I clear?"

He studied her, then said, "Haven't you always been, Janice?"

And before he could see how much she was shaking, Janice hurried out, fleeing into the brilliant winter day.

# 25

This was ridiculous, waiting around like this in the snow, freezing his rear, not to mention his feet. His gun bouncing in the pocket of his wool coat, Paul paced back and forth near the bus stop on France Avenue and tried his best to look as if he were waiting for a bus. Instead, he was peering down the block at one specific car: Zeb's. Buried nearly up to the hood in snow, there was no way anyone was driving that vehicle anywhere, at least not in the near future. Which was why Rick felt comfortable leaving Paul out here while he took off to meet with that woman.

"We might as well face it, Zeb's not going to come freely with us," Rick had said earlier this morning. "So maybe I can convince Janice to come back with me. And then maybe we can use her to lure Zeb either back to her house or somewhere where we can get our hands on Ribka."

But that was stupid, thought Paul, his arms wrapped around his thick chest. Zeb was inside this minister's house. Zeb had the baby. That was why they'd come all the way out here to this ghastly, freezing place. To rescue Ribka. To return her to The Congregation where love and godly attention would cure her ailment. All they had to do was go right up to the house, force their way in, and settle this. All the talk, it was pointless. Inane. Paul could take care of it in minutes.

Something moved up the street and Paul glanced toward the church. A couple of kids were pulling orange plastic sleds through the deep snow, and someone else was moving toward Zeb's car. Paul tensed and shrank back behind a tree. It was Zeb. Tall and young and lean. And devil-possessed. That young punk had caused so much trouble. What a pain. What a fringer. But Paul knew how to take care of him and his bad attitude.

Paul surveyed the situation and noted that Zeb had no child with him. So what was that idiot going to do, try and dig his way out? If so, he was even stupider than Paul guessed, for these side streets hadn't been plowed at all.

Instead of taking a shovel and going to work, however, Paul watched as Zeb went to the vehicle, brushed off the driver's side, pulled open the door, and leaned in. A minute later he reemerged holding a car seat and then headed back to the small house.

Oh, this was worldly. Zeb wasn't going somewhere in another car, was he? He supposed that Zeb could be using the car seat inside, just for something in which to sit the baby, but that wasn't a safe guess. Paul had to assume the worst. And if Paul let Zeb and Ribka get away again, well, then he'd be laughed right out of The Congregation. He glanced up and down France Avenue. Rick was nearly as stupid as his kid. He should never have left. Zeb and Ribka were both right there, right in that house just a short block away. So who knew what was going to happen next? After all, Zeb could have done something crazy like contacted the police.

There was no way Paul was going to stand idly by waiting for Rick to show up. Who knew how long his little pancake breakfast would take. Besides, he could have run into trouble with that lady. So, knowing what he had to do, Paul pulled up the collar of his coat, bent his head forward, then slipped his hand into his right coat pocket and wrapped his gloved hand around the butt of his pistol. Enough with all this crap.

Paul stomped through the deep snow, his head bowed low. His immediate concern was this person Zeb was staying with, and hopefully it was in fact just one person living in that house—a minister or caretaker—because an entire family would pose a problem. So how was he going to do this? The front door was out of the question. Much too direct. Paul knew that now, right in the middle of the day with two people in that small house, was not the time to break in through a side door or window. No, he'd just have to take things a little more carefully. First he'd circle around the church, scope out the alley. And then? Then he would look for a heavenly sign.

"Now, you're sure about this?" asked the minister, seated on the edge of the piano bench. "You know, you're welcome to stay as long as you need to. No rush."

Seated in a rocking chair in the living room, Zeb nodded. This guy was nice and everything. He'd given them a place to stay, after all. He'd kept little Ribka—who was sleeping soundly on a blanket in the middle of the floor—and him from freezing to death in the storm. But Zeb just didn't want to be here. Mark wasn't like Suzanne's father, that supposed Apostle of Apostles, who always kept poking and prodding, asking questions and demanding explanations. This guy was definitely lower key, but still he kept looking at Zeb with inquisitive eyes, obviously wanting to know the who, what, and why of Zeb and his baby girl. And Zeb didn't like it. Enough of this church junk. After all, everyone at The Congregation had seemed real friendly and all when he'd first returned there three years ago, but then slowly, surely, they sort of tightened on him. Constricted like a snake or something.

"If you think your Blazer can make it through this," replied Zeb, "then that would be great."

"Oh, I'm the minister with four-wheel drive, who can get

through anything to anyone. That's not a problem at all. Rain or shine, snow or freezing temps, I can get there."

"Great. I'm sure our staying here is kind of a pain."

"Don't worry about that. I mean, isn't this what church ministers are supposed to do, shelter the weary?"

"Well, I just think Ribka will be more comfortable in . . . in her own place," lied Zeb. "I'll come back for my car once I get Ribka settled and once the roads are clear."

"I see." Mark rubbed his hands together in a slow, pensive manor. "And you spoke to your wife last night?"

"Right. I called her. Sorry, I forgot to say thanks."

"Everything fine?"

"Sure. Sure, of course."

"Okay, then," said Mark, rising, "I'll go get my car started. It's back in the garage."

"Do you need help?"

"No, just give me a few minutes to get the engine warmed up." Mark got up and reached for the car seat, which sat on the floor by the front door. "I'll take this out."

"Great. I'll start getting her ready."

Listening as Mark disappeared into the kitchen, put on his boots, and zipped up his coat, Zeb hardly moved. Only when Mark went out the back door did he huff a breath of relief. Maybe he'd get out of here with no problem after all.

Above the roar of at least two or three snowblowers down the block, Paul heard the back door open and immediately flattened himself against the side of the garage. He leaned forward just a bit and, peering around the corner of the tiny building, caught a glimpse of a tall, thin man stepping through the deep snow and carrying a baby's car seat. It had to be the guy who'd taken in Zeb and Ribka, and it was immediately clear that he was intending to drive them somewhere.

Over my dead body, thought Paul.

He stood quite still, listening as the guy progressed through the deep snow. Then Paul heard a jangling of keys, a door opening, and the hum of a garage door as it was electrically hoisted upward. It was all too clear, he realized.

Not wasting a moment, he moved quickly along the building, slipping around the corner and right into the open garage. As the other man opened the driver's door, Paul rushed alongside the vehicle.

Hurrying forward and pressing his pistol at the back of the man's head, Paul calmly said, "Just be quiet and move away from the car."

"What?"

"Keep your voice down and move back," instructed Paul, pulling the man to the end of the car.

"I . . . I . . ."

"What's your name?"

"M-Mark."

"Okay, Mark, I don't want to hurt you. Just tell me where the kid is."

"Zeb?"

"That's right. Where is he?" demanded Paul, holding the other man firmly from behind.

"In the living . . . living room."

"And the baby's in there too?"

"Yes. What kind of trouble is he—"

"Shut up. Is there anyone else in there?"

"No. No one." Mark was quick to add, "Listen, maybe . . . maybe I can help you."

"I'm not in need of help. The baby is. That's why I'm here."

"Okay. I see," said the minister, turning around slowly. "There's just no need to—"

"You don't listen very well."

"We can talk. Work this out. If you have a—"

"I said be quiet."

"Yes, but—"

The talkative type. Paul hated them. And he had no time for antics like this that might keep him from Ribka, so he brought back the pistol and clubbed the minister on the back of the head. With one swift blow to the skull, Paul knocked out Mark, who crumpled downward.

Paul eased the body down to the cement floor of the garage. ''Too bad you don't belong to the true church.''

Working quickly lest he be seen by any snoopy neighbors, Paul hurried to the wall and pushed the button. Now, he thought as the garage door rattled shut, onto the next.

If he were smart, thought Zeb, and if he had any sense of design, he'd come up with a whole new style of winter clothes for kids. The neighbor lady had brought over an old snowsuit for Ribka, but how could anybody make anything as difficult to put on as this nylon outfit with its awkward zippers, the stubby little arms, and the separate hat and mittens? He was on the living room floor nearly wrestling with his baby as he tried to get her properly bundled up, and all he could think of was how impossible this was. Trying to move Ribka's arm into one of the sleeves, he cooed and smiled at her. But that didn't help. And she let out a howl.

''Oh, come on, Ribka. I know this is hard.''

Her arms started shaking and quivering. Zeb stopped. Okay, okay, he thought, taking a deep breath. Just be patient. And get her pacifier. That'd help, that'd give her something to do while he tried to get her dressed. He glanced around—but where was it? He felt his shirt pocket. Checked all around the baby blanket. Sure, the kitchen. He'd fed her not too long ago and she'd been sucking on the pacifier while he heated her bottle.

''I'll be right back, little girl.''

Cutting through the dining room, he dashed into the kitchen, a small room with a low table by the rear window. The pacifier, however, was nowhere to be seen, and Zeb grabbed at his short hair, wanted to pull it right out of his head as he looked around the kitchen. Where the hell was it? The bedroom? Had he left it in there by chance? Quite possibly, and he started to dash off. Just as quickly, though, he stopped. Maybe he didn't need to be rushing like this. Maybe Mark was going to have to do a fair amount of shoveling just to get his car out of the garage. In which case the last thing Zeb wanted to do was get Ribka bundled up and then have her sit around and get all hot. Turning back around, Zeb crossed quickly through the kitchen and went right up to the back door.

Paul heard steps from within the house and froze, pressing himself against the outer wall. Okay, he thought with a grin, it would be only too perfect if Zeb just came out here, the baby cradled in his arms. He pictured himself just standing there as Zeb walked out. Praise Jehovah, he would say, for delivering the infant unto me.

A few seconds later, though, it was clear that wasn't going to happen. Oh, the baby was in there, right inside that house. Paul could hear her crying—a real wailer, that one. He waited a moment longer, and when he was sure Zeb wasn't on the way out, he clutched the gun in his right pocket and moved toward the back door. As quietly as possible he climbed the three outside steps, placed his hand on the doorknob, and turned it. Very good. It was unlocked, and he pushed, feeling the door swing easily. In one quick movement he shoved the door all the way open, pulled out his gun, and stepped inside.

The small kitchen, though, was empty. Paul eased the door shut behind him, stood there, trying to discern footsteps or any other movement. What he heard instead were not the sounds of a crying baby, but those of a baby laughing and cooing. And some faint music. Paul took several careful steps, moving toward a door that led into the rest of the house. Reaching the edge of that passage, he paused again. Yes, the child was here somewhere. He could hear her, hear what sounded like Zeb trying to calm her. This, realized Paul, was going to be pathetically easy.

He peered through the doorway, saw a large, empty dining room table, and proceeded. That room opened into the living room, a space that was filled with many chairs and there, right in the middle of the floor, a dirty diaper. Zeb and the child, though, were not to be seen. Paul realized there was another room, one just to the left. Okay, so they were right behind that closed door. Paul could hear them clearly now, could hear the baby, the hushing sounds of her father. Simple. And Paul, his gun drawn, slowly and quietly proceeded around the edge of the dining room table. When he reached the door itself he paused, heard the laughing of a child and the soft tinkling of some lullaby. With his free left hand he reached for the doorknob. Next he twisted the knob, threw open the door, and charged in.

The room, however, was completely empty.

"Shit!" he cursed.

On the bed was a small tape recorder, and from it emerged the baby voices and lullabies he'd heard. Realizing he'd been duped, he ducked back out of the room. No, Zeb couldn't have gotten out the back way, so Paul charged through the living room, running right across the soiled diaper. He glanced up the stairs, then hurried to the front door, which he ripped open. His eyes immediately went to Zeb's half-buried car, which was still sitting there. He glanced across the street, saw some kids shoveling.

Up the street he noticed a vehicle, a small Jeep with a black canvas top, that was stopped right in the middle of the road. And there was Zeb, clutching the baby and talking frantically to the driver. Paul rushed out, but just as quickly Zeb raced around the vehicle, climbed in, and then all that Paul could do was watch the Jeep chug away through the deep snow.

# 26

As soon as Todd drove his dark green Cherokee up the snowy street to the rundown building, he knew the answer. He checked the address they'd been given at the hospital personnel department and looked up at the small gray house, which was clearly falling apart.

"This is the place, but Zeb's not here," he said to Rawlins, who sat in the passenger seat.

"And what makes you say that?"

"Look at the snow. No one has shoveled and there aren't even any footprints."

"Actually, it doesn't look like anyone's living here, does it?"

The little building, located in a rundown neighborhood not too far from the old Sears store on Lake Street, did in fact look deserted. Unbroken snow not only covered the front walk leading to the house, but had also drifted up against the front door. Todd took note of three metal mailboxes tacked by the front door and assumed that this wreck of a house had been carved up into three apartments by some absentee slum lord. That this was all Zeb could afford didn't surprise Todd.

Parking in a drift, Todd and Rawlins climbed out and made their way up the steps and onto the front porch. The address they'd been given at the hospital claimed that Zeb lived in Apartment 3, but there was no name on that mailbox, only an arrow pointing to the side.

"Come on," said Todd.

Reaching the back of Zeb's house, Todd and Rawlins found the third apartment, a small ground-floor place. Rawlins put a finger to his lips and motioned for Todd to stop just outside the door. They stood still, trying to discern anything from within—a TV, a stereo—but there was nothing, least of all a baby's cry. Todd then stepped forward and peered through a small window in the door. Inside he saw a tiny kitchen with one chair and then a room beyond, on the floor of which lay a mattress, the sheets and blanket pushed all around.

"He's obviously not here," said Todd. "God, I wish we could take a look inside, see if any of that stuff is his."

"Good idea."

Rawlins nudged Todd aside, pulled back his gloved hand, and punched a hole in the small window in the door.

"Oh, shit, that hurt," said Rawlins, clutching his fist.

"I can't believe you just did that."

He nodded at the door and said, "Well, don't just stand there."

Todd glanced from side to side, saw no neighbors, and pushed in a few more shards of glass. He then reached through the small hole, fumbled around until he found a bolt. Within a matter of seconds he was pushing back the door and they were inside.

The apartment was as pathetic as it was small. What had probably once been a back hall was now filled with something that was supposed to be a kitchen: an old, dingy refrigerator on the right, a worn sink on the left, and a tiny electric stove just beyond that. Neatly placed on a counter were a single plate, a bowl, glass, knife, spoon, fork, and toothbrush, all laid out to dry on a dish towel. Todd took a couple of more steps, peered into a tiny bathroom with only a toilet and haphazard shower crammed into its crooked corners. A single brown towel was neatly folded on the only towel bar. Even before they moved into the next room Todd knew that this was in fact Zeb's place. While Zeb may have shaken a religious cult, he was still operating under their code of cleanliness and order. The only thing in the entire apartment that was disheveled was the mattress, which along with the chair in the kitchen constituted the extent of furniture. Todd and Rawlins stood on the edge of the main room, a space no larger than ten by twelve, and studied the orange shag carpeting, the flimsy fake-wood paneling on the walls, and the sheets and blanket that had been kicked and tossed this way and that.

Rawlins went directly to a small closet at the back and rifled through some shirts and pants while Todd just stood there, overwhelmed. This was the shadow of Zeb's life, his few possessions, his pathetic home. So just how was Todd related to all this, if at all?

Todd spotted a black canvas suitcase against the wall, lifted it, noted that it had some weight to it, then took the bag and sat down on the edge of the mattress. Unzipping it, he found a makeshift dresser: socks and underwear filling one side of it, some T-shirts and a pair of jeans in the other. In a small side pouch Todd discovered a manila envelope filled with papers. Looking inside that, the first thing he found was a color photograph.

"No doubt about it, this is Zeb's place," he said, studying the picture. "Here's a photograph of Ribka and him."

Rawlins had returned to the kitchen, where he was opening the one overhead cabinet, and asked, "Anything else?"

"Just a sec."

Peering into the envelope, Todd spied a stack of papers, which he dumped onto the mattress. It was a file of sorts, Zeb having gathered all of his important papers together. There were a couple of letters postmarked Santa Fe—hadn't Janice said that was where his mother lived?—some photos taken somewhere in the mountains, his birth certificate, a couple of old grade-school report cards, his social security card. And finally a blood-donor card, which Todd studied carefully. It was from a blood bank in Santa Fe, and it listed not only Zeb's blood type as AB but that he had twice given blood. The last time had been three and a half years ago, which Todd figured would have been just prior to Zeb's reunion with his father in Colorado.

"Nothing really in the kitchen or bathroom," said Rawlins, having gone over them a second time. "How about you, find anything?"

Todd stared at the blood-donor card, realizing that it could hold the answer to the most pressing question on his mind. Did he even dare mention it to Rawlins?

"No, nothing," said Todd, stuffing everything except the donor card back in the envelope.

"Not even any telephone numbers?"

"Nope."

"Then where did he sleep last night?" asked Rawlins. "I mean, he had a baby with him, and I'm just assuming or rather hoping that that was his own kid, that he somehow got her back. You don't suppose he knows someone else in town, do you?"

"I have no idea. Maybe we should stop by some of the shelters."

"That's not a bad idea." Rawlins checked his watch. "Shit, I have a deposition downtown in twenty minutes. Can you give me a lift? I think we found everything here that we're going to, don't you?"

"Yeah," replied Todd as he got up, for he'd potentially discovered far more than he'd hoped for. "Let's go."

# 27

Like the roar of an approaching jet, the deep, steady rumbling grew with each moment, and Janice was glad for it. She recognized what the sound meant: liberation. There was, however, no aircraft aiming right for her house or even approaching the nearby airport. Instead, Janice turned around at the kitchen table where she sat and saw the top of a huge blue truck barreling down her alley. The plows were out in full force, and quite obviously they were making good progress. At least now she'd be able to get her car out of the garage. Thank God for small miracles.

Less than ten minutes ago she'd walked in the door after meeting Pat, and the phone had been ringing. She'd charged in, grabbed the cordless phone, and dropped herself at the breakfast table. It was Todd, calling on his car phone to explain that they'd been to Zeb's apartment, not found him there, and that now he was taking Rawlins downtown to the police station. Todd then went on to say he was going to swing by his house, pick up some clothes, and head back to her place in little over an hour. Refusing to go into it over the phone, he said there was something they needed to talk about.

No shit, Sherlock, she thought, still seated at the small marble table.

Wearing her coat, not to mention her Sorrel boots, beneath which had already formed a good-size puddle, she tried to figure out a course of action. Todd was going to come back, and what was she going to do? Of course she was going to tell him she'd just met with Pat. She had to. Somehow she'd thought she might be able to mediate a solution to all this, but after seeing Pat she realized it wasn't possible. So she'd report all that to Todd and . . . and then, well, she couldn't put it off any longer. She simply had to tell him that which she'd been avoiding for so long, namely that Pat might be Zeb's real father.

She bowed her head, shook it. How had this turned into such a mess? Where were Zeb and Ribka? Were they all right?

She stared down at the phone in front of her. Come on, damn it all, ring! Come on, Zeb, call me! The phone, however, just lay on its side on the small marble table as if it were dead.

She thought back to last night when the intruder had broken in and taken Ribka, and Janice castigated herself for not having been tougher, fought harder. She'd promised Zeb that nothing would happen to Ribka, that she'd guard her with her life. Yet she'd failed. If he didn't already, surely Zeb would hate her for this. God, she'd really and truly blown it. What kind of mother was she? What kind of grandmother? She could take care of no one, protect no one, she thought as her eyes began to bead with tears. Whatever confidence Zeb had been hoping to find in her, she'd lost. He gave her a second chance, and she'd ruined it. Oh, shit, she thought, staring at the phone, she'd be surprised if Zeb ever spoke to her again.

Suddenly the phone rang.

She jumped in her chair, and at first she couldn't believe it. Then she lunged for the handset.

"Hello?" she said, unable to hide the desperation in her voice.

"It's me."

Her voice immediately started trembling, and she asked, "Zeb?"

"Yeah."

She bit her lip, could barely speak. Yes, that was his voice. Just get a grip, Janice.

"Thank God. Are you—"

"You've got to come get us," he interrupted.

"What?"

"You've got to pick us up."

"Sure. Of course. Anything. Anywhere. Do you have Ribka? Is she with you?"

"Yeah, I've got her." He hestitated, then asked, "You didn't . . . you didn't just give her to that guy, did you?"

"What?"

"Paul, this guy from The Congregation, had Ribka. I snuck up on him—that's how I got her back. But . . . but you didn't just give him to her, did you?"

"No! God, no!" She put her hand to her chest. "Zeb, believe me, please. He broke in and—"

"So I can trust you?" he asked bluntly.

"Absolutely."

"He didn't hurt you, did he? Are you all right?"

"What?" said Janice. "I'm fine. But what about Ribka? What about you? You're not hurt, are you?"

"No, but listen, we're at a phone booth in front of a gas station. It's cold. And something terrible just happened. I'll tell you all about it, but you gotta come get us now, right now."

"I've already got my coat on."

Zeb gave her the address, and within seconds Janice was out the back door, tearing through the sun and snow to her garage.

# 28

Todd drove into the dark, cavernous garage of his condominium building, removing his sunglasses so he could see. After he'd parked in his stall he headed to the lobby to check his mailbox, which he did in a daze, taking the staircase down and past the security desk, couch, and several chairs, then crossing to the bank of boxes at the far side. All he could think about was Zeb's blood-donor card. What should he say to Janice?

As Todd lifted his key to his mailbox a figure stepped around the corner and said, "Hello."

Todd barely looked up and replied, "Good morning."

He was in no mood to talk about yesterday's storm or today's sunshine, whether any of the snow would melt or if there was another blizzard on the way, and he reached into his box and grabbed a handful of mail. All he wanted to do was gather some clothes and head back to Janice's, for they had more than a few things to discuss.

"I recognize you," said the voice of the nearby stranger.

It wasn't so much the voice but the manner of speech that gave Todd's heart a jolt. He stopped still. The guy had an accent, a very slight one, didn't he? Or was it the tone, was that what seemed familiar about it? Either way there was something unmistakably familiar about the voice, and Todd turned slowly to the side. A man was standing there, hair thinning and graying at the temples, face pale. His body none too thin, the face slightly round. White shirt, narrow tie, sport coat. He knew the voice, but not the guy, not really.

The man smiled just a bit and continued, "But you don't recognize me, do you?"

Todd's heart began to beat altogether too quickly. This man, this would-be stranger, echoed to the past, and Todd stared at him, saw a double image, one from the past hidden beneath this present vision. Oh, shit, he thought, staring at him. It couldn't be.

Todd cleared his throat and asked, "Pat?"

"Very good." He nodded and grinned slightly.

"What . . . what are you doing here?"

"I wanted to talk. Can we?"

"Sure." Nearly too stunned for words, Todd started to lead the way toward a sofa in the lobby. "Have a seat."

"I was hoping we could talk privately. Perhaps in your apartment?"

"My apartment?" asked Todd, unable to hide his hesitation.

"Don't worry," said Pat, sensing Todd's concern. "I mean you no harm. There are just a few things, well, we need to discuss."

"Okay."

Yeah, there were a few things, thought Todd. Like why Janice had called him. Like why he was now in town. Like what had really happened over twenty years ago.

Dear God, thought Todd as he headed toward the elevator, Pat a half step behind. Unbelievable. It was in fact Pat. The last time he'd seen him had been that fateful December at Northwestern—Pat had been some skinny kid caught up in the mysteries of sexuality and of death. And now, Todd realized as he stole a glance, here he was more than two decades later, the epitome of a middle-class, middle-aged man.

Entering the elevator car, Todd pushed the button. As soon as the doors closed and the lift started moving upward, he couldn't hold it in.

"You know, I've never forgotten about what happened. That was one of the worst times of my life."

Pat, his face serious and grave, looked up and asked, "What?"

"I mean . . . I mean what happened at Northwestern. You know, when Greg was killed and all the crap that happened afterward."

"Oh, that." He shook his head. "I've put it all behind me. Forgotten it. Much more important matters these days, you know."

It jarred Todd. He stood quite frozen as the elevator carried them upward, thinking, am I crazy? Didn't something truly awful happen, which not only left one guy dead, but altered both Todd's and this guy's lives? Of course it did. More than once over these long years Todd had thought that if it hadn't happened, if Greg hadn't spied on them that night, so much for both Todd and Pat would be different. The incident had driven Todd further into the closet; and wouldn't Pat have finished his education at Northwestern instead of fleeing his life at the university?

Instead, it was as if Pat and Todd had been in some huge car accident together, and Pat was not only saying no big deal, but dismissing its significance in the course of their lives.

Nearly at a loss for words as they got off the elevator and started for his apartment, Todd said, "God, Pat, I'm just so . . . so shocked to see you."

"Until this morning no one's called me Pat for years. I go by Rick now, but you can call me Patrick if that makes you more comfortable."

Okay, thought Todd, as he unlocked the door and ushered the way in. However you want it.

Strolling past Todd, Pat entered the sunny living room and glanced around. "Nice place."

Todd halted on the edge of the room and then watched as Pat surveyed the black leather couch, the glass dining room table, and then crossed all the way to the sliding glass door of the balcony. As the sun poured in on him he peered out, obviously eyeing the frozen white image of Lake Calhoun.

"I understand last year was pretty rough for you," said Pat, staring out, his back to Todd.

"What can I say—I'm out of the closet now."

"What?" Pat turned around. "Oh, yes. I understand. You're open about being homosexual."

"And you?"

"And me what?"

What was with this guy? Didn't he recall what they had done, how intimate they had been? Pat had not only begged for sex, in the case of their basement encounter he'd forced it to happen.

Todd asked, "Are you out of the closet or in?"

"Me, homosexual? Heavens no. That was a phase I was going through, back then, you know." He shrugged and looked right at Todd. "Lying with another man is a mortal sin. It's against Scripture. I worked on all this, studied very hard, and prayed very hard too. And it paid off. The Lord Jehovah had mercy upon me."

Todd stared at him. "What are you saying?"

"I've since been sexually rehabilitated."

"Rehabilitated? What does that mean?"

"It means the demonic spirits were cast out of my body."

"Pat, what are you talking about?"

"Simply that homosexuality is not the will of Jehovah, and through devotion and study I've been cleansed."

Todd didn't know what to say. "Gee, and all I tried was electric shock aversion therapy."

"Yes, well, my hands, my mouth, my anal canal—all of them were cleansed of ungodly deposits of semen."

"What?"

Pat glared at him, then said, "Perhaps you don't know, but I was married for a long time and we have a son."

This was crazy. Fucking crazy, thought Todd. And to make it even weirder, at the very same time Todd was aware that Pat or Patrick or whoever this guy was was looking him up and down. Checking him out. Their eyes met, and Todd's heart clanked.

Squinting into the glaring light, Pat turned away from Todd and looked back to the view of the oval lake. "Janice was right, you are looking quite well."

"You talked to her, didn't you? I know she called you last night."

"She called, and I just saw her, actually. In fact, I came right here after we met." Pat started to say something, stopped, then continued. "Todd, I came to see you today because I need your help with something."

The only thing that might have surprised him more than this visit was this request. And rather than pleasing Todd, a slow sense of dread began to fill him. This, he knew, wasn't going to be pretty.

"And what's that?" asked Todd.

"Then you'll help me?"

"What do you want me to do?"

Pat smiled. "You haven't changed much—still the cautious one, still waiting for others to make the first move."

"Perhaps. And I suspect you're just as manipulative, as driven to get whatever you want."

"I'm sure that's not meant as flattery." Pat cleared his throat. "Anyway . . . I imagine you're aware that many years ago Janice had a baby."

As if an enormous bookcase had just fallen over, everything crashed still inside Todd. He had a glimpse of the truth, and suddenly he was short of breath. It couldn't be, he thought. Yet . . . yet it made sense. Too much sense. All too easily it would explain why Janice had avoided telling him.

Pat was staring at him, a wry grin upon his face. "Ah, so you didn't know that Zeb was my son."

Todd went over to the couch and dropped himself down. Janice and Pat had screwed? He could barely imagine it, the two of them in bed together.

His voice by no means as strong as he would have liked, Todd said, "What the hell are you talking about?"

"You want details?" Pat smiled. "Before I devoted my life to God, Janice and I—how shall I put it?—enjoyed carnal pleasures."

"I can't believe it."

"Oh, yes. And from that union our son was born. When Janice decided to abandon the child, my new wife and I decided to adopt him."

There could have been other guys, maybe the entire proverbial football team. It was possible. But it wasn't, not really. First of all Todd knew Janice, knew she wasn't one to throw herself around.

"When?" demanded Todd, feeling betrayed.

"When what?"

"When did you and Janice have sex?"

"Um, let me see, it was that week I left Northwestern."

"You mean right after Greg was killed?"

"Yes, I suppose that's correct. I suppose it was just after he died. Right, that's when Janice and I drove out West."

Sure, thought Todd. They were talking about a few days in a woman's cycle. Either Janice had been fertile when Todd and she had slept together, or she had been a few days later when she'd slept with Pat. It was that simple.

Suddenly Todd was jumping to his feet. "God damn it!"

He stormed across the room, stopped at his coffee table. There were a couple of magazines. A book. Just as he'd felt at Janice's, he wanted to hurl them across the floor. Smash them. Throw them at Pat. He wanted to open the balcony door, hurl something right out the window and over the edge. Janice had been his girlfriend. Pat, his secret lover. And those two, the two people he'd been the most intimate with, had actually slept together?

Pat was talking. Todd turned and looked at him, this pale, aging figure who'd spoken of demonic spirits and sexual rehabilitation.

"Todd," Pat was saying, "I want to ask you if you'll tell Janice to back off."

"What?"

"I need you to do this. You know, of course, what's going on."

There could be no dancing around any of the issues, and Todd asked, "You're referring to Zeb and his daughter?"

"Precisely. It's a very serious problem, and I need you to convince Janice to drop the matter."

"What?"

"This may sound crass or overly blunt—I just don't know how else to put it," began Pat, "but Janice gave up Zeb over two decades ago. She got rid of him, Todd. She shed him and any and all decisions regarding his life. It was all legally done, so to put it simply, his problems today do not concern her."

"Oh, shit."

"Please, just listen to me. Zeb is my son, and his daughter is my granddaughter. This is a family issue—and whether Janice likes it or not, she's not part of the family."

Todd took a deep breath, realized how all too easily he could have ended up like him, like this Patrick, and said, "Pat—or Patrick—first of all, Janice is Zeb's birth mother, and if he comes to her for help then I'm sure she's going to do everything and anything in her power to help him. Second of all, Janice is no dummy and she never has been. She's amazingly sharp and she's amazingly moral. By that I mean she's always done what she felt was right, and neither I nor anyone else has ever convinced her otherwise."

"Please, Todd, we're talking about the life of a baby."

"We most certainly are."

"But you don't understand—"

"I'm afraid I do."

"No, you don't." Pat clenched his fists, turned back to the balcony door, stood there as the arrows of winter sun pierced him. "How you and Janice live is wrong. As I've already said, it's a sin against the Lord. But once we were friends, the three of us, and that's why I'm here today, to tell you that Janice should forget about all this because it's dangerous, because I can't protect her."

"Is that a warning of some sort?"

"Yes, I'm telling you there will be trouble for all if Janice interferes."

"And what about me? What if I do something?"

"Todd, please. There are some very powerful people involved in this. Very committed. And there's only so much I can do to hold them back, per se."

"And I'm telling you that's bullshit."

Pat turned and looked at him. "What?"

"You came here because you wanted to see me."

"Oh, please, don't be ridiculous."

Todd watched as Pat stiffened, and Todd knew he was right. By the subtle, hidden glances, Todd had guessed the truth.

"You came here to check me out." Todd hesitated, then said, "Don't think I haven't noticed how you've been looking at me."

"How dare you!"

"Don't worry, I'm not calling you a faggot. At first I didn't understand, but now I think I do."

"Is your life that ghastly, is sex all you think about?"

"Patrick, you're not listening—I'm not calling you queer."

"God have mercy on you, you sodomite!" Patrick started for the door. "Even though you've lost your values I came here out of concern for Janice and you."

"Bullshit. You came here out of concern for something else."

"And what might that be?"

*  *  *

*Todd was shivering, his entire body shaking, but he barely felt the cold. Holy shit, he thought as his breath steamed into the wintry night air, what was going to happen now? Greg had seen everything, he was going to tell everyone! Standing behind his fraternity, his entire life went shooting through his imagination. Homo. Everyone was going to call him a homo.*

*It caught his attention as if it were a single giant snowflake falling from the sky through the dark night. But of course it was on fire. That's why he noticed it. The glow. Bright and orange. His eyes automatically focused on it and watched as the mysterious object slipped through the air to the ground. A cigarette, he realized. Big and thick. A hand-rolled cigarette that hit the snowy ground with a faint hiss.*

*The next moment a desperate noise struck his ears, and he leaned back, slumped against the cold, dark, brick building, and at first thought it was a siren. It was a voice, though, and then he thought someone was doing a football cheer. Something like that. Then he wondered if someone was just goofing around, all stressed out before final exams. Todd glanced toward Sherman Avenue, looked around. But the courtyard was empty. Empty and black and cold.*

*He heard the desperate sound again, realized it was a scream, and looked straight up.*

*The fire escape hovered right above Todd. All this iron grating, black and bolted to the back of the fraternity. It climbed all the way to the top of the building, back and forth and back and forth, a landing on each floor. Todd could barely see anything, but looking straight up he saw something moving on one of the platforms way, way up there. Shit, what was Greg still doing outside Pat's window?*

*Panic surged through him, and Todd ran away from the building for a better look. Someone was up there, someone was screaming. And . . .*

*"Oh, fuck!" muttered Todd.*

*Someone was hanging off the fire escape, dangling there, flapping around like a flag. He was hanging by one hand, but it was immediately clear he couldn't hold on. Too cold, too icy. And a split second later the figure fell, screaming and tumbling all the way down, all the way to the ground, where it ended with a thud. And frigid silence.*

Todd waited a moment and said, "Somewhere in the back of your mind you've been worrying that I figured it out."

"What are you suggesting now?"

"That you're afraid I know what really happened that night Greg was killed." Todd waited a couple of seconds. "And maybe I do."

Pat started for the door. "I'm leaving. I've said what I wanted to. Perhaps someday you'll repent for your homosexuality."

As the other man brushed past him Todd said, "There was a second person out on that fire escape, wasn't there?"

"What? What worldly things are you talking about?"

Todd watched Pat's every step, every flinch, studied him as his hand froze on the doorknob. For a long moment there was silence between the two men. So, thought Todd, he was absolutely right.

"I don't know how I could have been so stupid, why it didn't occur to me before," continued Todd. "But when I was beneath the fire escape I looked up and saw someone moving right above me, someone stepping around on the grating. Then I moved away from the building and someone was already hanging by his hand. That couldn't have been one and the same person. I mean, I heard the screaming before that— which, after all, is why I looked up—and the person, Greg, was screaming because he was hanging by his hands and about to fall." So now he knew for sure, thought Todd. "Greg didn't slip that night on the fire escape, did he? Someone pushed him, right? And if it wasn't you—"

"My window was stuck!"

"Well, if that's really true, then you saw it all, you know who did it, you know who pushed him. And all this time you've been protecting someone." Todd added, "Who was it, Pat? The other guy you were screwing at the frat house?"

Unable to bear the situation, Pat ripped open the door, and his voice boomed like a preacher as he shouted, "I'm sorry you don't realize the danger you're in!"

# 29

On her knees before the wooden chair, her hands clasped in front of her, Suzanne bowed her head in the dim light of the prayer closet. Oh, please, God the Father, show me the way. Lead me to the best decision. The correct one. My baby's gone, I'm worried about my husband, and here I kneel, begging for Your mercy, Your understanding, Your wisdom. Show me the divine path. I've been Your obedient disciple. I'll always be Your humble slave. Just give me a heavenly sign, show me what to do. Guide me in Your divine way.

Ever since her father had left earlier this morning for a meeting of The Elders, Suzanne had been in the tiny room, a space not more than three by four feet. She'd been in here— the dim bulb burning, the door shut—praying for insight, begging for help, hoping the right decision would come to her. If she was going to do it at all, now was the time. Her knees burned with pain, but she wasn't going to get up, she wasn't going to leave this holelike room until she knew, until she'd been given an answer. And it had better come soon, because what did she have, another twenty minutes before her father returned? He'd already been gone almost two hours.

She moved her right knee across the wooden floor, felt a splinter slide into her skin. "Ouch!"

And then she slumped to the side and fell against the wall. Raising her leg, she picked at the tiny sliver of wood, pulled it free.

But that was it, she realized. The signal she'd been looking for. The divine sign. God had chosen to prick her with a little piece of wood. He'd pierced her skin, even drawn blood, to break her concentration. Then He'd allowed her to pull the sliver free from her body. So she was meant to pull herself free from this place, right? Well, wasn't that what God the Father was trying to tell her?

Of course.

She pushed herself up, barely able to stand on her numb legs. As she shook her limbs and tried to get the blood flowing, she knew what she had to do. Opening the door, she flicked off the light and stepped out of that stuffy little room into the bright light. She hesitated, listened, but heard no sign of her father. So she was right. God had been sending her a message; He had pricked her with that sliver to wake her up, to tell her this was her chance, the only one. Given the way her father was watching her, she certainly wasn't going to get another opportunity as good as this, at least not for the next few days.

Happy she'd been given such a definitive answer to her prayers, Suzanne crossed the small hall and entered her father's bedroom, where she walked around to the bedside table. For a second she feared it might not be there, but when she opened the drawer there it was, the shiny black pistol. Suzanne ran one hand through her thick blond hair, stared down at the weapon. What choice did she have?

She snatched up the gun and grabbed the small box of bullets. Clutching them to her breasts, she ran out of her father's room and into her own, where she threw open her closet door. First she pulled out a big blue sweater—dark blue, of course, because The Congregation frowned on bright colors—

which she spread flat on her bed. Next she placed the gun and bullets right in the middle of it, then carefully pulled up the sleeves and bottom and neck of the sweater. A tidy little bundle, she thought, smiling, the gun and bullets wrapped snugly inside. Next she dove back into the closet and pulled out an extra pair of shoes and a small canvas duffel bag. This should work, she thought. Her dad had done the same thing last year, packing away a gun when he went up to visit those people in Idaho.

"You know, I think someday the government's going to come after us," he'd explained more than once to his little girl. "They could lay siege upon us, you realize, for after all, God's true church was prophesied to be tortured. And if you need to, you run, Suzanne. Take some money and take a gun—we'll meet up later, just like our emergency plan says. But if you get on an airplane, be sure, baby doll, that you don't take the gun on board the plane. No, they'll catch you if you do that. Instead, you put the gun in your luggage and check the bag. That way they won't discover you got a way to defend yourself."

So now she dumped in some shoes and more clothes. And that was it. A full bag, which she zipped up.

Money. The duffel draped over her right shoulder, Suzanne raced down the hall and into the kitchen. From the narrow spice cabinet just to the left of the stove, she took a large coffee can. No one at The Congregation had credit cards—they were far too worldly, and Suzanne had seen one only a couple of times in her entire life—and when she popped off the lid of the can, she found the whole thing stuffed with money, thousands and thousands of dollars crammed in there. She reached in, peeled off eight or nine one-hundred-dollar bills, thought better of it, and left that money on the shelf and took the entire can for herself. There was no sense running short; she'd need plenty for the ticket, and the three of them would probably go through the rest pretty quickly. Besides, her dad could always just dip into the coffers of The Congregation and get more. In fact, she thought, snatching the short pile of hundreds, he didn't even need that.

The last thing she took was the sheet of paper with the names and the telephone numbers her father had written down. If she were caught at this point she'd be in deep, deep trouble. She had a vision of her dad walking in and figuring out what she was doing—he'd rip open the bag, hurl the money against the floor, scream, maybe even wave the gun around. And lock her in the prayer closet. She just had to get to the airport.

She snatched her dad's car keys from a hook by the door and grabbed a jacket. She paused by a window, peered out over the compound. The bakery looked quiet, so did the meeting hall and the family dormitories. Okay, so her dad was still in his meeting down there and everyone else was making dough, literally so. As if she were scurrying through the rain, Suzanne bowed her blond head and darted outside to the car, her father's prized white Cadillac. Jumping in, she jammed the keys into the ignition, stomped on the gas, and the engine came to life like a tiger. Okay, okay, she told herself. Don't be too nervous. She just had to get the car in reverse, back out of here, and—

Suddenly she was shooting backward, right out of their drive and onto the paved country road. She stomped on the brakes, brought the car to a screeching halt, then moved the gearshift to drive. Almost instantly she was flying down the road, whooshing away.

"Wow!" Suzanne screamed with delight.

She swerved over to the right side of the road, saw the speedometer quickly climbing. Great, she thought, she'd be at the airport in Denver in no time, whereupon she'd catch the very first plane. With any luck, she realized, she'd be in Minneapolis in a matter of a few hours.

# 30

"Oh, great."

That big blue snowplow had done a fine job of cleaning the alley, but it had plowed the snow right up against Janice's garage door. When she pressed the button and the garage door rumbled upward, the first thing she saw was this white wall about two feet high. She knew she'd never be able to smash her Honda Prelude through it, so she grabbed a shovel. As if she were frantically digging through an avalanche in search of some buried soul, she worked as quickly as she could. Zeb had the baby—thank God—but they were in trouble. They needed her. She had to be there *now.* Huffing, Janice carved out a narrow path for her car, hurling the already crusty snow aside. By the time she'd shoveled from the very edge of her garage to the cleared alley, a distance of only three or four feet, her brow was blistered with sweat and her heart was racing. What if Zeb didn't wait? What if he gave up on her?

Her body trembling, Janice finally climbed into her small car. She jammed in the keys, revved up the engine, then put the car in reverse and gunned it. She blasted out of the garage like a bullet, then shot down the narrow alley.

Zeb had said he was in trouble, but who knew what that

meant? Given the recent events, Janice feared everything and anything, particularly that thug. But Zeb was okay, right? The baby too? Isn't that what Zeb had said on the phone? In her mind she replayed the conversation, tried to remember each and every word, tried to fish out any kind of truth. Good Lord, she drove as if she were insane, her red car swerving and sliding on the slippery streets. She just had to get to that stupid gas station. There weren't that many cars out, but everyone was merely creeping along. At the corner of 50th and Bryant the traffic came to a snarled halt and she leaned on the horn.

"Move it!"

Almost twenty-five minutes after Zeb had called, Janice drove up France Avenue and finally spotted the large red sign of the gas station near 44 Street. Please let him still be there, she chanted silently. Please let them both be all right. What if something was the matter with Ribka? What if she needed her medication? Maybe Zeb should have called 911 directly. She turned off the street much too quickly and managed to steer her car toward a towering outdoor display, the car sliding to a stop only inches from the display. Next Janice was throwing open the door, jumping out. Zeb came charging out of the gas station's small building, cradling a bundle inside the big parka.

"Is Ribka okay?" asked Janice as she rushed toward him.

"Yeah."

"Thank God."

"Come on, we can't stand out here."

"Sure, sure. But . . ."

There was everything to say, but only one thing to do. She didn't merely embrace Zeb, she clutched him and Ribka to her. Bit her lip. Swallowed. And tried not to burst into tears.

"Just . . . just believe me," said Janice quietly. "I didn't give her to him. He had a gun."

"I know. It's one of the guys from The Congregation. He just came after me again."

Janice pulled at the top of Zeb's coat, peered in through the opening, and saw Ribka cradled warmly inside. Zeb, however, wouldn't linger, and he nudged Janice back and started toward the car. Flooded with relief, Janice couldn't move for a moment, but then she dashed toward the car, climbed in, started it up. As she sped away from the gas station Zeb kept staring out the back, trying to ascertain if they were being followed.

"I don't get how they've been tailing me," said Zeb, searching behind them. "I mean, how did Paul find me this morning? And last night these two guys showed up at the hospital and chased me."

"Wait a minute," said Janice. "This isn't making sense. I think we have a bit to sort out."

"Okay, but just don't go back to your place. That's probably the first place they'll look for me."

So, as Janice drove along, she and Zeb pieced together the events of the past day and a half, from Zeb talking to his mother in Santa Fe, to the break-in at Janice's house, and then to the events at the hospital last night. Janice not only explained that the two guys at the hospital had been her friends, Todd and Rawlins, but that she had seen Pat this morning.

"Oh, shit," moaned Zeb. "I knew it. I knew they'd send the whole posse after me."

Zeb went on to tell Janice all about getting stuck last night, staying at the church, and then spying Paul out by the garage this morning.

"Who knows what happened to that minister. I saw Paul and took off. There's no messing with him."

"No kidding." Janice shook her head. "We've just got to put you someplace for the next day or two. Someplace that's safe and where they wouldn't even think of looking."

"I could stay at a hotel. I don't have any money, but—"

"No, I've got a better idea." She wanted Zeb not only somewhere safe, but where he could be watched as well. "You don't have anything against drag queens, do you?"

# 31

Todd was driving around the south end of Lake Calhoun when his car phone rang. As he picked it up he glanced to his left across the bright frozen surface of the lake, a white plain of winter. Beyond that rose a relatively new crop of glass and concrete, the sparkling towers of downtown.

"Hello?" he said.

"Hi, it's me," said Rawlins over the line. "Where are you?"

"Just circling Lake Calhoun. I'm on my way to Janice's."

"Listen, something's come up."

Recognizing the seriousness in Rawlins's voice, Todd tensed. "What's the matter?"

"We've got what looks like an attempted murder."

"Oh, shit."

His mind immediately flashed to Janice's house. He should never have left her alone. Or Zeb—had he been harmed? The possibilities came charging at Todd and he nearly drove off the snowy road.

Todd began, "It's not . . . not—"

"Hey, don't panic. It's some guy you don't know, a minister in south Minneapolis."

Rawlins went on to explain how the call had come in not too long after he'd arrived at the station. One of the members of this church had stopped by the parish house to help with the shoveling. Finding the front door wide open but no minister, the concerned churchgoer went out back, peered into the garage, and saw someone in a pile on the garage floor. He immediately called 911, and the police broke into the garage and found a guy unconscious and hypothermic.

"So why are you telling me all this?" asked Todd as he turned right on Xerxes and headed directly south.

"Well, the guy's still unconscious at the hospital, so we don't really know what happened. He'll probably be okay, but when the cops were at the garage this other neighbor comes along, this woman, who says she was over the night before. She'd brought over some baby clothes and stuff because some kid's car got stuck out front and the minister was letting this guy and his baby spend the night."

A deep sense of dread plunged through him. "Zeb?"

"Right. She even mentioned him by name. A very polite young man, she said, but there was something odd about him. Like he was scared or something. The minister had taken her aside, said he thought the boy was in trouble and that he was worried about the baby. Our guys are searching the house right now, trying to see if anything was stolen, but—"

"But what?"

"But a car with Colorado plates is stuck in the snow right out front. There's no question that it's Zeb's. From the description it sounds like the same one we saw last night out at the hospital."

Todd pulled to the side of the road and let a car pass. This didn't make any sense. For one thing, if Zeb were in fact guilty of any wrongdoing, why would he be so stupid as to leave his car there?

"Something else is going on," said Todd into the phone.

"Let's hope so. The crime lab is over there right now. They're checking for footprints in the snow, but there's already been a slug of people walking around. They probably won't be able to get anything clean."

"Well, listen, I'll be at Janice's in a few minutes, and if we think of anything we'll call. Or call us if anything comes up."

Rawlins cleared his throat. "Something already has, Todd. That's why I'm calling."

"What do you mean?"

"We're putting out an arrest warrant for Zeb."

"You're kidding."

"At this point we just want to talk with him, that's all." Over the line Rawlins already sounded exasperated. "If you're in contact with him, if you know anything regarding his whereabouts, then you've got to give us a call; otherwise you'll be in trouble for conspiring to hide a fugitive. Do you understand?"

"Sure," replied Todd, driving on, "but I wish I didn't."

# 32

"Don't worry," said Jeff, his voice hushed as he and Janice stood in the small kitchen of his bungalow. "He'll be perfectly safe here. I'll be gone most of the afternoon, but I'm sure he won't have any trouble."

Janice stepped around the corner of the white refrigerator and peered into the living room, where Zeb was still seated on the couch feeding Ribka. They'd arrived only ten minutes ago, and Ribka had cried until she had a bottle.

"It's not just that," whispered Janice. "I want you to keep an eye on him too. I don't think he'll bolt, but I really don't know."

"Girlfriend, what is it with you and this kid and his baby? You're really hung up on them, aren't you?"

As she leaned against the white Formica countertop, Janice felt Jeff's suspicious eyes upon her and she glanced back in the living room. Avoiding his inquisitive, gossipy look, Janice turned and looked past the tiny round breakfast table and out the rear window. No, Todd wasn't the only one she had to tell about Zeb. Todd was the first, but then there were all her friends and even a few business associates.

"I'll tell you about it later."

"There's a big secret there, and don't tell me there isn't," replied Jeff, a catty twinkle in his eye as he took a quick sip of diet Coke. "I just love dirt, particularly by the truckload."

"Sorry, now's not the time. For now I just don't want you to take your eyes off Zeb."

Jeff stepped over to the sink, peered into the other room. "That shouldn't be difficult."

"Knock it off, Jeff. This is serious, very serious."

"Okay, okay, but we're opening a new show tonight and I've got a rehearsal this afternoon. Blizzard or not, I can't miss it." Jeff looked at the clock on the microwave. "The guy who does the lights, Pedro, is coming by in fifteen minutes to pick me up. He's got one of those cars like Todd's. You know, one of those macho things with four wheels that all spin at the same time. Unfortunately, that means Zeb'll be here by himself."

"Can't he go with you?"

"Well, well, well, aren't we the little Ms. Mother Hen. I guess he can. I mean, the more the merrier. He can either watch and applaud or stay in my dressing room."

"Good. Do you have a phone down there?"

"How about a beeper? I'm sure we could get one and padlock it to him."

"I just want to be able to reach you in case anything comes up."

Jeff rolled his eyes, grabbed a paper napkin, and scribbled down a number. "This is the phone in the dressing room. Let it ring a long time. Or call back if I don't answer."

"Thanks. Let me talk to him and straighten this out." She leaned forward and kissed Jeff on the cheek. "Thanks. You're worth your weight in gold."

"Then that must mean I'm priceless," he replied, pinching his big waist.

Janice slipped out of the kitchen and into the living room, where Zeb held the baby against his shoulder. She walked around the television and sat down next to him on the couch, sinking into the deep white cushions.

"Sometimes it takes her forever to burp," said Zeb as he patted Ribka's back with a sure, steady movement.

"Did she eat much?"

"The whole bottle. She must have been starved. Do you think I should give her more?"

Janice wished she had more experience in these matters, and she said, "Actually, I think father knows best. This is all a little bit new to me, you know."

Suddenly this rumbling started, and then a huge belch erupted out of the baby's tiny body. Janice and Zeb looked at each other and burst out with laughter.

"Wow, that's the best one I've ever heard her do," said Zeb in amazement.

"I never got anything close to that when she was at my house." She reached over and gently rubbed Ribka's back. "Do you know what a great dad you are, Zeb?"

"Thanks. Even though I was raised with a bunch of religious nuts, Mom was really great and—" He stopped, his brow tightening into a mass of deep furrows. "I'm sorry, I . . . I didn't mean to offend you."

"Don't worry, you didn't." All of this was so hard; Janice wanted to both do and say everything right and at the same time not show how much she hurt inside. "She is your mother, and she did a wonderful job raising you. You're supposed to call her 'Mom.' "

"Then what do I call you? 'Janice' just sounds so . . . so distant."

"Well, we'll have to work on that, the distant part. After all this settles down I hope we'll spend a good amount of time together."

Zeb smiled. "Me too."

"Good." Janice hesitated, then said, "We've got a lot to talk about. Or I do anyway. There's a lot I'd like to try to explain."

"Okay."

Looking at him just now, she saw that there was still so much of a young boy left in him. "Okay" meant yes, he wanted to hear it all, he wanted to know everything, wanted to understand just why he'd been given up for adoption. And Janice would try her best to put it all into perspective for him. After thinking so much about it all these years, after reading so many books and articles, she hoped she'd have something intelligent and comforting to tell him.

"Unfortunately," said Janice, "we don't have time right now. Jeff has to go downtown to a rehearsal, and I'm hoping you'll go with him. I'd just feel better if you and Ribka weren't alone. There've been so many problems already that I don't want you here by yourselves." She hesitated, then added, "Plus, to be perfectly honest, I don't want you taking off. I . . . I just don't want to lose you again."

"Sure, we'll go."

"Jeff's rehearsing for a drag show. It's at a gay bar, the Gay Times, but at this time of day it'll be empty. Is that okay? You won't have a problem going in there with him, will you?"

Zeb shrugged. "That's fine."

"Trust me, I know a bunch of the queens down there and they're all real sweet. They'll probably fight over who's going to baby-sit Ribka."

Zeb started to laugh, then stopped. "Can I ask you a question?"

"You can ask me anything."

"Well, are all your friends gay?"

"I guess a lot of them are." With a grin she added, "But some of my best friends are straight."

He obviously failed to see the humor, and asked, "What about those two guys last night, the ones who came out to the hospital?"

"Yes, Todd is a very old friend. One of my closest and . . . well, most important friends." She put her hand to her head, told herself to leave it at that for now. "He and Rawlins are dating, actually."

"Oh."

She saw the seriousness wash back over his face. He's not, she prayed, drifting away, is he? I'm not losing him over this, am I? He'd said he didn't have trouble with her sexuality, but maybe he did, maybe he simply couldn't identify and articulate it. Janice sat there, trembling inside, fearing that she was losing him even as she was watching. Mother has baby. Mother loses baby. Mother finds baby-who's-now-a-youngman. Mother loses him again because . . . ?

"Does it . . ." Zeb started to talk, stopped, tried to formulate his concern. "Does it matter to you that I'm . . . well, you know, different than you?"

She studied him, wondering, Is he asking what I think he is? "Zeb, I'm not sure I understand what you're saying."

"Janice, I'm . . . I'm straight. Do . . . do you care? I mean, does it make a difference to you?"

Staring at his beautiful young face, so innocent, so desirous of love, the question took her by surprise. What he wanted to know was just so simple, so honest, but at first Janice couldn't think what to say, merely because she'd never pondered the issue from that side of the fence.

"Oh, my God, Zeb." She reached out and took one of his hands in hers, felt herself choking up. "It doesn't matter who you are or who you love, whether you're gay . . . or straight." Then she had to stifle a small and incredulous grin, for she never, ever expected to be saying these words. "Sweetheart, I just want you to know how incredibly proud I am of you. You don't even know how much I love you." She paused and added, "And how much I hope to one day earn your love as well."

"But you already have," he said. "Earned it, I mean."

At the same moment they were both reaching out, birth mother and son, embracing each other with the small baby cradled in between. Janice felt her granddaughter squirming against her, felt the strength of her son holding on to her, and was amazed. To her it was a miracle, this sense of fullness that she thought she had so long ago abdicated.

"Ahem. I'm sorry to break up this little love fest, kiddies, but this girl's got a song to sing. My pal Pedro will be here any minute."

Janice and Zeb pulled back to see Jeff standing in the doorway, a small cosmetics case in hand.

Janice wiped her eyes with the back of her right hand and said to Zeb, "Okay, you stick with Jeff and he'll make sure everything's all right."

"That's right, if anyone tries to hurt you," interjected Jeff, "I'll beat them with my pearls and tie them up with my feather boa."

Zeb asked, "But when am I going to see you again, Janice?"

"Soon. I hope all this will be over real soon."

# 33

Todd had been sitting on the living room couch for over ten minutes when he heard her key in the rear door. He didn't move, just sat there in his beige down parka and listened as Janice stomped her feet and took off her coat in the kitchen.

"And where were you?" he finally called.

"Todd, is that you?" she responded, unable to hide her surprise.

"No, it's just your friendly neighborhood thug come back for another violent assault."

"You scared me." She appeared at the edge of the living room. "How did you get in?"

"You left the back door open. You must have been going somewhere in a hurry, huh? I checked and saw that your car was gone. And don't tell me you just went to the post office."

"I didn't." She came in, crossing through the large room and dropping herself in an overstuffed armchair alongside the couch. "Actually . . . actually, my dear, Zeb called."

Little could have surprised him more, and Todd sat up and demanded, "What? Where is he?"

"He phoned from a gas station."

"I can't believe it."

"I went and picked him up."

"So where is he? Outside?"

"No, I took him somewhere."

"Such as?"

"Somewhere safe."

"Janice," said Todd, clasping his hands and his voice growing tense, "don't hold out on me. We need to start being real frank with each other. This kid's in serious trouble."

"No, he's in serious danger."

"That too, but you haven't heard. Rawlins just called me on my car phone. Some guy was attacked—it just happened a couple of hours ago—and they have a warrant out for Zeb's arrest."

"Oh, no." She put both her hands to her face. "Not the minister."

"How the hell did you know that?"

"Zeb told me."

"So he did it?'

"No, of course not." Janice took a deep breath. "Zeb's car got stuck in the snow last night, and this minister took Zeb and Ribka in for the night."

Todd had been holding on to the hope, however small, that the police were somehow mistaken. But quite obviously they weren't. Todd shook his head, unzipped his coat, wondered how much worse it could get.

"First some religious kooks are after Zeb, and now the police," Todd said. "What else did he tell you? Like who went after this guy, this minister?"

"Maybe."

Todd sat there in disbelief as Janice recounted the entire sequence of events, from getting the phone call, to picking up Zeb, to Zeb's story of what had happened at the minister's house. Piecing it all together, Todd was relieved that it made sense, particularly since Todd had come face to face with this guy, this Paul.

"So what do you think?" asked Todd. "Do you believe Zeb? Do you trust him?"

"Implicitly."

He sat back, glanced around the large room with its tall ceiling, then gazed out at the sunny, white day. He didn't even know Zeb, barely knew what he looked like.

"Call me nuts, but I guess I trust him too." The next moment Todd eyed her and asked rather lightly, "See anyone else today?"

"Actually, yes." Janice stared down at the floor as if in shame. "I saw Pat—Pat from Northwestern. He's here in town, and I met him just a little while ago. I'm sorry I didn't tell you sooner, Todd, but I was trying to keep it as simple as possible."

"So what happened?"

"I ended up telling him to go to hell."

He couldn't help but grin. That was just like Janice. Always moral. Always—well, almost always—forthright. Relieved that she had told him and that finally, perhaps, everything else was being laid out, he knew he had to tell her too.

Todd said, "I saw him too."

"What?"

"When I stopped by my place he was waiting for me in the lobby."

"You're kidding. What did he say to you?"

"Among other things that he had a son, namely, specifically, Zeb."

Completely silent, Janice bowed her head and lifted her right hand to her eyes. She looked as if she were about to say something, but instead she just sat there, completely silent.

"Well?" asked Todd. "Is it true?"

Janice shrugged.

"So he's possible dad number two?"

She nodded.

"Any other candidates?"

She shook her head.

He said, "That's kind of what I assumed."

"And that's kind of why I didn't tell you. I didn't know how," she finally said. "What happened between Pat and me, well, it wasn't pretty, I can say that much. We were—"

"Later," said Todd, standing and walking toward her. "I don't need the gory details, but if you want to tell me, tell me later."

"Are . . . are we still friends?"

"The best. That is, if you can forgive me and my temper."

"Well, it is something you need to work on."

Janice pushed herself up from the overstuffed chair, and Todd wrapped his arms around her thin body, holding her tightly against himself. Outside of his small family—his mother and brother, who both lived in distant states—he shared more history with Janice than any other person in the world. They'd gone from youthful love and lust to avoidance and distance, then all the way back to a profound kind of respect and love, a familial kind that could never be broken. As he held her in his arms, his face nuzzled in her thick hair, her face pressed against his chest, Todd couldn't help but wonder if the thing that had always been binding them wasn't cosmic destiny, but simply and actually a child.

Janice asked, "So you want to know where Zeb is?"

"That's kind of a loaded question. We're not only legally obligated to contact the police with any information we have, but I'm dating a cop. I promised I'd give Rawlins a call as soon as we spoke."

They broke apart. There just wasn't any easy way of doing this, thought Todd, as he drifted into the center of the room. Glancing at Janice, he not only saw the worry on her face, but knew she was contemplating all the legal ramifications as well.

She said, "Todd, don't you see how easily this could get out of control? My God, it'd scare Zeb to death if he thought he was wanted by the cops. And what if Rawlins can't control all this, what if the police descend upon Zeb and haul him down to the police station for questioning? You of all people know how terrifying that is. What if they want to hold him overnight? Not only would he be separated from Ribka, I might not be able to take her.''

"I hadn't thought about that."

But she was right. The authorities could easily insist on placing Ribka in a foster home, which would shatter the already spooked Zeb.

"Todd, you and I both know that Zeb didn't try to kill anyone, so how can we protect him as much as possible?"

Todd thought for a moment. "Okay, let's do it this way. Let me call Rawlins down at the police station. I won't tell him anything, not over the phone anyway. I'll just get together with him and then bring him to talk to Zeb. No one else involved. Zeb's going to have to talk with the police sooner or later, so it might as well be sooner and it might as well be Rawlins."

"I don't think we have any other choice." She rolled her eyes. "I guess that makes me not only Zeb's birth mother but his birth lawyer too."

"So dispense with the secrecy—where's Zeb?"

"Down at the Gay Times."

"Oh, great, so much for maternal instincts, sending your son and granddaughter down to a gay bar."

"Listen to yourself, Todd, you sound like Rush Limbaugh."

"Gee, thanks."

They discussed the logistics and decided upon a reasonable plan, which Todd hoped to God made sense. Janice then gave him Jeff's dressing room phone number and dashed to the upstairs bathroom.

"Just call and check on Zeb, will you?" she asked as she hurried out of the room.

Of course he would, replied Todd, as he sat down on the living room couch and picked up the phone. He dialed the number and a deep voice answered on the first ring.

"Miss Crystal's dressing room."

"Hi, Jeff, it's me, Todd."

"Well, hello, my darling Mr. Manly Man. What a wonderful treat to hear your suave voice. Do you miss me or are you just calling for a fashion tip? On a bright wintry day like today I recommend blazing blues to go with your brilliant eyes."

"Thanks, Jeff," began Todd, "but Janice just wanted me to see how everything is."

"Just fabulous. You can tell that dyke hen that we arrived at the Gay Times a few minutes ago and I'm doing my makeup—brilliant red lipstick, some nice rouge, and great eye shadow, a nummy evening blue. My rehearsal starts in fifteen minutes."

"I think she's more concerned about Zeb and Ribka."

"Well, you tell her that I think she should spend as much time worrying about her cosmetics as she does about them. Father and daughter are wonderful though. Not to worry. In fact, they're right here dozing."

"Great." Todd wondered how much to tell him and decided the less, the better. "If Zeb wakes up you can tell him that Janice is on the way down."

"Oh, fab. I love an audience. Ta-ta."

Todd had hung up when, his hand still on the receiver, the phone rang again. Although he wondered if he should, he impulsively answered it halfway through the first ring.

"Hello?" he said.

"Yes, Janice Gray, please."

"Who's calling?"

"This is Denise from her office downtown."

Great, thought Todd. That was all they needed, a call regarding some court case or divorce settlement or whatever. He could easily imagine her getting tied up on the phone over some petty issue.

"Listen," said Todd, "we're on the way out. Can Janice call you back on my car phone in just a few minutes?"

"Of course. Just make sure she calls. It's urgent."

"Right."

He hung up, and by the time he had his coat on she was on her way down the stairs.

"I thought I heard the phone," she said. "Was it a hang-up?"

"No, I answered. It was Denise from your office calling on some business."

Janice rolled her eyes. "Being a lawyer is just so much fun I can't stand it."

"I told her you'd call her back on my car phone. We should get going. I'll call Rawlins from the car too. That way I can keep the conversation short and not explain much."

Janice went to the front hall, where she put on her coat and boots again. Just as they were about to leave, Todd eyed the control panel of her security system.

"This time," he said, "I think it would not only be advisable to lock the doors but also set the alarm."

Giving him a snide look, she said, "You sound like my father."

Janice went up to the panel, a small plastic box with a keypad in the center, and punched in her security code. Immediately, however, the system started squawking and a digitized voice began barking.

"Warning, system error! Phone lines not accessible! Warning, system error!"

"God, I'm sick of the way this thing yaks at me," muttered Janice.

She reentered the code, but the same thing happened again, the system sounding the same warning.

"What's that mean?" asked Todd.

"Beats me. It's never done that before."

"When did you last set the alarm?"

"I don't know."

"Have you set it since that guy broke in?"

"No." Janice paused in thought. "No, I guess not. You guys were here last night, and I didn't set it earlier today."

Todd rubbed his forehead and tried to recall what little he knew about these things. Last summer when he was still at Channel 7, he'd done a special report on security systems and how they operated. He'd not only talked about the different types—from the standard models to the newer wireless ones—he'd also pointed out what the consumer needed to look for in a good system.

"Don't these things usually have a main panel or central box?" he asked.

"Sure, it's downstairs in the laundry room."

Exactly where that guy had broken in the other night. Had he tampered with anything?

"Maybe I'm being paranoid, but let's check it out," said Todd.

From the front hall Janice led the way through the kitchen and down the basement stairs. Todd followed her as she flicked on a light, continued past a small storage room, and then entered the laundry room, a large space with a pile of dirty clothes mounting beneath the spout of the laundry chute. The first thing Todd did was check the window, which looked just as he'd left it, still covered with plastic and nailed board.

"The main panel's right here," said Janice.

A gray metal box fastened to the wall, it looked like a fuse box except that it was locked. Several wires came out of the top and were connected with another that led to the outer wall of the house.

"Is that your phone line?" Todd asked.

"Um, it looks like it, doesn't it?" Janice's eyes followed the wire to the wall. "Yeah, that's it. I think the phone box is just outside on the side of the house."

Janice reached up to a ledge, felt around, and then pulled down a hidden key, which she used to open the panel. Inside were a variety of wires and connections, all of which looked reasonably confusing yet orderly. Todd studied the mass of electronics, but couldn't make sense of any of it.

"Well," said Todd, "at least it doesn't look like anyone's pried open the box and tampered with anything."

"Let's try it again."

Janice led the way out, turning off the lights as they went. Upstairs, they returned through the kitchen and to the front hall. And when Janice punched in the security code a third time it worked.

The digitized voice said: "System armed, level three."

"That's weird," commented Todd.

"Yeah, well the electronics world baffles me," replied Janice. "Come on, we've got thirty seconds to get out the door before the alarm system is activated."

But it was more than weird, thought Todd as they hustled out the door. Something was striking him as wrong, yet he couldn't figure out what. When he'd done that piece on security systems he'd compiled a list of cardinal rules, and something about Janice's system violated, Todd was sure, one of those.

"What's the matter?" asked Janice as she locked the door behind them.

"I don't know, but you should get the security people over here to take a look at it."

"Sure."

Squinting as the bright sun reflected off the snow, Todd hurried down the front walk to his Cherokee. As they climbed in his vehicle and he started it up, he realized he had one more question for Janice, this one of an entirely different nature and one he needed to ask before he dropped her off at the Gay Times.

Pulling into the street, Todd said, "You know, there's something else I've been meaning to ask you."

"Such as?"

"What blood type are you?"

''My blood type? B.''

''Oh.''

''Why?'' And then she understood. ''Wait a minute, this is about Zeb, isn't it?''

''Of course.''

# 34

She'd never thought about it, but Suzanne had no idea how hard it would be to rent a car. First of all, she was only nineteen, so every one of the girls—they couldn't have been any older than her!—at every single one of the car rental agencies said she was too young. Secondly, they all said she had to have a major credit card, which Suzanne most certainly did not, her father and every one of The Elders considering such things far too worldly. And thirdly, she needed to have a driver's license, which of course she didn't have either because, after all, whoever needed let alone wanted to leave The Congregation?

It was just so frustrating. She'd managed to get her dad's car to the airport, fly all the way to the Minneapolis/St. Paul airport, and now how was she going to get to her husband and baby? This couldn't happen. When the very last of the car rental places turned her down, Suzanne, in desperation, had pulled out her wad of cash and dropped it right on the counter.

"Here," said Suzanne, shoving a pile of bills at the girl, who like Suzanne had a thick mane of bright blond hair. "I've got lots of bucks. Why don't you just give me a car and keep the extra money for yourself?''

On one of the very few television shows Suzanne had ever seen, some crook had bribed a county clerk and gotten some secret information. And Suzanne now saw the temptation burning in the other girl's eyes as that young woman stared at the pile of one-hundred-dollar bills. After a long moment, however, the girl shook her head and snapped herself out of it.

"No. No, I can't. That . . . that wouldn't be right.''

"Oh, come on," begged Suzanne, looking as desperate as possible and trying to force her eyes to well up with tears. "I need to get to my baby. She's just a few months old. And . . . and she's sick.''

"But you don't understand. I can't take your money, because the computer won't release a car to you unless I enter all the proper information and numbers. I'm really sorry. I'd love to help you, but there's nothing I can do unless I put in a credit card and driver's license number.''

"But . . . but what am I going to do?''

"If you've got so much money, why even rent a car? It just snowed a whole lot last night and the roads are terrible. Why don't you just take a taxi?''

"Oh.'' Suzanne, who'd never even been in a cab, hadn't thought of it. "How do I do that?''

The girl at the desk looked at her as if she were from Mars and said, "You just go outside to the taxi stand. There's a whole line of 'em.'' The girl hesitated, then added, "Are you from outstate?''

"Out what?''

"Outstate. You act like you don't know anything, like you're from the country. You know, you better watch where you flash that money around. This isn't Chicago, but it's not Mayberry R.F.D. either.''

"Mayberry what?" asked Suzanne, wiping her eyes.

"Listen, just be careful with all that money.''

"Oh. Oh, okay.''

Dragging her duffel bag with her gun packed inside, Suzanne headed out into the cold. Even though there was a double-decker road up above and it was dark down here, they'd liberally spread salt, so it was damp and slushy. Noisy too, noted Suzanne, as she dashed through the traffic, following the signs to the taxi stand, where a guy ushered her into a yellow cab.

"Where to?" asked the driver, a burly guy with dark hair and a dark, stubbly beard.

"Minneapolis."

"Very good, dear. That's where you just flew into—the Mini-Apple. So don't keep me in suspense. Where do you want to go in this fair city?"

"Oh."

Suzanne reached into her purse and pulled out the piece of paper, which she calmly unfolded as the cab sped away from the terminal. On it was simply written a name.

"I want to go to the Fourth Church of Christ."

"That's very nice that you want to go to church. Very, very nice, but where the heck is it? I don't even know where the First or Second or Third Church of Christ is, let alone the Fourth. Don't you got, you know, the address?"

"Actually, I don't know. But here—here's the phone number."

"Oh, brother. You from outstate or something?"

"No. No, I'm from out in Colorado."

The lack of address was a problem that proved only a minor delay. The driver took sympathy on Suzanne and called his dispatcher, who in turn looked up the church's address in the phone book. And then they were on their way, speeding along the slushy freeway and into south Minneapolis.

"Sorry, I don't know much about this stuff," apologized Suzanne. "I've never even been in a taxi before."

"Well, isn't this a grand day in paradise."

Suzanne kind of liked this, sitting in the back and being driven along. It was as if you were famous or something. Here she had a driver and all she had to do was tell him where to go and he'd take her there, no questions asked. She didn't even have to try to figure out which direction to go. And with this guy driving she didn't have to worry about the slippery roads either. The girl at the car rental place was right, this was the thing to do. Peering forward, she saw the little machine up front, saw the numbers adding up. So what. She had enough money to keep this taxi for a whole week, maybe a month. Zeb was going to like this, her arriving in style and everything. It wasn't taking that long, really. Maybe only fifteen minutes later the driver was steering off the freeway and into a neighborhood.

"I'm gonna stick to the main roads 'cause a lot of the side streets haven't been plowed yet. It won't take too long though. Don't worry."

She didn't, and he was right, it didn't take long. Ten minutes later they were speeding up a street named after a country, France. Cool. A smile blossomed on Suzanne's face. Zeb was right to leave The Congregation. And she was right to follow him. Everything was going to be different—namely, her dad wasn't going to be telling her what to do every second of every day—and everything was going to be good.

The taxi driver turned right on a small street that had been plowed, but then he immediately began to slow down.

"Whoa, what's going on at this church of yours, young lady?"

"Huh?"

"Looks like the police have suddenly found God too."

Suzanne leaned forward and peered out the windshield. Down the block she could see a small, snow-covered church, but instead of presenting a picture of serenity, Suzanne saw a street of chaos. There were three or four police cars parked in the snow and cops standing all over the place. Bright yellow tape was strung from tree to tree, and off to the side a bunch of people in puffy winter parkas were standing around in the drifts, pointing and watching and gossiping.

"Dear Jehovah," she gasped.

She immediately panicked. She'd been right there last night when her father had called Zeb's father and given him the name and telephone number that Zeb had called from. So what had happened? Surely Rick had gone after Zeb. And for sure Paul had gone along too. But they wouldn't have hurt Zeb, would they? Suddenly Suzanne felt herself wanting to burst into tears. From time to time disobedient members of The Congregation had gotten into trouble for things like reading forbidden books or listening to rock music stations, and those punishments had ranged from scrubbing the bakery floor to washing dishes for a month to being locked in the prayer closet for up to six hours. But . . . but what would Zeb's father do to Zeb for taking Ribka and running away? Would he find forgiveness and love, or . . . or would he hurt him?

A woman in a big tan coat and blue Moon-Boots was walking away from the church, plodding through the deep snow. Suzanne lunged toward her window and desperately cranked it open.

"Hey, lady! Lady! What happened at the church?" begged Suzanne, leaning out of the taxi. "Why are the police here? No one was hurt, were they?"

The woman looked back at all the commotion and shook her head. "I've lived here for over twenty years and nothing like this has ever happened. Minneapolis used to be such a safe place. Now just look at what's happened! I mean, what's going on in this country of ours?"

"But what happened?"

"Why, someone was attacked and nearly killed!"

The cab driver muttered, "Oh, charmed, I'm sure."

Suzanne stared out the window of the taxi. Oh, no. Oh, dear Lord. Zeb? Not Zeb?

Almost too afraid to ask, with a faint voice Suzanne asked, "Who?"

The woman said, "The minister, of all people. They found him in the garage, knocked out and just about frozen stiff.

Such a nice man. Three or four people had seen him out shoveling this morning. He was all friendly and everything. We're just hopin' he doesn't die.''

Her hands trembling, Suzanne somehow managed to close the window. The piece of paper. The one with the phone numbers on it. Where was it? Crap. What had she done with it?

"Oh, Lord Jesus," she whimpered, her eyes beading with tears. "Please protect my Zeb and Ribka. Please keep them safe from harm."

She snatched the scrap of paper from the seat next to her. Where else could she go? How else could she find them?

"Here!" she said, pushing the piece of paper at the taxi driver. "Go there! Go to this place!"

"What?"

"Take me there, to that address, the one that's written down! Take me now!" she demanded.

"Okay, okay. Just hold on. I'll get you there," he said, reading the scrap. "I know the place."

"Hurry before someone else is hurt!"

"Not to worry, ginger, we're on our way."

# 35

"You know, the situation isn't just nearly out of control," Rick said as he led the way into his hotel room and locked the door behind them. "It's completely out of control. And no thanks to you, I might add."

Rick threw his coat on a chair and stared at Paul, who didn't reply. In fact, since Rick had picked him up Paul had offered little except that Zeb was gone. Disappeared. No longer at the small house attached to the church.

Finally, Paul said, "Perhaps this isn't meant to be."

"What a ghastly thing to say! Don't tell me you're losing faith?"

"Of course not, it's just that—"

"We're talking about my granddaughter, don't forget. About her health, about her life. We need to rescue her and bring her back to the fold."

Staring at the floor, Paul said, "Yes, sir."

"So get busy!"

Rick now watched as Paul crossed the hotel room, took his thick briefcase, and placed it on the bed. His movements quick and precise, Paul snapped open the case, pulled out several wires, and turned to the telephone on the bedside table. Using suction cups, he attached the wires to the phone, then dialed a number. As soon as the line was ringing, Paul pressed a series of keys on the phone itself, thereby dialing in a code.

"I pray to God we're able to learn something. Or maybe I should pray for something more simple," said Rick. "Like I hope to God this contraption of yours still works."

Rick sat on the opposite bed and waited to see if there would indeed be a miracle. In theory, at least, the small device that Paul had attached to Janice's telephone line—identical to the one placed on Zeb's mother's phone line in Santa Fe—was supposed to digitally record every one of her phone calls. Just as important, it was supposed to identify the name and telephone number of every incoming and outgoing call. And Rick now waited as the small contraption in Paul's briefcase seized Janice's phone lines and downloaded all of the information regarding Janice's calls. It took little over a minute.

"Is there anything?" asked Rick finally.

Paul nodded as he disconnected the suction cups from the handset and hung up the hotel phone. He pressed a button on the small electronic box in his briefcase, and the recordings of Janice's phone conversations began to play. First was Rick's call that morning when he asked to meet Janice. Then there was another call from a friend. And then a very important one.

The recorded voice from the box said, "It's me."

Recognizing Zeb's voice, Rick lunged forward and said, "He called her after he left the church."

The two men listened to the rest of the recording as Janice nervously said she would pick him up, she still had her coat on, she'd be there in minutes.

Rick checked his watch and said, "She's picked him up by now. Maybe she brought him back to her house."

Paul held his hand up to silence Rick. To their surprise they next heard the voice of Todd Mills speaking to a man called Jeff about none other than Zeb and the baby. From the conversation Rick and Paul learned everything they needed.

Rick smiled. "Praise Jehovah."

"Thus is His will."

So the sodomites had hidden his boy and granddaughter at a gay bar. He should have guessed they'd do something disgusting like that. And Janice was on her way down there. Perfect. From the conversation it sounded as if only Janice was going to be there, which should make things slightly less complicated.

"Very good," said Rick, standing up. "My apologies. This thing of yours does work. Quite well too."

He stood up, started pacing. They had to act quickly, for this could very well be their last chance and—

Just then there was a knock on the door. Rick looked at Paul, who froze. Who the hell, wondered Rick, could that be? Not the maid. The room had already been cleaned. The knock turned into pounding, and Paul started stuffing the wires into his briefcase, which he snapped shut.

"Just a minute!" called Rick.

He crossed through the room and nodded to Paul, who withdrew his gun from his coat pocket. No doubt about it, this could be serious trouble, and he motioned Paul into the dark bathroom. Once the other man had slipped out of sight, Rick went right up to the door.

"Who's there?"

"It's me! Let me in!"

It was a young and thin voice, that of a woman. At first Rick thought he recognized it, but then he realized he was being ridiculous. That was impossible. It couldn't be her. He leaned up to the small peephole, looked out, and saw blond hair and a slender body.

"Oh, my word!"

His hands fumbled for the lock and he threw open the door. What next could go wrong?

"Lord Almighty!" he said upon seeing her. "Suzanne, what in the world are you doing here?"

"I'm looking for my husband and your son, who just so

happen to be one and the same," she said as she barged past him, a small duffel bag slung over her shoulder. "Where's Zeb? What have you done to him? Have you hurt him? And where's my daughter?"

Rick demanded, "How did you get here?"

"How do you think? On the back of a little angel."

"Does your father know you're—"

"Of course not. Now where's Zeb?"

Rick pressed a hand to his forehead—this was the last thing they needed—as Suzanne marched into the main part of the room. Seeing that it was empty, she dropped her duffel bag on the floor and then crossed to the mirrored door of the closet, which she slid open. Her husband, though, was not hidden in there, and as she turned Paul emerged from the bathroom, his pistol hanging from his hand.

"You fat pig!" shouted Suzanne when she saw him. "What did you do to Zeb? Where is he?"

She lunged at him, pushing Paul back against the wall and beating on him with both fists. Rick went after her, grabbing her by the shoulders and pulling her back.

"Stop it!" he shouted.

"You big thug!" she screamed at Paul. "Did you hurt Zeb?"

Rick demanded, "That's enough!"

He dragged her away from Paul, hurling her onto the bed. She jumped up, and when he grabbed one of her wrists Suzanne lunged forward with her mouth and bit him as hard as she could.

"You little slut!" shouted Rick as he brought back his hand and slapped her on the left cheek.

Suzanne fell back on the bed, clasping her face and sobbing. Rick couldn't believe this. There was no time for such antics. What in the devil's name did she think she was doing, coming here like this? She was going to foul everything.

"Suzanne," snapped Rick, "you were stupid to come here! And you're stupid to bother us!"

She sobbed, "My baby . . ."

"Stop it! We don't have time for your hysterics!"

He walked to the window, his fists clenched. What he should do now was take her right back to the airport and put her on the first plane to Denver. There wasn't, however, enough time. Which meant that unless they wanted to tie her up here in the motel room, they had no choice.

"I'm sorry, my dear, but things have gotten complicated," said Rick, his back to Suzanne. "Paul and I were just about to leave to get Zeb and your baby. We know where they are, but we don't have much time. What that means is that you're going to have to come with us."

Paul demanded, "What?"

"We can't leave her alone," Rick said to Paul. "We have to keep an eye on her."

"But—"

"Suzanne, you won't mind coming with us, will you?"

She wiped her eyes. "No."

"And you'll be good, you'll wait in the car while we go get Zeb and your baby?"

"Y-y-yes."

"All right, then let's go. Time is wasting."

She nodded, then leaned over to pick up her bag.

"We'll be coming back," Rick said. "You can leave your bag here."

"No," she said, picking it up and holding it tight against her body. "I might need it."

"Very well. Let's go."

# 36

It wasn't far from the Gay Times to City Hall, only a matter of a few blocks, and the streets downtown had been well cleared of snow. Five minutes after Todd had dropped Janice off he was pulling up to the towering red granite building that occupied an entire block. But Rawlins wasn't waiting inside the arched entry as promised. Todd stopped in the slush along the curb, put on his flashers, and prepared to wait. If there was one thing that bugged him about Rawlins, it was his sense of time—he was always late. After five minutes of just sitting there and wondering where in the hell Rawlins was, Todd picked up his car phone and dialed Rawlins's number.

"Nope, he isn't around," said Jack, one of the other detectives who picked up the phone in the bull room where they all worked. "He left—I don't know—something like ten, fifteen minutes ago."

Great, thought Todd, hanging up. Rawlins could appear in just a couple of seconds. Or, knowing him, this could take forever. Todd closed his eyes, clenched his right hand into a fist, and pounded lightly on the steering wheel. There wasn't time for this right now, and he tried to remember Rawlins's beeper number. Recalling what he hoped was it, he dialed and did in fact receive a message to leave his own number, which Todd did, pressing in the number of his car phone. Todd hung up, but nothing happened. He just sat in his Cherokee staring at his phone, willing it to ring.

Trying not to get too bent out of shape, Todd started thinking about Janice's security system. There was something not quite right about it, he was sure, but what that was exactly he didn't know. He thought about the initial message the small speaker had given, tried to imagine what it could possibly have meant. Perhaps the storm had somehow affected the phone lines. Maybe snow and ice had built up on the wires outside.

Fifteen minutes after Todd had arrived, Rawlins finally came trotting out the arched entry of City Hall. Todd took a deep breath. Just be cool, he told himself.

"Sorry," said Rawlins as he climbed in and shut the door. "I got called into Captain Letzen's office—there was nothing I could do."

"Didn't you get my call on your beeper?" asked Todd, trying not to sound too irritated.

"Yeah, but like I said, I couldn't break away, not even to make a quick call. So what's up?"

As he started up his car and drove off, Todd said, "I've got some info we need to discuss."

"How nice. And here I thought we were getting together for a friendly cup of coffee. Do tell."

"I didn't want to go into it over the phone, but I know where Zeb is."

"Very good. The plot thickens."

Todd turned the corner. "Zeb didn't attack that guy. You're right, though, he was there. At that house, the minister's. After we saw him at the hospital Zeb got his car stuck in the snow, so this minister let him spend the night at his house. But like I said, Zeb didn't hurt anyone. He was there this morning and this other guy, someone from the cult, started stalking the house. Zeb can not only give a complete description, he has a name too.''

"Excellent.''

"And the guy just so happens to be the same one who broke into Janice's and attacked the both of us.''

"Which means you can give descriptions as well.''

"Exactly.'' Todd asked, "So does that mean you're going to have to take Zeb in for questioning?''

"Well, there is this warrant out for his arrest, you know.''

"Right, but . . . well, both Janice and I are afraid that Zeb will panic if he's separated again from his daughter. We don't know if he'll clam up or just try to get away. Can't I just take you to see him and then you can do an informal interview of sorts?''

Rawlins thought for a moment. "Okay. I shouldn't do this, but for you . . .''

"You're wonderful.''

"I hope you mean that.''

"I hope I do too.'' Driving back toward Hennepin, Todd changed the subject by saying, "Do you know anything about security systems?''

"Not much. Why?''

"Because something's screwy about Janice's.''

Todd reviewed the situation, explaining what had happened, how they hadn't been able to set it, and how they'd gone down to the basement to check it out. Everything—all the wires and such—had seemed in order, he went on.

"Wait a minute,'' said Rawlins, "you say the phone wires went right out of the basement?''

"Yeah.''

"Well, that could be the problem right there.''

That was enough to make him remember. In the piece he'd done for Channel 7 one of the tips was that phone lines should leave the house via an attic or the top of a house and never at ground level. The experienced burglar could simply and easily cut the lines, thereby rendering a security system virtually impotent.

But wait a minute, he thought. If someone had cut Janice's lines, as the first warning on her system had suggested, why did it work later?

"It could have been something like snow on the lines," Todd said. "Or maybe when that guy broke in he caused a short in the wiring. Something like that, because just a few minutes later we were able to set it."

"Well, she should still have it checked out just to make sure no one tampered with it."

"Right." Coming to an intersection, Todd turned left. "She should have the security company go over the whole thing."

"Hey, where are you going?" said Rawlins, pointing to the right. "The Gay Times is that way."

"I know, but Janice used my car phone on the way down and something has come up. We've got to make a quick stop, a very important one."

# 37

"So that's how the police see it," Janice said as she finished relating to Zeb the trouble he was now in. "You're the only person that any of the neighbors saw at the minister's house, which makes you, of course, their prime suspect."

"But . . . but I didn't hurt anyone!"

"Of course not."

In the distant background an old disco song pounded on and on as a half dozen drag queens went through their dress rehearsal on the stage of the Show Room. Here in Jeff's dressing room, however, the atmosphere was far more serious as Janice and Zeb discussed the most recent events. It was a small room with a rack of gowns on one wall, feathers and wigs scattered all over another, and a makeup table covered with cosmetics and brushes off to one side. Janice sat on an old, drooping love seat, the baby Ribka cradled in her arms. Just maybe, she thought, everything was going to be all right. Just maybe the intensity of the last few days would begin to back down. She brushed her hand through Ribka's dark curls, then looked up at Zeb, who sat at Jeff's dressing table.

"I think we've finally got things under control."

"But it was that guy, Paul! It had to be him! He must have attacked the minister out in the garage or . . . or, I don't know, something like that."

"I'm sure it was. If nothing else, though, you're a witness, and I'm afraid you're going to have to talk with the police at some point."

"You mean down at the police station?"

She shook her head. "I don't think so. We might be able to avoid that. You remember Todd and Rawlins, the ones who were out at the hospital?"

"Yeah," said Zeb, meekly.

"Rawlins is a cop. He's going to come over here, if that's okay. He just wants to talk and see how much he can get straightened out. Is that all right?"

"I . . . I guess. When?"

"Actually, he's on his way over now. The sooner we deal with this, the better."

Janice went on to tell him how she, as a lawyer, thought this was the best way. The easiest. If they could keep it nice and simple, if Zeb could tell them everything he knew, then this might be over within a few hours. Not only might the authorities be able to apprehend whoever attacked the minister, Zeb might no longer have anyone pursuing him.

He shrugged. "You don't know my dad."

Oh, but I do, thought Janice. She bent over, kissed Ribka on the forehead. Oh, but I do.

"Zeb, we've got a lot to talk about," began Janice. "There's a lot you don't know and a lot I'd like to—"

The door quickly opened, and Janice looked up, expecting to see Jeff swirl into the room, draped in a shimmering gold gown. Instead, two men burst in, both of them quite familiar and one of them holding a pistol.

"Dad!" shouted Zeb, jumping to his feet.

"Speak of the devil," said Janice, clutching Ribka against her chest. "What the hell are you two doing here?"

"I'm afraid this is what it's come down to," said Rick, his

voice stern and authoritative. "Now, my son, I'm afraid your little escapade is over. It's time to come back home. We've all been terribly worried about you, especially your young wife, and it's time to return to The Congregation."

"But—"

"No, the decision has been made."

Zeb ran one hand over his short hair. "But Ribka—she's sick, she needs medicine."

"Ribka will be fine. She just needs your faith."

"Oh, cut the crap, will you?" snapped Janice. "She has a bad ear infection, that's all."

"Oh, ye of little faith." Rick stepped toward her and reached out. "Give me the child."

"You can't do this!" she said, cowering back in the old love seat.

"Just watch."

Janice's mind whipped through a flip chart of possibilities, excuses, lies. She tried to conjure up some lawyerly trick. If only she could stall them, delay them in some way.

"Paul," she said, "do you know the police have a warrant out for your arrest?"

The large man grinned. "Oh, really?"

"For murder?"

His face became serious. "What?"

"You attacked someone, a minister, who's in the hospital and may die. I thought one of the commandments—one of the biggies—was 'Thou shalt not kill.'"

"Don't listen to her, Paul. She's being ridiculous," interrupted Rick. "Just give me the child and we'll be gone, right, Zeb?"

"No way. I'm not going back to that funny farm."

Janice said, "The police are on the way here."

"Right," replied Zeb. "A cop's coming over to talk to me."

"If they're on the way, then I guess we'll have to hurry."

Paul raised the gun, started to step forward. "Do like he says, lady, and give him the baby."

"Like hell I will, you murderer."

Janice clutched her granddaughter, sank back. There was no way she was giving up Ribka, not again.

"Fine," snapped Rick impatiently. "Then we'll have to take all of you. Paul, you get the boy."

Paul lunged across the room, grabbing Zeb and twisting his arm behind his back. Zeb bucked, tried to pull away, but then his face collapsed in a wave of pain.

"Leave him alone!" shouted Janice, rising to her feet.

"Zeb, my son, you really must start behaving. Please, I implore you, do as your elders tell you." Rick reached out for Janice. "Now come with me. No one's going to get hurt as long as you do as you're told. Please, Janice, just stay nice and calm. Our car is right outside."

"Oh, great," quipped Janice, realizing she had no choice. "Road trips with you have always been a barrel of fun."

"I . . . I don't get it," said Zeb as Paul pushed him out the door. "How did you find us down here?"

Paul replied, "God the Father showed us the way."

"Bullshit," said Todd, stepping into one end of the long, narrow hallway and blocking their exit. "They had Janice's phone bugged."

Rick paused for a second and then jerked Janice, who was clutching Ribka, in front of him. Todd couldn't tell how immediately dangerous the situation was, but recognized the guy behind Rick as the one with whom he'd fought at Janice's house. Todd's eyes flashed over Zeb for the first time and he felt a jolt.

Rick said, "Too bad you didn't figure that out sooner. Now, get out of our way. Like I told you before, this is a family matter."

"Of course it is, that's why I'm here."

"Move before Paul is forced to shoot you."

"Oh, I wouldn't do that," called Rawlins from the opposite end of the hall, where he stood, a gun trained on Paul. "Todd's special, if you know what I mean. I don't think you want to hurt him."

A few silent seconds crept by, and Todd hoped this battle was already won. But then he watched as Rick grabbed the gun from Paul and placed it against Janice's temple. Her grasp on Ribka firm and secure, Janice's body went rigid, and Todd could see the panic sweep across her face.

"Dad, no!" screamed Zeb.

"Shut up, Zeb!" Rick glanced at Rawlins, then at Todd. "You let us go or I'll shoot her!"

"Dad, stop it!"

The desperation clear on his face, Rick dragged Janice toward a door and shouted, "Come on, Paul!"

Zeb twisted and bucked in Paul's grip, but then they started down a side hall. The Gay Times was a labyrinthine place, complete with everything from a piano bar to a pool hall, and while Todd knew the main parts pretty well, he had only a vague idea of the dressing room and stage areas. He was pretty sure he could cut them off, though, and he dashed down another hall and into a room, which was full of stacks of chairs but no other way out. He retreated, found another door, through which he tore. The music from the Show Room blared away, louder and louder, and Todd only hoped he'd find some way to circle around and cut them off.

He came around a corner and this tall, skinny thing in a green sparkling dress crashed right into him. One of the drag queens, Todd realized, a black man, sleek and elegant and struggling to maintain her balance on her tall, spike heels.

"Did you see a guy with a gun?" demanded Todd.

"You bet your sweet ass I did," said the queen, straightening her long black wig, then pointing up a few steps. "You go right up that way, doll, and you'll get a bullet right through your heart, I'm sure of it."

"Thanks."

"Oh, a real hero. I think I'm gonna cry."

Todd bounded up the short staircase and found himself backstage, a cavernous black space full of ropes and a few paltry pieces of scenery. As the music blasted away, Todd cut around, emerging on the far edge of the stage on which his friend Jeff, à la Tiffany Crystal, was prancing and dragging around to the sounds of Diana Ross.

And there, emerging from the other side, were Paul, Zeb, Janice, and Rick, the gun still at Janice's head.

All at once the music stopped, and Tiffany was left mid-swoop, mid-song, and as awkward as a lumberjack in a skirt.

"Hey, you bonehead," she called to the technician in the back as she straightened up, "I got a song in my heart, but no music in my throat. What's up?"

His voice low, Todd said, "Get out of here, Jeff."

She turned around, her gold gown glimmering in the lights. "Why, hello there, big boy. Come to sing a duet with me?"

From the opposite end of the stage, Janice, her voice trembling, said, "Do as he says, Jeff."

Tiffany Crystal turned around further, saw the full situation. "Oh, fuck. I mean . . . I mean, oh, my word."

And with that she went scurrying down the front steps and into the tables, which were clustered at the base of the stage. Todd took a step forward, hesitated. What could he do? How could he stop this?

"Pat . . . or Rick . . . you've got to realize that Zeb doesn't want to go with you. And if his daughter is sick, then how she's treated is his decision."

"Get out of our way, Todd!"

Clearly that tack wasn't going to work. Think, he told himself. Figure something out. Glancing to the side, he saw Rawlins enter the room, and Todd held up his hand, motioned for him not to come up any closer.

"You used to be a pretty nice guy, Rick. We were friends, remember?" ventured Todd. "I don't know what it was, but there was something kind of charming about you. You were full of life, full of energy.''

From out in the dark audience a woman's voice called, ''Fragile too, wasn't he?''

Todd peered out into the darkness and saw a blond woman leaning against a column.

''There was something about him,'' she said, ''that just made me want to take him in my arms and tell him everything would be all right.''

Zeb tried to pull away from Paul, but couldn't, and he shouted, ''Mom!''

''For God's sake, Martha,'' snapped Rick, ''what the hell are you doing here?''

''What kind of mother wouldn't come to help her boy and granddaughter?''

Desperate to find and see Zeb, Martha had flown up here, and it had been she who had made the emergency call to Janice's office. Using Todd's car phone as they headed downtown, Janice had then called her at the Holiday Inn. After getting Rawlins, Todd had swung by and picked her up as well.

''Do you remember him back then, so pretty, so young-looking?'' she asked.

''Sure I do,'' said Todd. ''You could look him right in the eye, see a person who knew . . . who knew right from wrong.''

''Exactly.'' Martha continued, ''I'd been living at the ranch, the communal one, for almost two months when he came. And I think I fell in love with him that first night he was there.''

*She'd been sitting on the back porch steps, staring up at the stars, when she heard the screen door squeak open.*

*''Hi,'' said Martha, her long blond hair swishing as she turned around and saw him, Pat, the guy who'd just arrived that afternoon. ''Isn't it beautiful? I mean, it's just so clear.*

*All you have to do is look up and see all those stars and you know that's where Jehovah and all the angels live.''* She wrapped her arms around her knees. *"Maybe this sounds awful, but sometimes I just can't wait to get up there, to be with Him. Won't it be wonderful?''*

*"Probably, but I'll never get to heaven.''*

*"Don't be silly.''* She scooted over. *"Come here and sit down next to me. Hold my hand, otherwise I might just turn into an angel and fly away right now.''*

*"I mean it.''* Pat sat down, hesitantly took her hand, and then looked upward at that great promised place. *"I'll never get there. I'm going to hell.''*

*"Hey, don't talk like that.''*

*"But I'm bad. You know, evil.''*

*"Then you've come to the right place. If you give yourself to God then you'll find love and happiness. That's what we're doing here in this house, coming together in love.''*

She glanced over at him, saw tears welling in his eyes. And so she couldn't stop herself. He needed help. He needed a true friend. He was in pain, pain that was honest and sincere. She leaned over, kissed him on the cheek.

He blurted. *"I . . . I had sex with another guy.''*

It took her by surprise, and at first she didn't know what to say. She didn't even know him, they hadn't even spoken five words before this, but she'd never seen someone open up so quickly, so deeply.

*"We all make mistakes,''* said Martha. *"God the Father is infinite in His mercy.''*

*"Then . . . then a few days ago I wasn't very nice to a friend of mine. A girl. We were in a motel. I was drunk. I . . . I made her have sex with me.''*

She squeezed his hand. *"You don't need to tell me this. You need to—''*

*"But I want to. I have to. I have to tell someone at least.''*

*"You need to find God the Father and tell Him. We can help you—find Him, I mean. All of us can. Don't worry.''*

*"It's too late. Something worse happened. Something at college. I need to turn myself in to the police. I did something horrible. I . . . I need to tell the authorities."*

*"No, silly," she said, amazed at his agony. "You don't need to tell anyone but God."*

*"But you don't understand."*

*"Of course I do. I understand that the police can't help you. And I understand that God can." She glanced upward at the dark sky. "Look! Look a falling star! It's a sign, Pat! A sign for you to reach out to heaven."*

*"What happened was horrible, I—"*

*"Shh. Whatever it was is between you and God. Find Him and you'll find eternal love and forgiveness."*

"Do you remember that night, Rick?" said Martha, wiping tears from her own eyes. "You just started weeping. Sobbing. And I thought I'd never seen anything so pure, so honest. That was the man I fell in love with, that young man who was drowning in a sea of despair, who was reaching out . . . reaching out to me."

"Stop it, Martha!" snapped Rick.

"And that's what I grew to loathe about you. After that night you never really gave yourself to God or anyone else, particularly me. Whatever was burning inside you never turned into love. No, gradually, bit by bit, it just turned bitter, and over time it turned into hate, didn't it?"

"Now's not the time for this kind of nonsense!"

Suddenly it was all so clear, thought Todd, staring across the stage at Rick. He understood. What had happened so long ago had kept Todd in the closet for years; Rick, on the other hand, had hidden elsewhere.

"You didn't join that church to find God or to be sexually rehabilitated or anything like that, did you?" said Todd. "Hell no, that's not what you've been hiding from, is it?"

"Spare me your accusations!"

"It was just like you said, you didn't see anyone else on that fire escape, did you?"

"Of course not."

"You didn't see anyone else because, of course, it was you out there. You got that window open, didn't you? Somehow you went out on that fire escape."

"God's wisdom is all-encompassing."

"It was you—you out there with Greg. I saw you, didn't I? And what did you do, push Greg? Is that the truth you wanted to confess to Martha, that you killed someone?"

Rick stared at him, hesitated, then blurted, "You were the coward, not me. At least I didn't run away."

*He ran to the window. What a bastard, that Greg! He'd tell the entire fucking fraternity! And Pat reached for the window, tried to pull it upward, but it didn't budge.*

*"Todd, I can't get the window up! Help me!"*

*When Pat turned around, though, Todd wasn't right there. He was standing in the doorway, ready to run. Their eyes met, the terror mutual, but instead of coming to his aid, Todd turned and fled. Vanished, just like that. Todd was gone, he'd fled, abandoned him. For an instant Pat just stood there, overwhelmed with shock; he'd never felt so alone in his life. Then he turned, saw Greg laughing out on the fire escape, pointing at him, mouthing the word:* Faggot!

*Something in Pat exploded. Burst. He grabbed the window, gritted his teeth, gathered strength he didn't know he had, and shoved it upward. The cold air flooded in, constricting around his nearly naked body.*

*Greg stood out there on the black metal fire escape, laughing and pointing, a cigarette in one hand. "I was just out here having a smoke when I thought I heard something in your room. It was pretty dark in there, so I took a peek, and what do I see but a couple of faggots!" He laughed. "Man, wait till I tell the guys about this—you and Todd! Holy shit, we're gonna have us a wienie roast! I always thought you were a queer. I*

*always knew you didn't belong in our fraternity. But Todd?*
*Wow, wait till the guys hear about this!''*

*''Fuck you!'' said Pat, scrambling out the window in his*
*underwear.*

*''Oh, help me, help me, a sissy!''*

*Pat swung, but Greg was quicker and quite a bit stronger, a*
*star hockey player in the peak of fitness. He flicked his ciga-*
*rette into the air, then caught Pat by the wrist, just like that,*
*just that quickly.*

*Not releasing Pat, Greg softly, gently taunted: ''Faggot!''*

*Pat wasn't going to take this. No! And summoning his*
*strength a second time, Pat twisted his body in an attempt to*
*jerk his arm free. That was when it happened. Greg lost his*
*balance, that was all. The fire escape was so narrow, so*
*flimsy. He started to fall back and he reached out, grabbed for*
*something, anything. Found nothing. Greg tried to catch him-*
*self, but the railing was low, and when he went over he only*
*managed to grab on with one hand.*

*''Help me!'' Greg pleaded, hanging desperately from the*
*grating.*

*Towering above him, Pat looked down at Greg's fingers as*
*they clutched the slippery metal bar, and then said, ''Fuck*
*off.''*

"Okay, so I went out there," said Rick calmly, "but Greg
fell."

Todd stared at him and knew the truth. "Bullshit. You
pushed him, you killed him, didn't you? That's the truth that's
been eating you all these years."

Paul demanded, "What's he saying, Rick?"

"Nothing! Nothing at all!" he shouted, pressing the gun
against Janice's temple.

"I'm saying you killed someone," said Todd. "Or at the
very least you contributed to his death."

"You're filled with the devil, Todd Mills, you sodomite!"

Todd said calmly, "There are just some things that can never be cleansed, namely, the truth."

Suddenly Ribka started to cry, and Zeb said, "Dad . . . Dad, please let Janice go."

"We have to leave! We have to get out of here, get back to The Congregation where we'll be safe!"

"Dad, please!"

"Rick . . . the baby," begged Janice. "At least let Zeb take her."

Paul released Zeb and stepped forward. "Give me the gun, Rick."

"What? But Paul, we—"

"This isn't right," continued Paul.

Quite abruptly, a high voice shouted out from the back. "Why's everyone always treat me like a dog?"

"God Almighty!" thundered Rick. "I told you to stay in the car, Suzanne!"

"That's exactly what I mean—I'm supposed to wait in the car like a good dog. And here all of you are, up here in this bar, every one of you, including my baby!"

Shocked, Zeb looked out, then in a small voice said, "Hi, Suzanne."

"Oh, Zeb . . . are you all right?"

He nodded.

"And Ribka?"

Still tight in Rick's grip, Janice asked, "Please, Rick, just let me give the baby to her mother."

"No!"

"Rick—" began Paul.

"Don't come any closer, Paul. All of you just stay where you are! Anyone touches me and I'll kill her!" he shouted, pressing the barrel firmly against Janice's head.

Todd could barely breathe. He saw the pistol buried against Janice's head, saw the fear strip her face of any color. Sweat burst across Todd's brow. He glanced sideways, saw Rawlins out on the main floor, tense and ready to dart forward. But they were too far away. There was nothing they could do.

"This is not God the Father's way," said Paul.

"Shut up!"

"You've strayed, Rick. You no longer stand on The Promises."

"How dare you!"

"Give me the gun!"

Maybe he'd really do it, maybe he'd really shoot, and Todd's voice, little more than a whisper, said, "Wait, I—"

"You pull that trigger, Rick," continued Paul, "and you will have the wrath of the Lord upon you."

"Stop!"

"No."

"I'll shoot her!"

"Then we'll know where Satan truly lurks."

"Stop it! Just stop it!" shouted Suzanne, running forward and reaching into her bag and pulling out a pistol of her own. "Anybody hurts my baby and I'll kill him!"

Swinging his gun at her, Rick yelled, "You ignorant slut!"

"Dad, no!" cried Zeb, lunging forward.

But it was too late. Rick took aim at Suzanne and squeezed the trigger. Todd flinched, expected a blast. There was, however, none. Rick pulled the trigger again and again. Still not a single bullet fired, and Rick was paralyzed.

Paul calmly said, "I've never had it loaded. Never."

"You fool!"

Rick threw Janice and Ribka aside and darted toward the edge of the stage, rushing at Suzanne and her gun.

"Don't!" shouted Suzanne. "Don't! Stay back!"

Charging her, he leapt off the stage. Suzanne focused the gun right on him. And fired.

# 38

---

Todd ripped up one of Jeff's old gowns, a white cotton summer dress, and Rawlins, using a first aid technique he'd been taught down at the police station, held the bleeding in check until the paramedics arrived. Nevertheless, the loss of blood was extreme, for the bullet had struck Rick just beneath the left shoulder. Bending over the wounded man, who lay on the floor between a couple of round cocktail tables, Todd first feared that an artery had been pierced. When Rick had trouble breathing a few minutes later, Todd guessed that a lung had been punctured.

"Just hang on, Dad," begged Zeb, clutching his father's hand and trying to hold back the tears. "Help's on the way. The ambulance is coming. You're going to be okay. Just . . . just hang on."

Rick tried to speak, stared at Zeb for several seconds, then closed his eyes and nodded.

"One of the best trauma centers in the country is only a few blocks away," added Todd. "We'll get you there in a few minutes."

Relieved, concerned, amazed, Todd stood up and glanced

across the room. Not too far away, Paul had his big arms around Suzanne, who was sobbing, horrified that she'd actually shot someone, while the grandmothers, Janice and Martha, tried to calm Ribka, who'd been so terribly startled by the gun blast and the ensuing commotion. At least, thought Todd, no one else was hurt.

In a few minutes the ambulance arrived and two men and a woman came bounding up the stairs of the Gay Times and into the Show Room. They took over then, slowing the loss of blood even more, putting an oxygen mask on Rick, then lifting him onto a gurney.

"I'm here, Dad!" shouted Zeb, refusing to let go of his father's hand. "Dad, I'm right here!"

This time, however, he got no response, not even a nod.

"We've got to take him now," said one of the medics, a tall guy with red hair.

Zeb demanded, "He's going to be all right, isn't he?"

"I think we've got him stabilized. We'll do all that we can."

Janice came up behind Zeb, placed a hand on either of his shoulders. "Do you want to go with him in the ambulance?"

"Yeah."

"That would be great," the female medic, an athletic woman with brown hair, said to Zeb. "Your father's going to need a transfusion, and blood from a relative is always best."

"Sure, but . . . but . . . I can't."

Todd saw this ripple of panic wash across Zeb's face. Or was it helplessness?

"What are you trying to say, Zeb?" asked Todd.

"I can't give him blood—he's not my birth father. His blood is type O, mine's AB."

Janice, clearly shocked, demanded, "What? How do you know that?"

Zeb stated simply, "When Mom told me I was adopted, she gave me a whole file on me. The letter from you and all the legal stuff was in there. Everything, including Mom and Dad's wedding certificate. They got married by a judge, and their blood types were written down."

Todd looked at Janice, the shock shooting through them both. Todd knew what Zeb was saying, what it meant. Janice was type A, Rick was O. They couldn't have produced a child who was AB. But Janice and Todd could have, because Todd was type B.

As the medics started rolling Rick out, Zeb called across the room to Martha, "Mom, I'm going to the hospital. Are you okay with Ribka? You and Suzanne can watch her?"

"Of course, dear. She'll be fine."

Without hesitation Zeb hurried after the medics and the gurney, but Todd didn't move. Nor did Janice.

Once Zeb was out of earshot Todd asked, "If he knows that much, does he know about me?"

"No. Not yet anyway." She reached over and took him by the hand. "Come on, Zeb shouldn't be alone at the hospital. You'll drive me over there, won't you?"

"Absolutely. And I'll stay too, that is, if three won't be a crowd."

"Don't be ridiculous. I think this is going to be a long night, and hell, we've got to talk about something, don't we?"

Todd glanced back at Rawlins, who'd overheard most of the conversation and assured Todd that things were well taken care of.

"I had Jeff call the station, so there'll be a couple more cops here in a minute." Rawlins grinned. "Hey, good luck, man. I want to hear all about it—I'll be waiting."

"You'd better be." Todd reached over, pulled Rawlins into his deep embrace, and into his ear whispered, "I'm scared."